CLAN OF THE ARCHANGEL SERIES

BOOK 3

# True Strength

GRACIE MITCHELL

True
Strength

This book is dedicated to my husband, who encourages me to follow my dream.

To my amazing friends and family for their endless support. Lastly to the reader, who stays up late, trying to finish one more chapter.

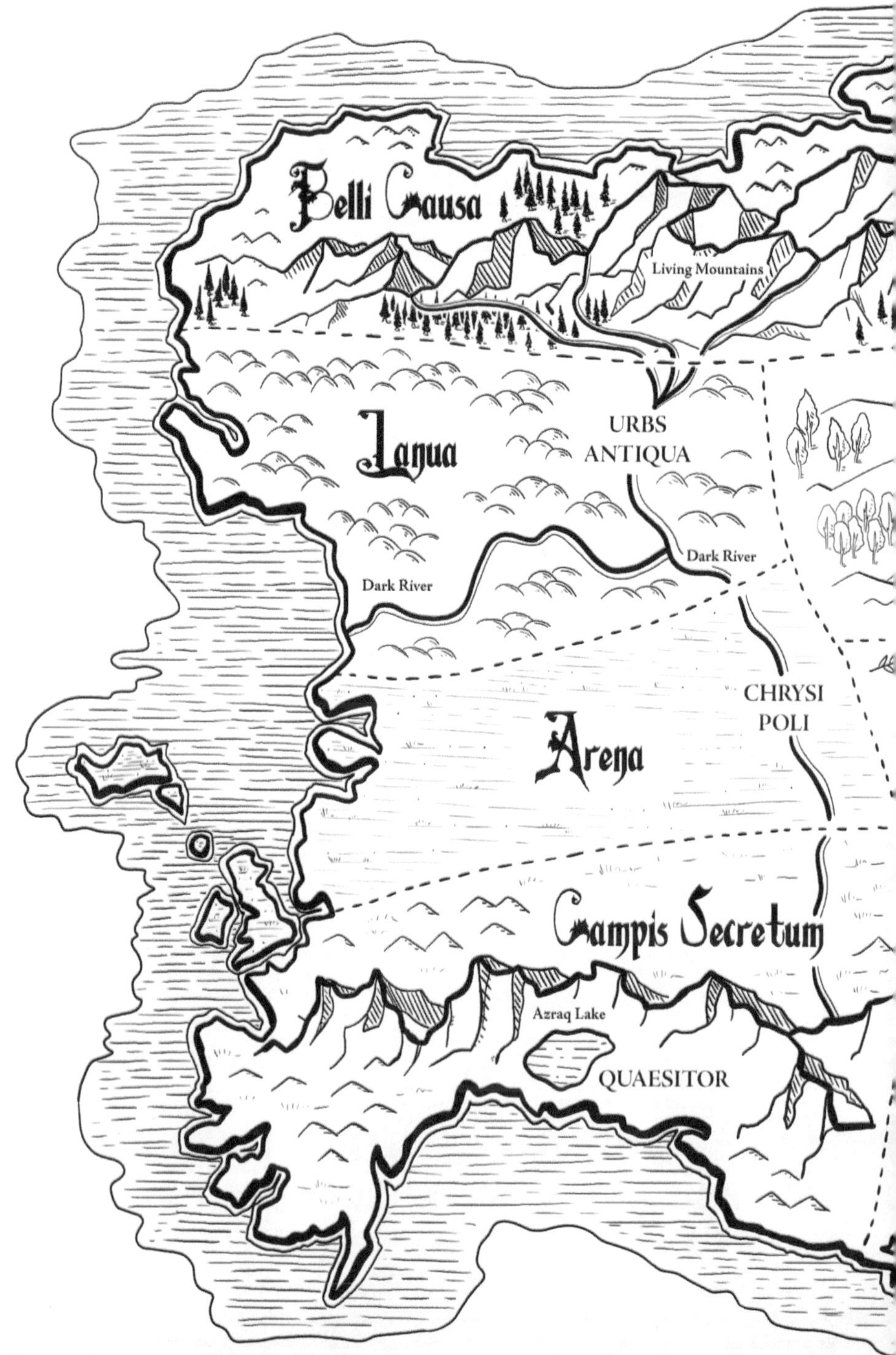

Belli Causa
Living Mountains
Janua
URBS
ANTIQUA
Dark River
Dark River
CHRYSI
POLI
Arena
Campis Secretum
Azraq Lake
QUAESITOR

Silva
VENTUS
AQUAM
CAPUT
Elementa
Vallis
Coal
Mountains
MORTEM
N
W
E
S

MIRAGE
Satan's Domain
RED CITY
Decimate Mountains
IANUA
CYPRIUS
Mt. Nofri Sai
UMBRA
West River Basin
Leviathan's Domain
TALIA
FUN CITY
East River Basin
South River Basin
ATLANTIS
the Demon Realm

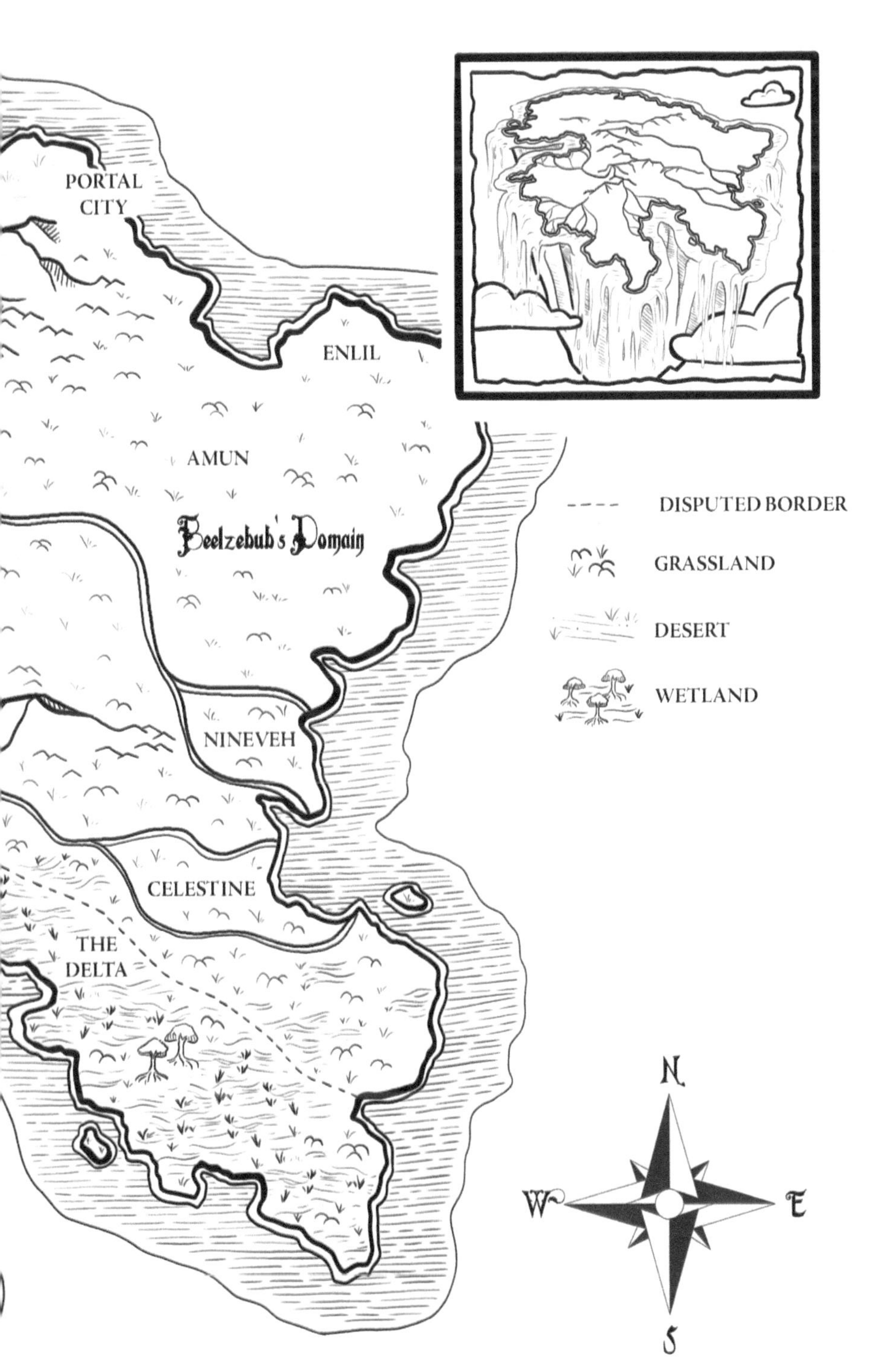
PORTAL CITY
ENLIL
AMUN
Beelzebub's Domain
NINEVEH
CELESTINE
THE DELTA
DISPUTED BORDER
GRASSLAND
DESERT
WETLAND
N
W
E
S

# Chapter 1

Ava stretched out as she stood. She had been sitting awake all night to make sure her mother was safe. Within her parents' bed chamber lay a king size, four post-bed in which her mother slept. Long, flowy drapes lined the bed as the morning sunrise peeked through the windows. Elizabeth slept peacefully but she would need to eat. Ava grabbed her dagger before quietly leaving the room. Down she ventured to the kitchen, only to find her parents' long-time servant, Kinsley.

"Oh!" he crowed. "Good morning, lost princess."

Ava grinned. Kinsley was the oldest angel she knew. He had been with the family for years, from when her father was young. Kinsley's white hair was slicked back and his sleeves were rolled up while he cooked. She grinned at the adorable apron he donned. It was a green apron with a badly drawn orange flower in the middle and one of the first pieces of clothing she had made as a child.

"After all these years you still kept this old apron." Ava chuckled as she joined him at the island countertop.

"Of course!" Kinsley replied, sincerity shining in his eyes. "This is the first time in many years I have been able to take it out of the closet. So help me Trinity I will never take it off again!"

"What?" Ava furrowed her brow, "Why would—"

Her sentence fell off as she slowly realized the gravity of his words. Tears and shame welled up within her. How arrogant of her to walk in here as if nothing had changed! Ava turned to Kinsley with an apology ready.

"Now, now. Don't you do that, princess," Kinsley chided her.

Tears continued to well up in her eyes, threatening to pour over. He came over and cupped both hands around her face tenderly.

"None of that regret or shame in here, princess," he continued.

"Your mother had a hard time seeing this apron after you were gone, and none of us blamed her." His old, dark hazel eyes gleamed. "No one in this house or city blames you either, you understand?"

A single tear spilled over, but Ava nodded.

"That is the past anyhow," He gently released her and went back to chopping. "Now I am proud to wear this apron and to have you back in this kitchen. I will not take this moment for granted like before, and neither should you."

Ava nodded once more as she wiped the tears from her face, sniffling. Kinsley silently passed her a tissue, before moving onto the next vegetable to chop up.

"Ok," Ava said determinedly. "How can I help? Mother will be up and hungry soon."

"Can you get started on some dough, dearie?" He inclined his head behind him. "I want to make you and your mother's favorite cookies, qullupu."

"Oh," Ava replied softly as a smile bloomed on her face. "I haven't had them in such a long time."

"I am almost finished with cutting up the dates. Once these cookies are done, I was gonna try to find a recipe that your…uh…Michael friend would like." He pursed his lips in concentration. "It is hard to get a read on that fellow."

Ava chuckled. She gathered all the ingredients she needed for the dough. She grabbed her spices, flour, milk, and butter to start to work.

"Most Michael angels are. They are a very…..stoic bunch I would say," she mused.

"Did you enjoy living amongst them and their…strange ways?"

Ava added all her wet and dry ingredients together and began to knead the dough.

"It was…" She trailed off as she thought back to those early years in the mountains. "It was quite a culture shock. I felt quite like a fish out of water, and very uncomfortable for many weeks when I first arrived. Looking back at it now though, I wouldn't trade that experience and growth for anything in the world. So overall yes, I do enjoy living with the Michael clan."

"My lady," a deep voice murmured to her left.

She looked up to see Atticus, the general who accompanied her home. He hunched his whole body over the door frame and barely fit in the kitchen. He wore his black and indigo uniform with all of his weapons on display. He had insisted upon staying on guard duty outside since they had arrived days ago, despite her pleas. She finally relented the last few days because he said the house was too small for him. Now, seeing him ducking into the kitchen, she saw how right he was.

"Welcome, Atticus," Ava greeted as she finished creating the cookies. They were now ready for the oven. "What's brought you in?" she asked, wiping her hands.

"A message came from your husband," he replied softly.

Ava froze.

"It is about the heirs." His voice took on a tone of concern. "It is about your children, my lady."

*Weeks earlier….*

A gentle breeze blew across the beautiful sand dunes, creating strings of dust along the wind. As Ben sat in the private desert garden of his family's estate, he practiced. He relaxed with his eyes closed in the sand, with his own thoughts and feelings, along with a few others. After another few minutes, Ben smacked at the sand in frustration.

"Couldn't even hear me coming, could ya?" A familiar voice called his attention.

Ben turned his head to see his older brother Canaan. His stocky frame showed despite his loose-fitting white tunic. Ben noticed his brow was glistening with sweat as he approached.

*He must've been training too, Ben thought absentmindedly.*

"Not training no. I just got back from my trip," Canaan replied to his thoughts. Ben tried hard to mask his jealousy, but nothing could be hidden in this family.

"I came out here to get some training in. Alone," Ben said as he turned away from his brother.

He closed his eyes again and tried to concentrate. He could hear the sand shift as his brother came closer to him. He attempted to ignore him and focus on the other occupants of the house, the staff scurrying around the kitchen and laundry room.

A finger tapped on his forehead, startling him out of his concentration. Canaan sat in front of him cross-legged with an annoying grin.

"Come on, little bean." He tapped his fingers on Ben's head again. Ben clenched his jaw as he jerked his head away.

"Focus on me," Canaan continued undeterred. "I am closer by. See what you can hear."

Ben groaned but gave a reluctant nod. He focused on just his brother, trying to sense what he was thinking and feeling. He felt the familiar aura his brother carried around him. It was a soft blue color and reminded him of the vastness of the sky. However right now, he sensed his brother was tentative yet determined.

Ben fixated harder to find the thoughts that explained his feelings. Listening to someone's thoughts was like concentrating on the sound of white noise. There was a mess of noise, but within it all there was a message to be found, and that message was the person's thoughts. Many Selaphiel angels were able to tune out all the unnecessary noise, but Ben struggled.

He closed his eyes to help him focus. His brother's blue aura stayed the same, but a new sound came forward, out of the noise.

*Silva...summit meeting...alliance with...Raphael...*

The white noise shrouded again as Ben released his concentration. He exhaled deeply.

"An alliance with Elijah." Ben furrowed his brow at his brother. "The Raphael family is not my first choice of a powerful family alliance. Plus, we have bigger problems to deal with. The demons are still spreading up from the south."

Another thump on his forehead from his brother.

"Ah!" Ben rubbed the offended spot, "Enough Canaan! You're gonna leave a mark."

"You talk too much, little bean," Canaan leaned back on his hands and regarded him with a shrewd expression. "The Michael family joined the summit meeting."

That caught Ben's attention.

"Oh?" he inquired. "How did it go?" Ambition got the better of him.

The Michael family had hidden themselves away for close to twenty years. Now they had ventured out of their mountains to talk with the other clans.

Canaan grinned as he squinted against the sun. At least he would get more details from Canaan compared to Amos.

"It went about how you'd expect," Canaan drawled. Ben resisted the urge to roll his eyes. Canaan always liked to tease the information he knew over him, ever since they were little. Like a carrot dangling above his head.

His brother raised an eyebrow at him, mockingly. Ben gritted his teeth together, frustrated. He took a deep breath to calm down before searching for the answer in Canaan's mind. Sweat dripped down the sides of his face as he concentrated.

*Elijah wants help in securing one of Mikael's heirs away. Specifically his daughter, Canaan thought. He's so bent on 'getting his family back' he's even willing to give some dominion over Silva.*

Ben turned his face away so his brother couldn't see the fire burning in his eyes.

*Power! True power over not just Silva, but if I can trick that sheltered little brat into marrying me, I'll have sway in Belli Causa too!* Ben's mind swirled with all of the possibilities. He could have influential power over Arena—his birthright, Silva, and Belli Causa. More than he could ever hope for if he had been born first. He'd finally have all the power he deserved.

Ben eyed Canaan suspiciously.

*Why are you telling me this?*

Something changed in Canaan's eyes for a moment. Ben tried to read his mind again, to see if he had any ulterior motives. His brother's blue aura turned a darker, sadder shade of blue.

"You have more…ambition and freedom than the rest of us." Canaan explained. He leaned forward and put his hand on his shoulder. "Reach out to Elijah…and Barmen. Learn as much as you can."

The clan's traditional goodbye. With that Canaan left, but Ben was already thinking ahead. Planning for the future. Cultivating the power he would soon have.

# Chapter 2

*Present day....*

The sound of the crashing waves used to soothe Ben. Now, the sound irked him as he paced around the enclosed room. The air tasted salty as the ocean breeze floated through the balcony. The space was within a coastal villa in the Elemental region, just outside of the capital ruins. The building was made up of smoothed granite and rhyolite minerals. Constructed from a reddish rock, the building stood out along the green foliage. The back of the villa lined along a coastal cliff, thus the endless symphony of waves was inescapable.

Ben slumped into the chair beside Atarah's bed. His light green tunic itched along his collar, irritating him more. He released a heavy sigh as he tried again to reach inside her mind for any form of conscious thought.

Nothing.

Ben rubbed his face. Charlotte said that all of her vitals were fine and stable. Atarah needed time to heal. He expected it would take some time for her to heal, but a day or two. Not seven days! This was with the help of an advanced healer!

Ben slowed his breathing as panic crept in. What if he hadn't been fast enough? What if he had grabbed her earlier?

When they had encountered Matthew in the human realm, it was his worst nightmare come true. Ben barely got everyone out of there in time. On that fateful day, he had managed to get all of the rangers through the portal. However, dragging an unconscious Gabriel Jr and Atarah through a closing portal physically drained him. Seeing Atarah's once again mangled body within his arms shook him.

Ben used to pride himself on his ability to control any given situation and plan around most outcomes. Ever since he had met Atarah nothing had been in his control. His hands shook as he realized that another person he loved could've been taken away from him.

He studied Atarah's sleeping face, praying to see those mesmerizing eyes again. To hear the soft melody of her voice. To sense that complex mind and beautiful purple aura. He went to her bedside and carefully sat down, worried that the slightest thing could injure her again. He leaned in close and caressed her cheek.

"Please," he whispered. "I'll work hard every day for the rest of my life to earn it, Atarah. Just please, don't leave me," he pleaded.

*Weirdo.* Clarissa's unwelcome thought came at him as she peered at him through the glass window.

So what if he was a weirdo? The only thoughts he cared about were Atarah's, which were disturbingly silent.

"What do you want, Clarissa?" Ben spoke loud enough for her to hear. He held Atarah's hand as Clarissa's thoughts turned to the night they arrived.

Clarissa Ignis and her family had been planning their capital city's rebuild when Ben came crashing through a portal onto their property. She ignited flames in her hand, ready to fight the strangers until she realized they were the rangers she had always heard about.

*What are they doing here?* she had thought. She turned to her father to ask, but his eyes were on something else. His eyes were wide in disbelief and horror. She had seen that look on his face when their city had been under siege.

She turned to see Ben, his eyes were wild, cradling Atarah's bloodied form. "Help!" Ben had screamed. "Please help!"

"Can you please not think about the past?" Ben said through gritted teeth. Clarissa blinked out of the memory.

"Oh, sorry. I forgot." Clarissa spoke in a flat tone. "Besides, I thought you had the weakest ability to read other's minds?"

She wore her light green tunic, the clan colors, with her clan's insignia on the upper right shoulder. She walked further into the room and kicked one of the round chairs out to sit in. She plopped down and crossed her arms to assess him.

While the room was not massive, it wasn't small either. Within the room centered a large bed Atarah slept in and a small table right next to the outdoor patio facing the ocean. The chairs consisted of woven fabric and wool that sank when sat on. More for lounging than sitting upright. Despite Ben pulling the curtains shut, the sheer curtains did little to dampen the room. Only his mood stayed dark in this room.

"My brothers can hear other people's minds. Reading is deciphering others' emotions. These are two different things. Some memories are easier to see, especially if the memory is shared," Ben explained.

He didn't bother explaining that his ability to read people strengthened when Atarah was by his side. Something about her brought out the best in him because he wanted to be better.

"Well it was quite a scare when all of you just showed up out of nowhere," Clarissa continued. Her dulled thoughts pulled his attention just as much as the waves outside.

*Flynn...Father...and injured...Gabriel...*

"What has changed?" He sighed. Her thoughts were another puzzle piece to solve.

"Well..." Clarissa hesitated. She glanced at Atarah as orange clouds of uncertainty surrounded her.

"I am not the best mind reader but.." Ben pinched the bridge of his nose. "Spit out whatever the bad news you need to tell me."

"And I thought I had a short fuse," Clarissa scoffed. "With Gabriel still recovering from Matthew's attack, Flynn has been up my father's ass about sending messages back to Luke and the others about what you have discovered."

*Ah, yes,* Ben thought.

The first night, Flynn had been frantic about sending messages to all of the Head Archs, especially Gabriel Sr, about the experimentation Matthew had done on his people. It was still unclear how many soldiers were missing and how many potions he had to travel the realms. Over the last few days, Malachi and Flynn had been sending messages out while the rest of the rangers aided in the city's rebuilding. Several of the rangers were from the Elementa region, including Flynn.

Ben raised his eyebrow in a silent question. The reports should have gone out by now, what had changed?

"Flynn wants Gabriel Sr to come to the villa and transport the rangers back to the human realm." Clarissa continued. "Fine by me to be honest. Those rangers have no real etiquette or appreciation for culture." She frowned slightly.

The angels of Elementa were the ones with no real appreciation, Ben thought.

True, the rangers were not as embracing of the social order in the Spirit realm, but they still helped rebuild several buildings while stuck here. Ben wanted to roll his eyes at such snobbish behavior but resisted. Atarah needed someone better than that.

"I wanted to come and tell you in case you had somewhere you needed to go…" Clarissa trailed off.

In the past week, Ben hadn't left Atarah's side. Not once. When he had to wash up and change clothes he had done so from the adjacent bathroom. Close by in case she woke up. Tempted to say no, Ben mused over the option.

He still hadn't told anyone he had gotten a look into Matthew's mind. Not the rangers, Malachi, or even Gabriel Jr. The only person who knew was Atarah, and he didn't divulge everything. He brought Atarah's cold hands to his lips.

The vague look into Matthew's mind told him enough. Though Matthew went after Gabriel and took Arick, that monster had plans for Atarah and Charlotte. When listening to his mind, Matthew believed he was doing what was best for all of the realms. That was worrisome. For many people could die from those "good intentions," including Atarah.

Ben feared not for his own life anymore, but for Atarah's. Twice now, her life was nearly forfeited because he hadn't done enough. Maybe he needed to take advantage of this opportunity. He needed to start thinking ahead instead of reacting. He would make a plan to keep Atarah safe.

What were his options? Who were the puzzle pieces he could move? People were just chess pieces, and he needed to know who could be moved or manipulated.

Clarissa shuddered.

"This is why I never trusted you. You get that glazed over look in your eye from time to time, and it freaks me out," she said.

He knew what she thought of him. From the first day they met, he had an idea of how suspicious she grew but he didn't care. You were either an angel he could use or an angel that was in his way. That was the way it had always been before Atarah came into his life. Instead of building an empire for himself, he would create one for Atarah. He never understood why rulers wanted to build an empire for anyone other than themselves until now.

What could he do now for that goal? Sitting here for the past week hadn't helped either of them. If anything, his anxiety worsened. The big pieces were the Head Archs and beneath that were the heirs. With the threat from Matthew, he needed leverage from the demon realm. A new playing field.

Ben's eyes widened as a plan formed in his head. He stood up abruptly, startling Clarissa.

"I do need to speak with Gabriel Sr. I have a place I need to go." Ben told a wide-eyed Clarissa.

"If that's the case, let me go with you," a voice said from the door.

Ben and Clarissa turned to see an exhausted-looking Charlotte. She wore a darker green tunic with blue decorative accents that made her hazel eyes stand out more. She walked further into the room.

"I can help—" she started but Ben cut her off.

"No," he said with a sharp tone. "You're needed here to ensure Atarah gets better."

"And Gabriel," Clarissa chimed in.

"Him too," Ben agreed. He had nearly forgotten about Gabriel Jr., who had woken up the other day. A very good sign for the heir, but Atarah needed looking after.

"You can't go by yourself though," Charlotte murmured. Her eyes shined with worry. Ben gave a small grin at the heir to the Raphael clan. Her concern and gentle nature made him understand why so many people liked Charlotte.

"It will be all right, Charlotte," Ben said to comfort her. He worked better alone.

"That's right; it will be all good. Especially because Isabella and I will be with him," Clarissa said as she walked over to Charlotte. She put her arm and wings around Charlotte.

"We'll make sure he doesn't do anything too stupid," Clarissa said to reassure, but it irked Ben.

"Actually Clarissa, I—" Ben was cut off.

"That's a great idea." Isabella came in behind Charlotte. She wore dark green riding pants with boots covered in mud. Her light blue tunic was covered in mud as well from her day's work.

"Neither of you know where I want to go," Ben protested. He concentrated on their minds for a moment. Why did they have a sudden interest?

*I saw the wheels... turning in that head... He has a plan...* Clarissa had a purple aura of caution shrouding her, while Isabella had a rich blue aura of trust. Isabella was following along with whatever her older sister said.

*Great,* Ben groaned in his mind while his face remained passive.

*Two fleas trying to hitch a ride. No matter. I can make use of anything,* he thought as the girls chatted to themselves. He glanced back to Atarah's sleeping form. He would do whatever it took to keep her safe.

Amos panted as he ran around his city. The weight of responsibility thundered in each step he took as he made his perimeter run. His throat burned from the dust and salt kicked up in the air from his jog, but he refused to stop. Morning was still far away and most of the city's residents slept. Perfect for him. The millions of thoughts that swarmed his mind dwindled down to a few thousand. At night was when he was able to get most of his work done. No one disturbed him with their thoughts, intentions, or auras. The early morning to late night brought him the most peace.

A few more hours before the chaos of the morning.

Amos jogged past the south gate, still in the mix of reconstruction. His wings tightened as he kept his gaze forward. Avoiding the spot where his parents died. His fist clenched. No, he reprimanded himself. *Emotions will do you no good. Relax,* he commanded his body.

He had enough emotions to deal with once everyone in the city woke up. He launched himself into the sky. A sandy breeze from the surrounding desert greeted him. His sore back muscles protested as he flew higher. He had flown around the city every night since his parents died, and he exhausted his body and mind.

*When Elijah comes back north, I'll ask him to fix up my back,* he thought as he surveyed the city. The south side of the city needed repairs while the north side could use more cleaning up. The checklist of what had to be done grew in his head as he veered to the west side of the city. The Uriel refugees lived in the north and west side of the city, which came with its own challenges. He needed to replenish the food storage too. The extra mouths to feed took a bigger chunk out of the food reserves than expected.

Amos landed softly next to one of the west neighborhood water fountains. He sighed as he gathered a floating bucket from the fountain. The young angel from the bakery down the street forgot her water container again. The angel, barely past thirteen years, lost her mother during the serpent's attack on the south gate. Overwhelmed, she worked extra shifts to help her aging father. Amos heard the father's despairing thoughts every morning when the old angel realized his wife no longer slept beside him. Along with the stressed thoughts of the daughter. From the distance of Selaphiel's house, Amos heard every citizen's thoughts.

He placed the bucket on their porch before turning to his next task. The family a block down took in nearly a dozen Uriel angels when the siege happened. They had been generous in helping the other angels, but taking in all of the refugees, their pantry was nearly empty. They stayed silent about their struggle for food, but Amos heard the worried thoughts of the wife.

He grabbed the dried meat and bread loaf he packed before his run from his little satchel. He took the wrapped up food and placed it on their window sill. He knew they opened the curtains every morning, so they would see it soon.

He knelt by the fountain, staring at his reflection. His mind empty yet roaring at the same time. He dunked his head in the water, completely submerging it. The cool feeling of the water calmed him for a few seconds. *A few precious seconds is all I need,* he thought. He lifted his head out and shook violently.

*Ok, now for what comes next.*

Once Canaan came back home with his intel, he could move forward with his plan. In the meantime, he needed to get that young brat of a baby brother back in the city. Why did the youngest have to be so irritating yet useful? He could use Ben's eye for political strategy now.

He had sent message after message to Malachi to send Ben back to Chrysi Poli but received no answer. Matthew revealed part of his plan, but Amos craved to know his real goal. Once he knew what someone wanted most in the world, it was easy to figure out their next steps without having to read their mind. He needed to know what Matthew was after. He had sent Canaan as a spy into the demon realm to try to get such knowledge.

Unfortunately, Canaan went into the demon realm before Amos knew of Matthew's experimentation. He prayed his brother was all right. Canaan was the most sensitive out of them all. He could pick up other's intentions very well; he would be safe. Ben, on the other hand, had Amos worried. Ben was power hungry. His youngest brother was too smart for his own good and too stubborn to learn from his mistakes. But his behavior had changed.

His little runt of a brother sounded concerned in his thoughts the last time Amos had been around him. He debated about going over to Aquam Caput himself but knew he couldn't.

Amos launched himself back into the air. He pivoted toward his home, to his office. The wind chilled his damp head as he maneuvered around tall buildings. He needed to keep a cool, level head because he couldn't afford otherwise. He landed upon the steps of his home, listening to see if anyone was around him before entering. A late night conversation was the last thing he wanted.

The closest thought came from the kitchen staff in the basement of the house, preparing for breakfast. One house servant remained awake but not near his study. Good. He didn't want to be disturbed.

He dashed into his office. Everything on his desk had a place. Everything was neat and organized, just how he preferred. He opened his realm map and pulled up his reports. All of the moving pieces to be considered. Mikael and Elijah were in the Coal mountains, hunting down the Abaddon. Joshua and Malachi rebuilt their cities from the destruction. *Gabriel Sr…ahh,* Amos pondered. Gabriel Sr was traveling to Aquam Caput to take trapped rangers back to the human realm. The Head Arch of Launa would be close to his astute little brother. Amos grimaced.

While he didn't know what Ben's plan was, he had to trust it would be in the interest of Chrysi Poli. He drafted three letters. One to Gabriel Sr, another to Sewall, and a third to Joshua. He wanted to cover all of his bases if his plan was to work. He needed to hear from Canaan soon or else this plan would go up in smoke.

*I need to keep moving.*

# Chapter 3

*"Get up!"*

Metal scraped against metal close by in a slow methodical rhythm. Grunts and groans could be heard closer. Off in the distance, high-pitched screams rang out. Gravity pressed down heavier on Arick's body as he tried to pry open an eye.

*"Get up, you fool!"*

That voice sounded off again. Arick groaned as he tried to rouse himself. Pain laced up and down both of his arms so intensely, he debated knocking himself out again. His entire body hurt but his arms were the worst. He peered through one swollen eye to get a hold of his surroundings. Darkness greeted him first before light from a small slit underneath a door poked through.

A stale and musty scent drifted through his nose. His body slumped along a hard, bumpy surface. He shivered as he attempted to stretch his legs. His feet knocked against solid rock as he squirmed. He heard the jingle of keys and slamming irons somewhere on the other side of the door. If he had to guess, he lay within a cell, based on the pleading cries echoing outside.

A cell made up of a strange black stone, consuming all the light that emanated from a small square hole on the ground. He tried to lift himself up into a seated position and regretted it. Pain so strong gripped him, he could do nothing but struggle to breathe.

*Hell, even breathing hurts!* Arick thought, grinding his teeth.

*"Damn sure looks like it, halfling"*

There was that voice again. Arick glanced around to see if anyone was close to him. Despite the darkness, he knew he was all alone with barely enough room to stand or lie flat. His chest tightened, and his breathing became shallow as the space enclosed him.

*"You don't remember me already, kid?"* the voice scoffed, *"This is why I can't stand working with angels."*

*"Oh!"* Arick thought. *"You're that watcher fellow I made a bargain with."* Arick gritted his teeth together to keep from groaning against the pain.

*"Take it easy, kid."* The voice continued. *"You took a big beating even after you passed out, that Luciferian kept hitting you and tried to rip your arms off."*

"Ugh, my arms," Arick grunted.

Pain was too weak of a word for the state his body was in. He tested his arms again, to assess the damage. The watcher spoke the truth. His arms were not only broken but twisted around every joint. His wrists, his elbows, and his shoulders felt off.

*"This is gonna be hell to set back together,"* he thought.

*"First order of business, kid, is to set your arms straight and then get the hell out of here fast!"*

*"Wait, you never told me your name,"* Arick thought back, *"back in the desert when we made the deal."*

*"You remember that, but you forgot my entire existence, kid?"* the voice jeered. *"It is no wonder you got punched by that little Arch."*

*"Atarah! The others!"* Arick jerked up, his thoughts frantic. He moved to stand up and cried out from the pain that shot down both his arms. His chest tightened and his breathing became erratic as he tried to manage the pain. Slow, deep breathing was how Mikael taught them to work through pain. The agony, hardship, and suffering of training. Arick slowed down as he took in deep, shaky breaths.

*"Come on, kid!"* the watcher continued, *"You gotta keep quiet and set your arms straight. You DO NOT want to alert them that you're awake."*

*"What happens if I do?"*

*"I've traveled through the demon realm for centuries. It is never good to draw attention to yourself in this place."*

*"What is this place?"*

*"This is the demon realm, kid. Many parts of it are beautiful, but we are in the not so beautiful part of it. We're in a city called Ianua. It's a place where many....uh...disgruntled demons and monsters live. We need to get out of here as fast as possible."*

*"Why are you helping me?"* Arick wondered as he shifted with

caution. Moving his legs underneath him.

*"Because I am tethered to you now, fool! If you die I'll be trapped in the shell you leave behind. Now set those arms!"*

*"Aw, come on now, watcher,"* Arick thought with sarcasm, *"I thought we were friends."*

*"Don't call me watcher, kid, and we are not friends. I am simply a—"*

*"Parasite."* Arick rolled his eyes.

*"A **spirit**"* he emphasized, *"trying to get my end of the bargain. I can't do that if next time I take over, I am left with twisted noodle arms. Now fix them!"*

*"No."* Arick grinned, enjoying this distraction.

*"KID!"* The voice turned vicious.

That didn't intimidate Arick. He had grown up his whole life with far more threatening tones than the one this watcher had. Harsher consequences too.

*"I'll get to movin' if you tell me your name like you were SUPPOSED to do,"* Arick thought, grinning at the frustrated huffs coming from the watcher.

The voice sighed. *"My name is Azazel, kid. Now will you get moving!"*

*"Azazel."*

That name tickled in the back of Arick's mind. It sounded familiar.

*"Less thinking and more doing, kid!"*

*"The name is Arick, not kid,"* he thought as he turned to start on his right arm. He leaned against the jagged, stone wall to line up his shoulder first. It was out of place, so he needed to get it back in place, then move onto the elbow. He took a deep breath and braced himself. He raised his arm up with his leg and jerked forward. A loud crunch and snap resounded around the small cell as Arick bit his lips to keep from crying out.

It took a while for the nausea and faintness to go away as the pain pulsed. Once the lightheadedness faded away, Arick lined up his body to reset his other shoulder. He took a shaky breath before jerking the shoulder back in place. Another crunch resonated around his small cell as he ground his teeth against the agony. The metallic taste of blood coated his mouth. He bit too hard on his lip, and now blood pooled in his mouth.

*"Oh well,"* he thought, *"better than dead."*

With his shoulders in place, he evaluated his arms. They were in bad shape, but he could manage, as long as he didn't get into any more fights.

*"Ha!"* Azazel snorted. *"We'd be lucky if we got out of here unnoticed. Try not to make too much noise, kid. The guards will use any excuse to come in here."*

*"What more can they do to me? How much worse can it get?"* Arick scoffed. The walls closed in a little further on him.

*"You don't want to know the answer to that, kid,"* Azazel replied.

Arick ripped some of his clothing to create a makeshift brace for his arms. Focus on a task, that'll help, he thought as his heart palpitated.

*"How do you know so much about this place anyway?"* Arick questioned Azazel. For a moment Azazel was quiet. Arick wasn't sure if he was going to answer until a sigh caught his attention.

*"I've passed through here many times over the centuries,"* Azazel replied. *"It's not my favorite place in the demon realm but it has its purposes."*

*"Oh?"*

*"It's easier to jump into someone's body when their spirit has been beaten to a pulp."*

Arick frowned at his answer. *Why?* Arick thought.

*"Because a beaten body still feels better than no body at all."* Azazel sounded exasperated. *"Let's stop with the interrogation here, kid. We have more important things to focus on."*

Arick finished making braces for each elbow. It gave him room to move his arm but not enough to allow him to further injure himself.

*"You got any escape plan in mind?"* Arick thought with a smug smirk.

*"Yeah, but you're not gonna like it."*

Arick blinked, surprised. He half expected Azazel to not have a plan.

*"Whatever, kid,"* Azazel drawled. *"It involves getting the guards' attention. We draw them in. You stay crouched and low to the ground. Once they open the door, tackle them to the far wall. The guards down here are tieflings, so a Michael angel like you should have no problem knocking them out."*

Tieflings were large, horned demons with sharp teeth and cloven hooves for legs. They were lower ranked but nothing to take too lightly. Arick learned about them and a handful of other demons in his lessons growing up. This would be his first time encountering them, along with many others now.

*"What about after that?"* he thought, crouching forward.

*"Pray we don't encounter a golem,"* Azazel said sardonically.

*"What's a golem?"*

*"Not a beast to mess with,"* Azazel drawled, *"After we get out of here we need to get to Umbra City as fast as possible."*

*"What's in Umbra City?"* Arick wondered.

*"Trinity, kid!"* Azazel huffed.

*"You are literally in my head,"* Arick shot back, irate. They both released a deep breath.

*"You're right, kid,"* Azazel conceded. *"Umbra is a city at the base of the mountains. But more importantly, it has a portal and it'll be our safest ticket back to the spirit realm. It'll take a day's journey to get there."*

*"A day?!"*

*"Well, there are other portal cities, but the journeys will be longer and extremely dangerous. ALSO I just got this body. I don't want to screw it up."*

Arick wondered if he wanted to go back home. Damn, he longed for a drink.

He patted around the small enclosure for the door. He saw some light from underneath the door but no handle or hinges. He couldn't bust his way out of this door.

*"Of course, they lock from the outside,"* Azazel drawled, *"Is this your first time being locked up, kid?"*

*"How in the realm did you know?"* Arick thought sarcastically. *"You know my other cells didn't have such soft conditions as this one."*

*"All right, kid, I get it."* Azazel countered. *"Just stick to this plan. Knock on the door to get the guards attention. Stay low and tackle them to the far wall when the door opens. Then GRAB THE KEYS before running like a bat out of hell."*

*"Yeah, yeah, yeah,"* Arick replied. *"Should be a cake walk."*

Arick kicked his foot against the door a few times before yelling.

"Hey! Anybody there? I need a masseuse in here! My back's killing me!"

Arick heard the stomping of boots close in on his cell. He crouched low, ready. The guard stopped outside of his door, jiggling the keys into the lock. As soon as the lock turned, Arick moved. He pushed off with his legs and forced his way through the cell. The jagged metal shot more pain into Arick's shoulder, but he didn't let up. He burst through and tackled the guard onto the ground. His eyes strained to adjust to the new light while one of his attackers was down.

However he hadn't been prepared for another guard to be there. The second tiefling guard hammered down his club onto Arick's back without mercy. He cried out as pain shot up all through his back from the impact. Star formed along his vision as agony set in.

*"Come on kid! You gotta move fast before they call reinforcements!"* Azazel urged.

Arick swiftly kicked the tiefling guard in the knee to bring him down. Giving another grunt, he delivered another kick to the tiefling's neck, knocking him unconscious. Arick checked his surroundings for more guards as he struggled to his feet.

The corridor was lit with lanterns lining along the walls. Everything was carved from stone, leading him to think they were underground somewhere. Other cells lined the opposite wall with large locks hanging from the handles of the thick metal door. There appeared to be no one else around…at least for now.

*"Ok, grab his keys and head down that corridor,"* Azazel instructed. *"If we're lucky we'll hit the exit door."*

*"Heads up, Azazel, I am not that lucky of a guy,"* Arick thought.

Azazel sighed inside his head as Arick bent over to grab the keys off of the first guard. The plethora of rings had Arick doubting that they would be able to escape without notice.

Glancing once behind him to make sure there was no one else, he ventured down the hallway. The flames from the lanterns flickered as he walked with light steps. His dry throat and empty stomach begged for food and water, while part of his mind begged for ale. Arick shook his head.

*"One thing at a time,"* Arick reminded himself. Azazel scoffed.

Around the curved hallway, Arick slowed to a stop as the hallway split into two.

*"Left or right?"* Arick asked. Azazel came forward, from the

back corners of his mind and seemed to fill out his head. Arick felt his consciousness receding as Azazel took over his body. The sensation reminded him of falling asleep. It didn't last long though. Maybe a minute or two, before Arick surfaced himself back to a more 'awakened' state.

*"Did you just take over?"* Arick asked, bewildered.

*"Ugh,"* Azazel replied, *"Yeah, kid. You're in poor shape. Our body does not feel good to be in."* Arick received a mental impression of Azazel shuddering. *"Go right, kid. There are fewer guards that way."*

*"How could you tell?"*

*"The smell is more pungent in the left hallway versus the right,"* Azazel explained. *"Keep your knees slightly bent and be ready to perform axe kicks. That way you won't injure our arms any further."*

*"Wait,"* Arick mused. *"How do you know so much about fight moves?"*

Arick realized that Azazel had been directing him like one of his trainers back home. The reminder of home sent a sharp pain through Arick's chest.

*"No,"* he thought, *"Sanctum was never my home to begin with."* He never belonged.

*"Stop the pity party,"* Azazel scoffed, *"You're giving ME a mental headache. Once upon a time I used to be an Arch warrior. But now is not the time for a backstory, you gotta get movin,' kid."*

Arick turned right and drew his arms closer to his body. Azazel was right. He couldn't use his arms until they healed more. He widened his stance and kept his breathing even as he continued. He heard the shuffling of feet as the hallway curved. More guards were coming. He needed to immobilize them fast.

Two more tiefling guards came around the corner, each holding clubs in their hands. Luckily for Arick, they were not expecting someone around the bend, so he was able to deliver his first kick perfectly. Unluckily for him, there were two more guards behind the first guards. Two of the tiefling guards tackled him to the wall while the third lifted his club to beat Arick with it. He grunted as the club made contact with his stomach and then his head. The last contents of his stomach emptied onto the floor as the tiefling landed another blow to his stomach.

Disgusted, the tiefling jumped back, which gave him the opening he needed. Arick delivered a side kick to one of the guards holding him and then roundhouse kicked the other. Grinding his teeth against the pain, he grabbed the third guard, who had been beating him, and head butted him as hard as he could. The tiefling collapsed immediately.

A horn blared from one of the guards on the ground, sending alarm bells through his mind and the tunnels. Arick sprinted down the hall just as the guards jumped to their feet. Another sound from the horn screeched through the hallway, alerting more guards.

*"Crap, crap, crap crap!"*

The sound of stomping feet echoed around him. He heard guards shouting in a rough language. Arick didn't look back as he ran. Anytime he came to a turn, he simply chose the hallway that was quieter. Less boot stomping.

*"Keep going, kid! I think you're almost out!"* Azazel encouraged.

Arick barely registered his words as he sprinted, adrenaline pumping through him, spurring him on. He turned down passageways at random, not slowing down to see if the tiefling guards were right behind him.

Left, right, left, right, right, left, left, right. He didn't stop or hesitate. He darted around a corner so fast he plowed right past another tiefling guard, knocking him down. Slowly, the lanterns that lined the walls spaced further and further apart, limiting visibility.

After a while, the tunnels darkened, the sound of stomping boots and guards' shouts dwindled. Arick dashed into the darker depths of the tunnel, not caring as the light faded. The only thing that mattered was the sound of the guards disappearing.

Arick slowed to a stop as the underground channels shrunk in size, narrowing along each side of the walls. The only sound was his heavy breathing, and his light was a small flickering lantern far behind him. Before him appeared to be nothing but a pitch dark shaft with stale air and oppressive aura. Breathing became more difficult as he stared at the small dark hole.

*"Not that way,"* Arick thought as anxiety swirled within his chest.

*"No!"* Azazel urged. *"That's the way out."*

*"HELL NO! I'd rather be clubbed to death."*

Arick choked on air. He turned away from the exit as his muscles seized up on him. Panic caused his chest to tighten while he struggled to breathe.

*"Wait kid..."* Azazel paused, *"Breathe! Breathe, dammit!"*

Arick took a gasp of air. That first glorious breath after getting the wind knocked out of you.

*"Again, breathe, kid!"*

Arick took another deep breath in. Then another. *"Focus on a task,"* he reminded himself. "It always helps to distract."

*"Hey, I got a plan, Arick."* Azazel spoke in a lower tone.

Arick paused. That was the first time he used his name.

*"Close your eyes, kid, and relax as best as you can,"* Azazel instructed. Arick closed his eyes; with each breath he attempted to relax.

*"Take three steps, Arick."* he instructed. Arick stepped forward, his legs quivering.

*"Aren't you gonna take over?"* Arick panicked. His heart flipped in his chest.

*"Not with how messed up our body is right now. Keep walking."*

He continued forward, his arms twitching by his sides with his hands clenched. The urge to push against the walls to get more space became stronger with each step.

*"Keep your arms by your sides, and relax your shoulders. Relax your jaw. Keep going, kid."*

Arick kept moving, without opening his eyes. The sound of his shuffling feet echoing against the walls was the only indication of him advancing. Soon another sound resonated in the tunnel. The sound of wind and…waves. A breeze caressed his face. As he took another deep breath, fresh air greeted his tongue. Moisture danced along his tongue as he filled his lungs.

*"All right, kid. Open your eyes."*

Arick opened his eyes to see a curved tunnel, but there was now more light. The walls widened further apart as the light grew brighter. Arick ran toward the light coming from the end of the tunnel, while his chest loosened.

Just around the corner appeared a metal gate embedded into the rocks, but on the other side of the gate was freedom. Arick gripped the gate and peered out to see a large mountain range. Tall dark, mossy trees sprinkled along the ridges of the mountains as a large river rushed just underneath the gate.

*"That river will carry us most of the way to Umbra. Once there we should be mostly safe,"* Azazel explained. *"Now get the keys and*

*unlock the gate so we can get outta here."*

The keys…

Arick looked down at his empty pockets and torn, used-to-be white shirt and found nothing. He must've dropped the keys when he knocked into that last guard.

*"Trinity, kid,"* Azazel grunted in frustration. *"Use your head! You just needed to grab ONE thing."*

Arick jiggled the gate slightly and it wiggled. Arick glanced down at the long drop into the river. He didn't have his wings from the serum the rangers gave him. He wouldn't be able to fly his way out.

*"Could you not think of all of the ways we're screwed here?"* Azazel jeered. Nonetheless, Arick got an idea from his words.

He walked back further into the tunnel until the light faded and the walls closed in. He took a deep breath and tucked his arms in close, facing the exit. He crouched into a runner's position.

*"What are you doing, kid?"* Azazel asked apprehensively.

*"I'm using my head."*

Arick charged forward, sprinting as fast as he could. He tucked his chin and slammed his injured shoulder into the gate as hard as his legs could push. The gate groaned as it ripped out of the mountain walls. Arick catapulted out of the underground prison.

Sharp pain from the impact consumed him as he fell. He vaguely heard Azazel yelling in the far reaches of his mind. However Arick welcomed oblivion as he plummeted into the water and unconsciousness.

*"You better get me a beer, Azazel."*

The streets buzzed with sounds of bargaining, haggling, and trade as the red sun dipped along the mountain horizon. Demons of all shapes and sizes walked along the streets of Umbra, becoming more alert as the night approached. Thoughts of work, chores, and gatherings swirled around Canaan, like in any crowded room he entered into. He ignored most.

Canaan walked down the streets, feigning a limp as an excuse to listen to those around him. The air weighed on his lungs, though his steps were light. The thoughts of creatures sounded like that of a symphony orchestra. Some possessed a bass-sounding mind, which was heavy and burdensome. While others were like trumpets blaring as loudly as possible.

For today, he wanted to focus on the soft thoughts of the violins, cellos, and harps. The ones with the more subtle but commanding psyche. They had careful minds because they held the most responsibility, especially for the group he was spying on.

The assimilates, followers of Matthew the Luciferian, believed that the three realms needed to come together and combine into one realm. Every day, more and more demons joined this newly formed religion, answering Matthew's call. Canaan needed to collect as much intel as he could. He knew he was staying past his return date, but he refused to miss out on more intel that could save the lives of angels back at home.

*Tomorrow,* he concluded. He would go home tomorrow.

A soft crescendo of thoughts floated to him again. Canaan inclined his head toward two demons whispering to each other along the streets. Two malphas demons sat on the other end of the alley. Malphas were raven-like demons that possessed a clever mind and great stealth. One of the demons darted his blue eyes in every direction as his round form shifted nervously. Their wings tensed at their sides. An elongated, pointed beak snapped together as the malphas spoke to its companion.

Canaan was out of earshot and out of sight, but that mattered little if he kept focus. His ability to drown out everything else was what made him an invaluable asset. Most Selaphiel angels could "focus" on what others were thinking within a few feet, whereas he heard everyone within several miles. His record for hearing a being's mind was nearly unmatched, making him one of the best spies in all of the realms. The only one who bested him was Amos, his older brother.

*There are stirrings amongst the higher ranked believers,* One of the malphas thought.

Being as far away as he was, Canaan couldn't see who was thinking, or saying, what.

*Need to inform as many as possible. We cannot let the little princeling escape before the confluence,* the malphas continued. *The Great One wants to move forward as fast as possible. We need to start the next gathering.*

Princeling? Confluence? Next gathering?

More questions than answers. This had been his routine since entering into the demon realm. A familiar muffled sound reached his ears, signaling that the malphas were now talking instead of thinking their words.

Loud trumpets of thoughts reached him, coming from the opposite direction. The local law enforcement stormed through the street, itching to find anyone to turn in to their boss. Canaan turned to see two oxen demons sauntering down the road, with their star crest uniform. Their large, armored horns glinted against the last few rays of sunlight as they searched. Dark eyes scanned the faces on the street, daring anyone to meet the challenge in their gaze. Their minds blared, eager for a fight.

*Dammit!* he thought. When those demons acted rowdy, there would be nothing to stop those bulls. The skittish malphas would dart away at any hint of conflict too. This was probably his last chance to gather vital information on the assimilates. He turned back to the malphas, hoping to squeeze out a couple more minutes.

*My unease is growing. Is anyone around us?* one of the malphas mused. *We need to find a place with fewer ears.*

Another round of muffled sounds continued. From the demon's mindset, Canaan deciphered they were planning on meeting up at another time and place, both undetermined. Another dead end at this rate! Those two police officers made them more cautious.

The malphas' mind turned to thoughts of flight, dashing all of Canaan's hopes. While the thundering bulls stomped his way, Canaan saw his disguised face flash through one of their minds.

*Not good.*

He hunched over more and limped away. He needed to blend into the crowd, keep attention off himself. He pulled his brown hood over his head and leaned more heavily on his wooden cane.

Canaan hobbled past a corner to get further out of sight. He needed to find cover if he was to avoid their attention. At the far end of the street, an old rickety bar with few lights on caught his eye. Upon hearing the creatures in the bar, Canaan knew it was open. Run-down but open. He walked as quickly as he could, escaping from the boisterous thoughts of the guards.

He ducked into the bar just as some poor soul outside bumped into the oxen. He heard the indignation from the guards followed by the pleas of mercy, without the aid of his mindreading.

The bar was narrow and long with neon blue lights lining underneath each chair and bar stool. The red lights lined the backside of the liquor cabinets, leaving his vision poor. It didn't matter to him.

He shuffled over to an open chair at the long wooden bar. A large hunched over figure appeared to be unconscious and lying in his own drool. Canaan sat down. A small, bony imp trudged over to him. His over-sized, pointed ears and bat-like wings twitched every now and then as he regarded Canaan.

"Order?" Its voice was surprisingly high-pitched. Both the voice and thoughts sounded like cymbals clashing to Canaan.

"One ale, ple—" he ordered. "One ale."

He almost forgot that demons in the city disliked pleasantries. The imp flapped away, its thoughts on warming his drink, for the sake of messing with him. He didn't care. His thoughts traveled back to the malphas who were now well out of his range of hearing. He held his hands over his ears, as he gathered his thoughts.

*Princeling? Is there a new player in this game of war we have yet to meet?* he wondered. He needed to tell Amos of this when he got back. He had gathered quite a bit for now at least. The religion of assimilation was a relatively new one in the demon realm. Within the demon realm, three domains stood, each ruled under a different demon lord. The three lords: Beelzebub, Leviathan, and Satan; separated by the Decimate mountains. However, the lords fought with one another over border land placement and resources.

While the assimilates were confirmed within the demon lord Beelzebub's domain, Canaan didn't doubt that Matthew recruited in other places. He underestimated how huge the demon realm stretched. All of the spirit realm could fit within one of the domains alone.

Not every demon wanted to leave their realm. In fact many demons lived peaceful lives…as long as they remained unbothered. From his travels within Beelzebub's region, he noted that many demons wished to be left alone.

To have a new religion spread so fast was alarming, especially one that called for the unification of every realm. During his time here, he infiltrated one of the 'gatherings' of assimilates to see their recruitment strategy. They preached that a confluence of the realms would stop discrimination and hatred of demons and increase prosperity for all. If humans, angels, and demons knew and acknowledged each other, there would be no more killing, fighting, or economic hardship. They further proclaimed that doubters and naysayers held back the demon race, inhibiting growth and change.

All in all, Canaan understood the appeal this new religion brought to these demons. He heard the symphony of approval from the crowd. He saw the years of hard taxation from the demon lords, soldier drafts for more battles, and discrimination flash throughout all of their memories. The demons in the crowd were eager for a change, but outside of those rallies, Canaan heard a hesitancy in their voices. The shouts from the rallies turned into whispers between neighbors as the spread of the messages traveled.

A clash of cymbal-thoughts drew his attention, as the bartender returned.

"Here." the imp grunted.

He looked up to see the imp setting down a wooden cup with steam blowing up. Canaan wanted to groan at his warm ale but flipped a coin to the imp instead. He knew the imp wanted a reaction. He refused to give it.

"Iiifff, you're not gonna drink that…" Burp. "I'll take it," a deep voice drawled.

Canaan turned to see the hunched over figure had awakened. He looked up to see a severely battered face. An eye appeared swollen; a busted lip and a few gashes across his forehead, chin and cheek had only just closed. One golden eye looked at him questioningly and then back at the cup.

Canaan gave a simple nod and nudged the drink toward him.

The large male leaned forward with his head and bit the side of the cup. Tipping his head back, he gulped down the contents of the drink, undeterred by the warm temperature. Canaan looked down at his body which appeared to be just as bad as his face. His arms hung loosely bound to his torso, bloody. Bruises were painted all over this poor soul's body.

*What happened to him?*

Canaan glanced away as he focused into the stranger's mind, out of curiosity. Once he was inside, he almost fell out of his chair. The sonorous sounds of a cello with the bright sounds of a piano met his ears. Both were out of tune and out of sync with each other, creating a very off-putting sound. Canaan wanted to cover his ears at the chaos within his mind. As the stranger finished his drink, Canaan listened as the sounds of his mind grew dull.

*"Come on, kid! Let's get moving! I got you a beer. Now, let's get to that portal and get back to the spirit realm!"* a deep voice yelled.

*"Yeah, yeah,"* a younger sounding voice answered. *"Don't get your wings in a bind old man. The spirit realm will still be there tomorrow but when's the next chance to see the demon realm, eh?"*

*"Kid, that Luciferian is after you. There are eyes and ears everywhere in the demon realm. The safest place to be for both of us is the spirit realm."*

Canaan stiffened in his chair. The Luciferian was after him? Why? He peeked back at the mystery male. Canaan didn't recognize him. The stranger bore no wings, but mentioned them earlier. Did the stranger secretly have wings? Was he an angel or Arch?

*"What does it matter?"* the younger voice drawled. *"Safety is an illusion anyway. I mean...look at me...Everything I thought was safe... well it doesn't matter anymore...Let's find some river basin wine. The bar keeper said the best alcohol is in Leviathan's region."*

*"It's domains, not regions. And NO! We are not going exploring in the demon realm."*

*"Why not? It's not like there's anything special in the spirit realm?"*

The deeper voice sighed. *"I should've never given you alcohol."*

The large male appeared to chuckle a little.

*"Alcohol makes the daddy issues go away though."* The younger voice dripped with sarcasm.

*"Trinity, help me,"* the deeper voice murmured. *"Come on, kid. Let's head back to Sanctum. Then we'll—"*

*"Nope."* The 'kid' interrupted.

*"What about your sister?"* the voice pleaded. *"What's her name?"*

*"Oh yeah,"* A small grimace flashed across his battered face. *"Little cricket...At least she would drink with me."*

*"Yeah, I would want a drink too after the beating she got."*

The male visibly flinched. *"At least she got away."* His voice sounded quieter now. *"That's what matters."*

Canaan turned his head toward the male's profile. What was his role in all this?

*"Kid..."* the voice said reproachfully.

*"Okay, okay."* The 'kid' said, *"We'll head back to the spirit realm, but why do I have to be conscious to do it?"*

*"I'm the one that got us here from Ianua; now it's your turn to take over this messed up body. I signed up for a healthy, HEALED body when we did our bargain, kid."*

*"Oh yeah, thinking about our deal. How exactly are you supposed to help us against the Luciferian?"*

*"I can forage some weapons and teach whoever is willing to learn how to take down a luciferian... You weren't too bad yourself when you fought him, just lazy and sloppy in your fighting technique."*

The male scoffed.

*"I'd like to see you take him on next,"* the 'kid' replied.

*"Hey, kid..."*

*"Yeah?"*

*"Why is that male staring at you? He seems suspicious,"* the voice said, *"Get ready to fight again."*

The groan was almost audible. Canaan held up his hands.

"Do not worry. I am not here to hurt you." Canaan told the strange male.

*"Obviously"* the 'kid' thought, *"Like he could actually do damage."*

*"Don't get too arrogant, kid. Looks can be deceiving."*

"What is your name?" Canaan asked, leaning closer. He needed to know who 'they' were? What luck to stumble upon them!

"Um…" the male drawled.

*"Don't tell him your real name!"* The older voice commanded.

*"What about your name?"*

*"Definitely not!"*

Canaan listened to him struggle to come up with whatever name came first. The overall atmosphere of the stranger's mind was chaotic but kind-natured. He might come in handy with some much needed intel. Canaan decided to take a leap of faith. He scanned their surrounding area to ensure no one was around them.

He leaned forward and dropped his voice to a whisper.

"My name is Canaan Doctrina of the Selaphiel clan."

He watched the stranger's face transform from apprehension to relief.

*"Oh, he must be one of Ben's brothers,"* the 'kid' said. He knew Ben? How? Had they met?

*"He's an Arch Selaphiel?!?"*

Canaan grinned before giving a nod.

*"Great! He's been listening to us this whole time!"*

*"It's not so bad. After all he's on our side."*

Canaan shrugged as he whispered, "Forgive me for intruding, I have heard most of it. However I still haven't caught your names." Canaan struggled to remember who this Arch might be. With the golden eyes, a Michael angel, maybe?

"Oh," the male verbally spoke, "My name is—"

*"Whisper, dammit!"*

The large male rolled his one open eye. "My name is Arick Viribus, of the Michael clan," he whispered. "And inside me is Azazel, a watcher I made a deal with."

Canaan barely kept his face impassive. A watcher?! Not just any watcher at that but Azazel, the Azazel from their history textbooks. The one responsible for so many deaths of angels and humans. Why was the next ruler of Belli Causa being possessed by one of the worst watchers in all of their history? Why was Arick in the demon realm? Canaan met Atarah before departing for this mission but never Arick. Canaan remembered the rumors and gossip about the young Arch. A rumor of how handsome Arick was surfaced in his mind, but seeing this battered face he never would have guessed it was the Michael heir.

Canaan peered around as he heard the chimes of some curious looks their way. Not good. They needed to find a place where no one could overhear them.

"We need to find a place more private," Canaan whispered. "I have many questions to ask you."

"First time another male has asked me to leave with him from a bar," Arick said facetiously. "I have to say I am very flattered."

Canaan gave a small grin. He had heard rumors that Arick was a jokester too.

*"I should have insisted upon getting a Gabriel body instead,"* Azazel sighed from Arick's mind.

They both stood up from the bar. Arick moved stiffly but didn't utter any sounds of discomfort. Canaan shuffled toward the door he had entered, listening to any thought that concerned them. The imp made note of them leaving together, inwardly giggling at his prank of adding an aphrodisiac drug into his drink at the last minute.

Canaan coughed into his elbow to hide his smile. Arick looked down with a quirked eyebrow in a silent question. Canaan shook his head. No need to tell Arick he had been unintentionally drugged. Or that the barkeeper thought he was gay.

The hard part of being a Selaphiel angel was learning how to focus and listen for the silence. The absence of sound and thought as a way to tell if people were not around. This could be tricky because some creatures knew how to quiet their mind. He continued his limp out the door, taking his time so he could concentrate. They veered right down another street.

There were fewer demons walking along this street and, mercifully, no police patrolling. The moons shined bright tonight, lighting their way down the cobblestone street. Canaan hobbled down several streets, listening as closely as possible for any sentient beings. The roads leading away from the town's center gradually became steeper until they reached the stairs.

Stair pathways were carved in many directions from the mountains leading into town and roads. The stairs led into trails, leaving the city of Ianua and going into the mountains. Canaan wanted to get away enough so no one else was around. They reached the base of one staircase before Canaan relaxed. He heard no one except Arick and Azazel's thoughts.

"Now then," Canaan straightened up his posture and removed his hood. "When and how did you get here, Arick?"

Arick remained hunched over in pain and still towered over Canaan. Closer now, he saw the tattered remains of a shirt paired with shorts that reached a little above his knee. Canaan wondered if Arick was cold in these mountain temperatures.

"Well," Arick slurred slightly, "It is a long story."

Canaan noticed that he was swaying slightly side-to-side, not in pain but drunkenness. He had been so captivated by his thoughts he had forgotten the physical affect the alcohol would have on him. Canaan guessed he must've been drinking at the bar for a while before he had arrived.

What could have beaten down the heir of the Michael clan so

badly? Arick towered over most creatures and had the strength to compare. Mikael, his father, was a possibility but Canaan couldn't fathom why. He remembered his brush with Mikael before he had left on his mission two weeks ago.

Mikael and Elijah had stopped by their home in Chrysi Poli to track down an Abaddon. Both Head Archs' heads were filled with love and concern for their family. He thought back to what he had gleaned from them, but he only paid attention to the overall gist of their mind, not the details. He figured he could get the details later from Amos. Now, he regretted not digging deeper.

"First of alll…" Arick garbled, "I wa…was in the hummmaann realm and then…" Arick paused to hiccup. "Then…some purple-headed…seeker came along." Arick burped. "Ummmmm…then…" Arick furrowed his brow as if struggling to form the words. "I got beat up by…"

Canaan peeked inside his mind to speed up the process but was met with thoughts from Azazel.

*"Come on! Pull yourself together kid!"* Azazel chided.

*"I didn't realize how hard it is to talk until just now,"* Arick snapped back. *"Woah...my head is a genius, but my body is a dumbass."*

Azazel groaned. *"You're never getting another beer from me."*

*"We can switch anytime you like."* Arick quirked his eyebrow up and chuckled.

*"Your body feels like crap right now. Thought I would puke our guts out climbing the mountains."*

"Focus please," Canaan pleaded. "Just think about the events that led up to you coming to the demon realm."

*"Oh right,"* Arick mused.

Canaan became flooded with memories from both Arick and Azazel. So many flowed all around him, it took time for him to focus. He flashed through Arick's memories. His arrival in New York City with three other angels, looking for Charlotte and Atarah. Finding the rangers and being transported to the Mojave desert. The rangers 'recruiting' all of them to help against the Luciferian.

The plan was to strike a deal with a watcher in exchange for information. This was where the memories diverged between Arick's and Azazel's.

From Azazel's account, he remembered the impression Arick gave him. An angel that asked for his name out of heartfelt curiosity, which warmed his spirit. For the first time in so many centuries, Azazel connected to something. Connected to what? He was unsure but happy to be connected. After being in formless agony, that sense of touch was like feeling sunshine for the first time in thousands of years.

*"I'm not used to others being able to read my mind. When you're formless, no one can read you,"* Azazel told Canaan.

"What happened afterward?" Canaan pressed.

*"Matthew showed up,"* they thought at the same time.

The leader of the assimilates, the Luciferian, Matthew. Why did he appear before them in the human world?

*"I told this to the rangers, and I can tell this to you as well,"* Azazel continued. *"Matthew has been using a strange black serum to transport through the realms at will."*

*"The serum is made from Gabriel angels he's been experimenting on,"* Arick added. *"I remember that much before he beat the crap out of me. He was going after Gabriel Jr."*

*"He was after you too, kid,"* Azazel said.

Arick scoffed. "I don't w—wa" hiccup, "wanna talk about that," he drawled. The last image was from Arick holding Matthew down while Ben dragged a limp Atarah and Gabriel through a fast closing portal.

Canaan pursed his lips as he tried to draw everything together, all the information he gathered here along with what occurred in the human realm. Ben must've gotten Gabriel Jr and everyone else to a safe location. Hopefully? If Matthew could travel through the realms at will, no place was truly safe.

Also if Matthew was taking Gabriel angels and experimenting on them, where was he holding them? Canaan regarded Arick. While his arms were not in good shape, his wrists didn't appear to have been tightly bound together. He must've been held somewhere with a cell if they thought his arms didn't need to be tied.

*"After that we were transported to a jail cell in Ianua,"* Arick finished.

Ianua! Canaan thought. He had heard that city name from a few of the assimilates but it was not a city one could 'pass through.' How did they get out of the city?

*"Azazel knew the way out,"* Arick thought as he clumsily sat on a large stone.

He looked at Arick expectantly, waiting for Azazel's thoughts.

Oddly, the watcher kept his thoughts occupied.

"Azazel," Canaan started. "Does the word assimilates mean anything to you?"

*"Oh, that crowd,"* Azazel pondered. *"Why do you need to know? A curious Selaphiel angel like yourself hasn't figured it all out yet?"*

Canaan grinned.

"I don't know as much as I would like to know," he replied. "I'm not invisible after all."

Azazel scoffed inside Arick's head. *"Formless,"* he replied. *"Not invisible. It's very different and a lot more agonizing than being invisible."*

"Care to elaborate?"

Azazel sighed. *"From what I saw, the assimilates were a bunch of weirdos. Weirder than the rangers. They want to combine all of the realms together, which is completely insane."*

"Do you know how to get back into Ianua without detection?" Canaan asked.

*"Possibly, why?"* Azazel asked with suspicion.

Canaan didn't trust Azazel yet, especially if the stories about him were true. Azazel was given the harshest sentencing as a watcher for a reason. Canaan needed to be cautious around him.

"Why do you think? Given the spirit realms'…situation," Canaan replied.

*"You gotta give me more than that, heir,"* Azazel scoffed. *"You Selaphiel angels know way more than you let on."*

Canaan couldn't reveal everything he knew to an untrusted party. How could he get Azazel to be cooperative?

"We need to track down the Gabriel angels Matthew has been kidnapping," Canaan said with a pause. Something he already knew.

*"And you think they're somewhere in Ianua?"* Azazel said reproachfully.

"Didn't youuu…want a Gabriel body to begin with?" Arick hiccupped.

*"Eh, I still do! I thought your body would be worth the trade, but you treat it like crap!"* Azazel grumbled in Arick's mind. *"All right. I'll help you out to get in Ianua BUT be forewarned, I am not your friend, Canaan."*

Arick scoffed. "So doom and gloom, old timer."

*"When you get to be my age, everything* is *doom and gloom,"* Azazel replied.

Canaan nodded excitedly. "Thank you," he whispered.

*"Don't thank me yet. The road back to Ianua is dangerous and brutal,"* Azazel answered. *"You also need to get rid of that fake limp. Some demons love to prey on the weak."*

Canaan tossed his cane to some nearby trees.

"Done."

Azazel sighed. *"I'm gonna take over, kid, so hang tight while we do this mission."*

Arick raised his hand in salute. "Aye-aye, captain."

Arick's pupils oscillated back and forth rapidly, and his face went slack. A grave expression washed over him as Azazel took control. Canaan heard Arick's thoughts become quieter within their shared head.

"Ugh," Azazel huffed in Arick's body. "Now let's get going. As we get closer to Ianua you need to do exactly what I say or else we'll be killed. Do you understand?"

His voice sounded deeper than before.

Canaan nodded.

Azazel didn't say another word. Just turned around and started walking toward the mountains. He made it about two steps before tumbling to the ground. Canaan reached out a hand to steady him and almost buckled. He'd forgotten how heavy Michael angels were.

"Dammit, kid," Azazel whispered harshly. Their drunkenness had yet to wear off.

"Shall I go get that cane?" Canaan's lips twitched in amusement.

*"Ha ha, old timer."* Arick's thoughts drifted through.

"Shut up, the both of ya." Azazel shrugged him off before standing. He took the next few steps with no problem, but his stance widened past shoulder length, making him look ridiculous. "Come on!" Azazel called as he waddled up the trail.

Canaan bit his lip to keep from laughing. This was going to be a fun journey.

# Chapter 4

"You want to go where?" Gabriel Sr. asked with raised brows.

Ben glanced up at the Head Arch with a grim expression. Clarissa and Isabella appeared surprised as well. They all sat around Gabriel Jr.'s bed. Everyone, including the patient, regarded him as if he was insane.

"To the Court Hall in Quaesitor, please," Ben answered. Gabriel Sr. pulled his hand away from Gabriel Jr's shoulder to rub his neck.

"Yes, I can take you there," he agreed as his brow furrowed. "But I don't know how productive you will be there," he finished. *Why...go... there?*

The Head Arch's thought trickled in along with everyone else's confusion. Ben bit his tongue to keep from saying anything further. The less people knew, the less likely they'd screw up his plan.

"Oh, I nearly forgot. I don't think I can take you there," Gabriel Sr. replied.

"Why not?" Ben asked. He forced his face to remain impassive while irritation brewed within.

"Your brother has requested your presence back in Chrysi Poli," Gabriel Sr. answered. "He was quite…insistent to be frank."

Ben gritted his teeth. He had been ignoring his brother's letters. Now Amos sent someone to get him. *How annoying*, Ben thought. *I have my own plans to see through, Amos. Get some other pawn to play for you.*

"He has been sending a lot of letters to our father to send you back too," Clarissa spoke up. "It might be important for you to go see him, Ben," she suggested.

He loosened his face to ensure no one saw his frustration. The less they knew the better.

"Trust me, Gabriel," he began. "It is of utmost importance that I go to Quaesitor first. I'll go to my brother afterward, but completing this mission will help him too."

"What exactly is this 'mission?'" Gabriel Jr. asked from his bed. His head wound healed; only the faded bruise on his eyes remained. Gabriel Jr.'s thoughts swirled with genuine curiosity and the urge to go with him.

Interesting.

"I..." he began. He couldn't reveal too much about his plan nor did he want to create suspicion.

"What my job always is as a Selaphiel angel." Ben grinned. "To learn as much information as possible for my people."

"Then let me help instea—" Gabriel Jr. started.

"Absolutely not," Gabriel Sr. said in a harsh tone.

"But I—"

The father gave a stern glare at his son, stopping any further attempts.

*Son...all I have...too...danger...*

The thoughts came in bits and pieces, but Ben had an idea of how the Arch Head felt. Gabriel Jr. was his only living heir, nearly kidnapped and killed. Best not to involve too many people anyway.

"I will take you three there no problem," Gabriel Sr responded to Ben. "As long as you promise to see your brother, that is. In my old age, trust me when I say that it won't hurt anything to go see him." The Head Arch looked back at his son. "As for you, I'll be getting you home as soon as possible with extra guards posted. We still haven't recovered the fallen soldiers Matthew has taken."

Ben released a small breath as his wings relaxed. Gabriel was the only questionable part of the plan. He would find a way to Quaesitor no matter what, but the Arch taking him made his mission much easier.

"Thank you so much, sir." Ben sighed.

"Excuse me, sir." A voice drew everyone's attention. A servant wearing the lilac insignia from the Gabriel house stood at the door. "Another message has come for you. This one is urgent."

Gabriel Sr. gave a nod before standing. "The work of a Head is never done." He glanced at his son. "I'll be right back and then we'll all leave together."

The Arch Head left the room, shutting the door behind him. That was when other thoughts murmured in Ben's mind.

*Now...only...chance...escape...*

Gabriel Jr. reached out and grabbed Ben's arm.

"I need to get out of here." The heir spoke with a hushed voice and wide eyes. "Let me take you. Once I go somewhere, Father will be less scared to let me roam."

With the physical contact, Ben heard further into his mind. Waves of cabin fever rolled over in Ben's mind as Gabriel's thoughts came through.

*I've never been this still before in my entire life. Gabriels don't do well in confined places. I have to convince Ben to let me take him or else Father will keep me confined*, Gabriel Jr. thought.

"Gabriel..." Ben paused.

It wouldn't be in his favor to get on the Arch Head's bad side. However, it was important to remain allies with the next one in line to rule the region. Oh, decisions, decisions. Ben weighed the options.

He twitched as an idea came through his head. A reckless and very dangerous idea. Could he put the lives of others through such a disastrous situation?

Ben nodded in certainty.

"Very well then, Gabriel," Ben agreed. Gabriel Jr. sighed with relief before leaping out of bed. He dashed to the adjacent bathroom to change out of his bed gown.

"You better not make me regret coming with you." Clarissa hissed to Ben. Before he could respond, Gabriel Jr. came around the corner dressed in a moss green tunic with a belt tied tightly around his waist. He wore a dusty yellow flat cap on his head, which covered the fading bruise along his temple.

"All right let's go before Father gets back," Gabriel whispered. He beckoned them all forward.

"I have a bad feeling about this," Isabella murmured.

"I do too," Clarissa said. A purple aura shrouded around her as she turned to Ben. "You better not be putting us in too much danger."

Ben almost rolled his eyes. He didn't want Clarissa and Isabella coming along. Now she was complaining about being in danger? Ben sighed. This was going to be an exhausting mission.

A small light formed between Gabriel's hands. As he opened the portal further, the light grew to a blazing, white shine. He grunted and gave a satisfied nod.

"I still got it," Gabriel murmured before looking back up at them. "Hurry up before my father comes back. Quick!" he whispered with urgency.

Clarissa grabbed Isabella's hand before charging through the enlarged portal. The heiress gave one scowl at Ben as she passed by, blaring her thoughts.

*You...not betray...us...*

The sisters disappeared as the portal consumed them. Ben gave an eye roll before leaping into the portal himself. As blinding light and turbulent fall shifted him, the chaos of the portal overtook him.

The roar of the transport didn't last long. Like waking up from a falling dream, hot air swirled around him as he free fell for a few seconds, and then he was there. They all stood before the Burgundy Head Tree in the city of Quaesitor. Ben closed his eyes to concentrate on those around him, while Gabriel recovered his breath. He listened to one person at a time, so he needed to pick with care.

Ben moved toward the Court hall door, picking up the faint green-colored thoughts of his target. Gabriel and the Uriel sisters followed him, each curious. Ben walked past the Great Hole library further under the mountains. The stairwell walls were decorated with large lanterns and ancient carvings. Ben wondered how far the Hall went into the mountains as he came to a large open space with circular tables. The tables were made out of some sand-colored stone. Hexagons were carved along the ground, dividing each table and emanating some sort of light. Hexapods. Private meeting rooms.

The wide-open area appeared empty.

*Foreigners.*

The thought whispered in Ben's mind. Ben glanced to his left to see a slightly green aura, the exact person he was here to see. He walked up the far left hexapod, the one furthest from the exit. Within the hexagon stood an empty table, no chairs and silence.

"There's no one here," Isabella whispered, looking around the large room.

Ben was not so fooled.

He stepped to the last table, within the hexagon. Once he crossed the outlined shape, the lights shifted. The illusion of an empty table lifted. Now he saw and heard who he had come to see.

Barmen.

The heir of the Raziel clan sat alone with three large maps out before him. His blue eyes narrowed at Ben as his silver wings laid relaxed at his side. Everything about him creeped Ben out. While Ben's clan was given the stereotype of being elusive, it was the Raziel clan that was illusory.

"What can I do for you and your…companions?" Barmen spoke. Distaste coated his words.

Barmen's voice was deep with a mature tone. He was the oldest out of all the heirs, and by a few accounts considered a prodigy. His eyes looked beyond him, to take in the stragglers that came along on this mission. Clarissa's wings flared a little, while Isabella shifted on her feet nervously. Gabriel Jr. looked between Ben and Barmen, unsure.

"We don't have much time. We have some…unexpected parental pursuers," Ben said, glancing at Gabriel. "Is this a secured capsule?" Ben turned back to Barmen.

Barmen smirked at him.

"It is." He gave a small nod. "To what do I owe the pleasure?"

"It might not be such a pleasure for you soon, Barmen," Ben retorted.

"Oh." Barmen shifted the maps in front of him. Ben glanced down to see the map of their realm.

"Why don't you go ahead and lift the illusion?" he said to Barmen with his own smirk. "You're not gonna fool me with them."

*Illusion?* The heirs behind him thought collectively. Each of them grew up knowing the clan of Raziel had powers of creating illusions. Nonetheless, no one but Ben knew how powerful Barmen's illusions were.

"I should expect nothing less from the Selaphiel heir," Barmen snorted. "However I must say I did expect more. You are definitely not on the same level as your brothers."

Ben gave a plastic grin at the insult. Play with dirty players, one should expect to get dirty.

He sighed. "You're not in this pod are you, Barmen?"

Barmen gave a chuckle. "It took quite a long time for you to figure that out, didn't it?"

"We're talking to an illusion within an illusion?" Isabella asked incredulously.

"Woah," Gabriel whispered, amazed.

"Why must you be so dramatic? Not everyone is out to get you," Ben chided Barmen's illusion.

"Hmm." Barmen raised an eyebrow. "What is it you wanted again?"

"I need a secure hexapod to tell you," Ben replied.

"Security looks different for everyone."

"Fine then," Ben conceded, "We can stay in here. The security measure was more for your benefit than mine anyway." He pulled out a chair, opposite to Barmen, and sat down. He leaned back in the hard chair, pretending to be relaxed. "I've come to discuss the demon realm and…business." He emphasized the last part to get the message across.

The green aura grew stronger with Barmen's thoughts. Barmen's eyes narrowed onto Ben. Nothing was said out loud, but the silence was far from empty.

*How much do you know?* Barmen thought.

Ben grinned. "Enough."

It was a secret Barmen had been careful to hide. A secret kept from every Arch Head, heir, and citizen. Joshua, his own father, did not know what Ben knew of Barmen. Ben, also, knew Barmen would do anything to keep it a secret.

His underground trading business with those powerful enough in the demon realm.

It was how the city of Quaesitor lasted so long during the sieges. While many powerful Raziel angels held off demons with elaborate illusions, it was because of the secret deals Barmen had been making with demon lords that Quaesitor lasted for so long. When Ben found out about his little secret operation, it was like finding a jewel. A hidden gem for him to utilize. Months ago, he had plans to blackmail Barmen to include him in the money making business. Now, Ben wanted security and protection for Atarah.

"Please step this way." Barmen's illusion pointed due south with a grim expression.

"Much obliged." Ben nodded before getting up.

They all ventured further into the mountain, walking past all the 'empty' hexapods. All of the hexapods gave the illusion that the room was empty. Hexapods disguised all sights, sounds, and smells from any outsiders trying to eavesdrop on conversations. Illusions were the powers of the Raziel clan, but none had mastered them like Barmen.

Ben regarded Barmen in great respect, not because of how powerful his illusions were, but from how unimportant Barmen made himself appear without having to use his powers. That was a gift in and of itself. That was what Ben used to want. The ability to balance the entire world in his hand, without anyone realizing just how powerful he really was.

Now, Ben wanted that power, but for a different reason. A less shallow reason.

Leaving the open area to the only other door, they came to a dark hallway. The hall narrowed in width the further they walked. Forced to walk in single file, Ben led their team undeterred. He had been here once before.

They came to a small room with two stone doors. One to the east and the other to the west.

Ben coughed pointedly.

Another illusion lifted, revealing a third door in front of them.

"Thank you." Ben grinned.

He reached up to push the door and felt little resistance. The door was as light as pushing a curtain aside. He stepped through to find the real Barmen on the other side. Instead of sitting, he stood by a hologram with his back to Ben. The hologram looked like a trade map with routes outlining a zigzag pattern. Ben memorized the map, in case it would prove useful.

"Is this how you set up the trade route?" Ben stepped closer.

The map was a little difficult to read. Until he realized that all of the realms overlapped each other. One of the two cities that had drop off zones were Quaesitor and a spot near Mortem.

*Interesting,* Ben mused.

"What is it that you truly want Ben?" Barmen turned to him. The heir of Raziel was shorter than him and very lean. His short blonde hair glistened as he faced Ben. With high cheekbones and a raised brow, Barmen appeared intimidating and unimpressed with their arrival.

Ben sighed. Directness would not hurt in this situation.

"I want you to take me to one of the demon lords."

He heard someone behind him gasp, but he kept his eyes on Barmen. The older Arch eye's widened the slightest bit as the only clue to his surprise.

"Why is that?" Barmen asked.

"Why not come with and find out?" he replied.

Barmen gave a small grin. "You always did know how to keep things interesting, Ben." He paused. "Let's say I do this for you, and that is a big if, what do I get out of such a precarious situation?"

"Another beneficial deal."

"I need details, Ben," Barmen reproached, "I know how much your clan likes to skimp on the details." An undertone of contempt came in through his usual calm voice.

"Almost as much as your clan does," Ben fired back. "Alas, though no angel could ever compete with the Raziel clan when it comes to greed."

Barmen's face remained expressionless.

"I see no further point in conversing with you then." Barmen turned away.

"Wait."

Barmen peeked over his shoulder.

"I want to protect what's mine," Ben said with a clenched jaw. "So I plan to make a deal with Lord Beelzebub. I can't tell you all of the details, but I can strengthen your trading ties in the demon realm. This could make you extremely wealthy."

"Hold on," Clarissa chimed in behind him. "What do you mean by trading? That's…"

"Traitorous!" Isabella cried out.

"Double-crosser!" Gabriel hissed.

The news of a secret trading arrangement would send their realm into a civil war. However Ben had no plans to allow the public to know of Barmen's black trade market.

"How could you be dealing with the enemy while they destroy our homes, our cities!" Isabella cried out, pointing an accusing finger at Barmen.

"How could you do this?" Gabriel sneered. "You should be ashamed to bear those wings!"

Disgust dripped with every word. Ben glanced back at them to see all of their wings were flared and vibrating with anger. Clarissa studied Barmen and looked conflicted.

Ben focused his thoughts on all of them.

*How could this pathetic swine…*

*Low-life…despicable…*

*Why would he do such a thing?*

Ben opened his eyes to see Clarissa still staring at Barmen. She held more open-mindedness toward him compared to the others. *Interesting, that could be useful,* he thought. Ignoring his growing headache, Ben focused on Barmen.

*I know you are listening in on all of our thoughts, Ben. It really is impolite to do so.*

He saw Barmen, with his back still turned, but his mind fixated on him.

"Enough," Ben said softly. Isabella and Gabriel quieted, their outrage blared loud in their thoughts.

"Do we have a deal or not?"

Barmen faced him with a glare. "I still need more from you before I say yes."

"How about ensuring no one else learns of these deals you have made and not causing the next civil war between the clans?" Ben replied curtly.

Barmen grimaced. "Who would believe you?"

"Many, especially since I have witnesses." He indicated to Isabella and Gabriel.

"Hang on, Ben," Gabriel started, "I won't keep quiet about this."

"Yeah," Isabella chimed in, "Neither will I."

"You will if you want to help your people," Ben bit back. He turned back to Barmen. "And you will only have something to gain by taking me to the demon lord."

Barmen scoffed. "You obviously have no idea how dangerous it is to go before one of the demon lords. How ruthless and cunning they are."

"And yet here you stand. Not dead after striking a deal with them," Ben said. "Thriving in fact."

Suddenly Barmen stood before him, face to face. Mere inches separated them. A harshness took over Barmen's face as he spoke.

"You have no idea the toll it took. No idea, " Barmen whispered through gritted teeth. "Thriving is not a word I would use, not in the slightest."

Screams of terror and pain entered into Ben's head from Barmen. Images flashed before him so quickly, he couldn't make everything out.

Ben stumbled backward, clutching his aching head. He opened

one eye to glare at Barmen. The bastard was purposefully trying to overwhelm him.

"I'm staying firm on this Barmen. I *need* to see a demon lord."

Barmen regarded him up and down before speaking.

"What has you so desperate, Selaphiel?" Barmen murmured. "You've changed a little."

"Change can be good."

"I suppose I'll find out sooner or later." Barmen backed away. He looked at the others. "Are they coming along?"

"No—" Ben began.

"Yes," Clarissa interrupted.

He whipped around at her. "Absolutely not."

"Absolutely yes," Clarissa answered back. Isabella appeared as startled as he did. Clarissa moved toward Barmen. "The riches Ben mentioned earlier, that's how you were able to rebuild your city so quickly? Yes?"

Barmen gave a nod.

"That's all I need to know."

"But wait, Sissy," Isabella started. "This is the enemy we are talking about here! They destroyed our city!"

"Which is why I have no qualms using the enemy's money to rebuild our city," Clarissa explained. She moved to grab her sister's shoulders. "This will help our people. You do not know this, but the reconstruction of our city is at a standstill because our coffers are so low. We need the money."

"But from demons…" Isabella sighed. "Deals with demons never go well."

"Not if you're smart about making the deal and its rules." Clarissa released Isabella to glare at Ben and Barmen. "Neither of you are the only ones that are desperate."

Her eyes shone with the fire she possessed. Ben saw the memories of the struggle she and her father had endured with their people returning. It was indeed an uphill battle of recovery. Barmen's face remained expressionless. Ben heard Barmen's respect for Clarissa grow in his mind.

*She understands what it takes to lead*, Barmen's thoughts whispered.

Both of them gave a nod, agreeing for her to go. Next, they all turned to Gabriel, who still had his wings flared.

Gabriel groaned. "How am I supposed to support this madness?"

"It's either this or going back home to dear ol' Dad" Ben reminded. Gabriel paced around the small room, rubbing his hand over his head in frustration.

"Transporting into the demon realm is strictly forbidden and for good reason!" Gabriel argued.

"Don't you want to retrieve your brethren?" Barmen asked in a cold voice. Gabriel froze. That got his attention. He glared at Barmen.

"What did you say?" Gabriel said as he clenched his fist.

Wrapped in his own mission, Ben had forgotten that Gabriel angels had been kidnapped into the demon realm for experimentation.

"There is a rumor of where they might be held." Barmen paused. "But there are never any guarantees."

Gabriel's wings flared with anger.

"I need to try," Gabriel said, determined. "Alright, we will go."

Everyone sighed in relief.

"BUT," Gabriel continued. "We are hightailing out of there at the slightest bit of danger."

"Ok, Mr. Bossman," Isabella said sardonically. While Isabella and Clarissa laughed at Gabriel's chagrined face, Ben peeked at Barmen from the side of his eye.

There was another way to the demon realm. Barmen had been using it without a Gabriel angel. Having Gabriel Jr. here was a convenient excuse for him. Ben wondered how Barmen had been traveling to and from the demon realm. It would be another secret for him to uncover.

"Ok, everyone." Gabriel held out his hands. "Hold on. I've only learned about going to the demon realm in theory."

"So there is a chance we might not make it there?" Ben asked, with a raised eyebrow. He heard the wheels turning in Gabriel's mind. He could get them there, of that he was confident in, it was the process that made him hesitant.

"It's kinda like flying," Gabriel explained. "You know you could do it but for how long, ya know?" he asked rhetorically. He reached his hands out again. Everyone grabbed onto his arms tightly.

"You sure you can do this?" Ben inquired with a frown. Maybe he'd been wrong in his assessment of Gabriel.

"Yes," Gabriel huffed. "Don't worry. If I wasn't up to it. I'd tell you."

Gabriel closed his eyes and concentrated. A portal began to open, bringing bright light into the room. Wind came through the portal, whipping the air around them. Sweat formed along Gabriel's brow as he held the portal open, not fully recovered but doing his best. Now or never, Ben thought, steeling his courage. This would be by far the most reckless thing he has ever done.

Ben jumped through the portal first. Nerves careened through his whole body, causing his wings to shake. The weightless fall through space consumed him. His wings tried to expand to catch him, but passing through the portal constricted his limbs. Traveling through was quick.

He landed upon some rock. Kneeling, he struggled to breathe. The air felt heavy, and the sky was a deep red color. He checked his body for any injuries as he drew in a breath. All was well, for now. Despite his trembling arms, he forced himself to take in his surroundings. The sound of flowing water caught his attention first. Next was the rushing wind rolling off of the high grass that was all around. Tall green grass surrounded him in every direction. Three moons floated above the horizon while a few clouds passed by.

No danger yet.

He clenched his shaking hands. He *needed* to do this for Atarah. He took another breath to push back his emotions. Now that he was in the demon realm, the danger was real. *No.* He shook his head. *There's no danger yet*, he reminded himself.

He stood in a large field of tall grass that came to his shoulder. The bright green grass swayed with the wind, like waves on an ocean. He turned in the other direction. Large mountains with snowy peaks rose to the west. Where was the water? Ben turned around looking for the river he heard.

A groan caught his attention. He whirled around to see Clarissa and Isabella crumpled on the ground. Gabriel and Barmen leaned to help them up.

"My stomach never goes well with traveling." Clarissa groaned as she used Barmen's hand to stand up.

"Neither does mine," Isabella agreed. She yelped as Gabriel jerked her forward to sit her up.

"Come on," Gabriel ushered. "The faster you're on your feet the faster the queasiness will wear off. We call this travel sickness back at home."

"Well, I am about to be sick on *you.*" Isabella bent over again. She dry heaved, and Gabriel quickly moved away, his face turning a shade of green.

"Where did you drop us off at?" Clarissa asked, taking in the environment.

"If I had to guess," Barmen mused with a frown, "we're definitely in Beelzebub's domain."

"Where does the demon lord normally stay?" Ben asked. Barmen nodded to their north.

"He travels all over his domain, " Barmen explained, "but he favors Umbra City and Nineveh."

"Why those two?" Isabella fired off questions. "And how many cities are there? Which one is safest for us?" Her wings flared with each question.

"There are many large cities in the demon realm. Larger than our own cities in fact." Barmen explained. "While our realm is made up of regions, the demon realm is made up of three domains. The domains are named after the demon lord that rules them." He waved his hand around. "Right now we are in Beelzebub's domain, which expands larger than my region, Vallis, and Elements combined."

Gabriel swirled around.

"What?" he cried. "There's no way their land is that massive."

Barmen gave a small nod.

"I learned that the demon realm is significantly larger than our realm, but it wasn't until I traveled here that I understood how massive this realm is." He paused for a moment. "Or how diverse this realm is."

"Who cares how diverse they are?" Isabella cried out as she scratched her arms. "Tell us more about where things are."

Clarissa rubbed her legs, looking at Barmen expectantly.

"As I was saying, there are three large domains in the demon realm. Beelzebub's, Leviathan's, and Satan's domain. Beelzebub's domain is made up mostly of grassy plains, which is how I know where we are. Leviathan's domain has a combination of rainforest and marshlands. Very wet climates typically." Barmen sighed. "And then lastly, Satan's domain is mostly the red desert."

"The red desert?" Clarissa asked. She moved onto scratching her back. Ben scratched his neck.

"Yes, red desert. Tough terrain and tougher creatures live there," Barmen said, raising his eyebrow. He regarded them for a moment, confused. Then, his eyes widened in realization. "We should begin walking toward the mountains."

"Why the mountains?" Gabriel asked as he struggled to scratch his back. Barmen's mouth twitched.

"Because everyone seems to have caught some red mites."

"What are red mites?" Ben asked.

"Red mites are microscopic bugs that—" Barmen began.

"Bugs was all you needed to say," Isabella interrupted. She started walking, quickly, toward the mountains.

"Bugs that like to burrow under the skin and try to create a home for themselves on whatever poor creature they find," Barmen continued. He picked up a blade of grass. "They tend to like the tall grass, because it makes it easier for them to jump onto a host."

"Why aren't you being affected?" Clarissa asked. Barmen pulled something out of his pocket and showed it to her. "The lotion I use is made from lavender. Most bugs here can't stand the smell."

"Hey!" Gabriel said indignantly. "Share that!"

Clarissa lips twitched as she watched Barmen.

"Barmen," Ben drew his attention. He lifted his hand out and indicated to the bottle of lotion. Barmen poured some lotion in his hand before tossing the bottle to Ben.

"Come here, Gabriel," Ben said, "We'll share."

"Oh, thank the realms for bug repellant," Gabriel said with relief. Ben spread some of the lotion around all of his exposed skin.

"Isabella!" Clarissa called out to her sister, who was making a good distance away from them. "We have bug repellant!"

Isabella froze in her tracks for a moment before a wind flurried. Wind swirled around her, lifting her up, and soared her in the air back to them. A ball of wind that encased her slowly dissipated as she landed right in front of them.

Clarissa grinned at her sister. "Show off," she mumbled.

Isabella shrugged. "It helped get a few bugs off."

"Here." Barmen extended his hand with the lotion he had poured toward Isabella and Clarissa.

Clarissa and Isabella paused in surprise.

"Thanks," Clarissa murmured. Isabella scooped half of the lotion and vigorously rubbed it into her skin. Clarissa grabbed the rest of the lotion from Barmen's hand to follow suit.

Ben pointed to the mountain.

"Do the mountains have any other significance, Barmen?" he asked.

Barmen looked to where he pointed. "The Decimate Mountains divide the three domains. Umbra City is at the base of the mountains and provides a good access point for Beelzebub."

"Is that where Matthew opens his portals?"

Barmen gave a solemn nod.

"Matthew keeps his cult within the mountains. Staying in the mountains makes it easier to cross the domains' borders and recruit more members from all the domains."

"Do…" Gabriel began, confusion leaking into his voice. "Do the demon lords approve of what Matthew is doing?"

Barmen answered with hesitance. "They find him…annoying."

Ben focused on his thoughts, not trusting all of Barmen's words.

*The Lords have a bounty reward on that Luciferian's head. If I could get my hands on that reward…*

Barmen's thoughts faded out as a headache bloomed across Ben's forehead. So that was it. Barmen wanted the reward for himself. *Well, good luck trying to capture a luciferian*, Ben thought sardonically.

"Let's start toward Umbra then," Ben said to the group. "The faster we get this done the sooner we can go home."

Ben opened his wings wide and lifted himself into the sky. The sound of flapping wings echoed behind him, signaling that everyone was following. He peeked behind him to see red, black and silver wings flying in the sky behind him, the silver wings fast approaching.

"I hope you have a plan, Ben," Barmen called over the wind.

"Do I ever not have a plan?" Ben yelled back. Barmen grimaced.

"The demon lords aren't to be taken lightly. They are more powerful than the Head Archs, Ben. Bigger than cherubim and maybe seraphim."

Outwardly, Ben kept his face impassive, but inwardly he shuddered. His hands shook, and his heart raced as exhilaration thrummed through him at this chance. The higher ranking players meant there were higher stakes.

"Ben, you—" Barmen paused as he saw the grin Ben couldn't

keep off his face. "Crazy bastard," Barmen murmured.

Ben couldn't care less what he thought at the moment.

Even as he flew, his wings hummed with excitement.

"Ben, there's a high likelihood of death going to see a demon lord. Are you sure you know what you're doing?"

"The reason you're in this position, Barmen, is because you underestimated me," Ben said. "The demon lord probably will too."

*I hope you're right...*

Ben faintly heard Barmen's thoughts. More images of the demon lord's court flashed through Barmen's mind. Ben couldn't distinguish much other than the fact that violence, deceit, and brutality occurred frequently.

"When we get closer to the city, we will need to find disguises and hide our wings," Barmen continued.

Oh, Ben thought. He still had the ranger's serum coursing through his veins. He could hide his wings at will, but the others couldn't.

"You wouldn't happen to have any serum on you?" Ben asked. He glanced behind him and at the sisters. "More than one vial?"

Barmen frowned as he followed Ben's gaze. Clarissa and Isabella definitely needed to stay hidden.

"No," Barmen said in a hushed tone.

"I'm sure you know someone that has a few vials," Ben faced the front again.. "An Arch like you surely has connections in Umbra."

Barmen still gazed at the sisters.

"I do," Barmen agreed. "But he is not someone who is very friendly."

*We'll find a way to make him friendly*, Ben thought darkly.

The thunderstorm raged as many tried to take cover. The wind blew so strong, the rain came down at an angle, attacking more like needles than little water pellets. Lightning bolts struck across the sky and the ground. One struck dangerously close by at a tree. Noah clenched his teeth as the loud sound of thunder rolled over him.

# True Strength

*I hate this*, he thought as he crawled across the muddy rainforest floor.

There was no peace in this environment. Oppressive heat weighed them down with each step, while the air was so humid, it was like swallowing water with each breath. Insects larger than his head buzzed and crept alongside them. The infernal bugs were everywhere, driving him crazy. The only time they were safe from the bugs was during the afternoon, for thunderstorms plagued without fail. Noah hated this climate with every fiber of his being. A combination of all of the things he hated: hot, humid, and buggy. He missed the gentle cool breeze of his home region. The moderate, decent temperature that wrapped around you comfortably in the autumn woods.

Not this thundering hellhole.

Noah dragged on. Zewal and Tariel were behind him, making slower progress than him. While his father and Mikael, 'the lunatic' as Noah dubbed him, were far ahead of them. The portal they had found within the Maze of Uncertainty led them to the demon realm! The demon realm of all places! Noah had hoped the portal would lead them to where the seraphim or cherubim were, wherever that was. He pressed on anyway just on the chance that seraphim might be in the demon realm. All that he knew of the demon realm was that it was vast, diverse, and deadly.

Since they'd arrived, nothing but discomfort had plagued them. Mikael, the 'lunatic,' told them they had arrived in Leviathan's domain and that they needed to head north further in the Decimate mountain range. The past five days had been nothing but survival. Either hiding from monsters and demons or fighting their way out. Fight, hide, camp (very roughly), try to sleep, and then repeat. Noah hadn't gotten a decent night's sleep in so long, he almost fell asleep standing up. Still, they had to press on and keep hiking through the dense wetlands, marshes, and now this rainforest.

Mikael said that the rainforest was a good sign that they were closer to the mountains. When they had first arrived, dark murky water surrounded them. They had swum through into a marsh with little patches of grass. Large lizards, frogs, and mosquitos greeted them as they emerged from the water. Thick mud weighed down their arms and legs with each motion as they crawled out of the marsh. Oddly, the mud that coated Noah's entire body protected him from the sun's continuous onslaught. For while they hiked through the marsh, there was no hope of shade. No trees, no clouds, nothing but the beating of the sun's rays. Next were the wetlands, which had trees with expansive roots coming up from the water. Mangrove trees and tall grass surrounded them as they swam.

A cluster of small snakes watched them as they made their way through. Their beady eyes stared excitedly while another snake attacked them. A much larger snake that Mikael called the Titanoboa nearly succeeded in eating Noah. Thankfully, Zewal and Mikael were able to take the monster down while Noah and Tariel, who hated swimming, made their escape.

Now, they were on solid ground but had to stay low. Many large monsters roamed the forest, ones they wanted to avoid. Noah glanced back at Tariel and Zewal. Their faces had a grayish color to them and their limbs shook with effort.

Noah's eyes widened in alarm.

"Stop!" he called ahead of him to his father and Mikael.

He quickly made his way back to the Azrael siblings. They both slumped, face down in the mud, panting. Noah laid a hand on Tariel's head. She was hot to the touch. Not good.

He sat up and removed his water jug. He quickly dumped water around her head and neck while he reached for his powers. He grunted as his powers flowed into Tariel's neck and shoulders to offset the effects of heat stroke.

"What is it?" His father panted beside him.

"Zewal and Tariel are going through heat stroke," Noah explained. "We need to get them cooled down now."

Elijah didn't hesitate. He stripped down Zewal's tunic around his waist and poured water along his torso. Noah continued to put water along Tariel's body until his jug was empty.

"Here." The deep voice of Mikael called out to them.

Mikael moved large branches to reveal a water pool a few feet away.

"Dunk them in there," Mikael commanded, moving the brush aside. Noah lifted Tariel while Elijah carried Zewal to the pool.

"Gentle now, son," Elijah said while they lowered the siblings into the water.

Tariel and Zewal panted heavily. Their eyes were rolled back, and their faces still looked gray. They were pushed to their physical limits. Azrael angels were not physically fit and relied on their powers for battle. So the fact that Tariel and Zewal made it this far was inspiring.

"We will rest here for now." Mikael's deep voice carried behind Noah.

They had no choice but to rest while the Azrael heirs recovered. Elijah's hands glowed over both of their heads as he healed them. Noah lay down beside the pond, exhausted. The sounds and chitters of creatures echoed in the distance.

*When will this hell end?* Noah thought. Should they turn back?

*No.*

Noah shook his head. They didn't come all this way just to quit. They still needed to find the Abaddon and put a stop to Matthew. Also he needed to find out more information about luciferians and halflings. Any information that would help Arick's case.

Noah groaned. After all the crap he put Arick through and trying to get rid of him, this was the least he could do. Noah glanced at his father. Sweat poured down his face as he expended more energy to heal.

*All I want is my family back together.*

That was what Elijah had said to him all those months ago. He had never understood what his father meant by that. Growing up in isolation, Noah didn't understand what his mother and father meant by family. He grew up alone in a room with books, maps, and training lessons, with occasional visits from Charlotte and Mother. When Atarah and Arick came along, annoying and arrogant, Noah understood what it meant to build a relationship. Build a family.

Noah glanced at Mikael. The Archangel had his back turned, scanning the forest floor for any potential threats. His wings flared, ready to fight at any time. Noah saw a lot of Arick in Mikael's face; however they were completely different outside of their looks. Arick was more laid back and easy going in his demeanor, while Mikael was stern, closed off, and inflexible. Where Arick was sarcastic and arrogant, Mikael was serious and humble. Everyone saw them as carbon copies of one another, but Noah saw polar opposites.

"Mikael," Noah began. The Arch's head did a half-turn toward him, never taking his eyes off the forest floor.

"Yes?"

"Why did you send Arick with Atarah all those weeks ago at the summit meeting?" Noah asked.

Mikael spared a glance at Noah for a moment before turning back to the forest.

"For many reasons," he answered. "But none more important than giving Arick a chance to prove himself."

"Prove what exactly?"

"Everything," Mikael said. "Prove he wasn't a monster. Prove to you and Elijah you would grow to love him. Prove to himself that he has what it takes."

"He didn't strike me as having low confidence." Noah stood up to join Mikael in the look out.

Mikael gave a small grin. "He's a Michael angel." He glanced at Noah. "We are always trying to prove something."

Noah regarded Mikael, confused.

"They're ok." His father's voice drew his attention. Noah turned back to see Zewal and Tariel sitting up now, gulping water.

"You need to drink more water from now on and speak up when you need a break," Elijah explained.

"All of you are freaks of nature," Tariel murmured.

Noah pressed his lips together to hide his smile. He almost pointed out how bizarre Azrael angels were compared to the other clans, but held his tongue. Azrael were a prideful clan and wouldn't take teasing as lightly as he would.

"We will rest a little while longer before moving on," Elijah finished up.

"Are we in danger yet?" Zewal asked. Tariel sighed heavily.

"Not yet," Mikael replied.

"What I would do for a cold shower and dry clothes," Tariel groaned.

"I'd trade my favorite black tunic for a decent meal." Zewal joined in.

"I think I'd trade in my favorite horse just for one decent night of sleep," Noah said.

Tariel turned her black eyes onto him accusingly.

"How could you trade in your horse?" she protested vehemently. "They're family. You wouldn't trade in your sister for anything."

Zewal and Noah exchanged a slow look before glancing back at Tariel.

"You don't realize how annoying sisters can be then," Noah said, chuckling.

"I concur," Zewal chimed in. "Parents let you get away with everything."

"You take things without asking too," Noah fired back.

"You whine and complain," Zewal said.

"Everyone asks you how you're doing and caters to you."

"Well it's better than having an irritating brother," Tariel grumbled back. Mikael's lips twitched as he nodded along. Noah chuckled, thinking of Arick.

"Well at least you all have siblings," Elijah said with his own smile. "Someone to go to when you're in trouble or who to get in trouble with."

"More like they get you in trouble," Zewal grumbled. "Father's gonna have my head for letting you come with me to the demon realm."

Tariel shrugged. "Father's just scared. He needs to know that I can make my own decisions."

"You sound just like my daughter," Mikael said with a chuckle. He opened his mouth to continue, but a snap of a branch drew everyone's attention to the other side of the pond.

Noah's heart pounded wildly in his chest. He bent down as he drew his weapon. Out of the corner of his eye, Mikael did the same. His father helped Zewal and Tariel up to a crouched position. Noah struggled to keep his breathing quiet while he stepped closer to the pond. Mikael placed a hand on his shoulder, stopping him. Giving a brief shake of his head, Mikael advanced first. His weapons were drawn and wings flared.

"Noah!" Elijah whispered. Another strong hand gripped Noah's shoulder. This hand pulled him back.

"Stay put!" Elijah whispered again at Noah's bewildered expression. Elijah pressed him back while he crept behind Mikael. Noah clenched his teeth to keep from scoffing. His face flushed as he turned to Zewal and Tariel.

Another snap, this one closer by. He lifted his sword higher. His hands shook while his eyes searched for the unknown enemy.

A cry rang out as an explosion of movement occurred. One second, Mikael and his father were in front of him, the next gone. A large hoofed beast burst from the thick brush in front of them. The beast collided with the two head Archs, sending them careening over Noah's head.

Noah froze as the beast lowered its head to charge again. The demon bore one large horn on the top of its head along with a thick, white mane. Its red eyes stood out against the white fur. while four long legs carried the monster forward at a frightening speed. The elongated snout opened wide to show extensive rows of sharp teeth. The beast roared as it charged Noah, shaking him from his stupor.

Noah launched himself into the sky, narrowly missing the monster's sharp horn. The demon leaped from its hind legs, enclosing its jaws on Noah's dangling feet. Stabbing pain shot through his leg as he was dragged to the ground. Crying out, Noah stabbed his sword into the creature's eye, twisting the sword deeper.

Rearing back, the demon cried out in pain, releasing him. Noah crawled a few feet away, drawing his dagger when Mikael attacked. Like two boulders slamming into each other, Mikael tackled the demon to the ground. Faster than the blink of an eye, Mikael stabbed the demon. Cutting into its neck, Mikael never loosened his hold.

The cool relief of healing flowed through Noah as he sat up. His body healed itself. The demon groaned weakly as black blood poured from its neck. Noah turned to see Zewal and Tariel, hands extended and faces scrunched in concentration toward the demon. Mikael removed his sword, only to stab again into the dying creature. Satisfied by the demon's weakened state, Noah slumped to the ground, exhausted. Zewal and Tariel might as well have been the ones draining him of his energy, because he had nothing left.

A heavy hand smacked his chest, rousing him.

"Come on, son," Elijah urged. His father was crouched before him. "We can't stay—"

His father's words were cut off as large arrows appeared just mere inches from their faces. They froze. The black arrows, larger than his own sword, hovered in space aiming for his head, heart, and wings. Noah peeked at the rest of their team. He was not the only one surrounded. Mikael was immobile with arrows around his entire body. Zewal and Tariel had one arrow pointing at them, but their expression was one of agony. The Azrael Archs clutched their heads, pain lanced within their features.

*What was going on?*

Noah glanced around with his brow furrowed. His heart pounded in his chest. His hands shook as he slowly lifted them into the air. He kept his breath in long, drawn-out sighs, restricting any fast movements to not alert whoever was attacking them.

"What do we have here?" a deep, gargling voice called out. Bubbles emerged from the pond they'd rested in not too long ago.

A scaly head broke the surface of the water. Pale eyes stared at them. A burst of air shot through two slits from the sides of its head. Looming underneath the surface, the demon slithered out of the water toward Mikael.

"What are two Arch heads doing in my lord's domain?" it hissed. A black, forked tongue slid out as it spoke to Mikael.

"Our business is our own," Mikael panted out, undisturbed by the dozens of arrows that surrounded him.

The demon quirked its head to the side as if intrigued.

"It becomes our lord's business when angels come to our realm and kill our livestock."

"A unicorn hardly counts as livestock," Mikael replied back. The creature cackled in the water, causing bubbles to emerge from all around the pond.

"Still so," it wheezed. The arrows around them shifted into vines extending from the water. Within the blink of an eye, the vines wrapped around each of them tightly. Noah groaned as the threads cut into his side and wings.

"I think my lord will be…interested to see each of you."

They had no time to protest before they were dragged into the pond. Water splashed everywhere while they fought. He heard his father and Mikael fighting against the restraints to no avail. He swiveled his head to Zewal and Tariel; surely they could weaken this creature. His heart sank as he saw their faces withered in pain. Blood dripped from their eyes, noses, and ears. What was happening to them?

Noah gasped his last breath before plunging into the black water. Bubbles floating to the surface were the last thing he saw when the darkness closed in.

# Chapter 5

Thunder clapped above them, causing the ground to shake underneath their feet. The rain came down so hard, it hurt. The rocky terrain became slippery and uneven the further they traveled.

"This was a lot easier when I didn't have a form," Azazel grumbled before another roar of thunder echoed. His white knuckles gripped the mountainside as he led the way.

*"Remember to be careful what you wish for, old-timer,"* Arick's thoughts blared.

*"SHUT IT, KID!"* Azazel yelled back.

Canaan winced. Those two's inner battle raged on for the entire journey, and Canaan's head could only take so much bickering. Normally he tuned out others' thoughts, but with Azazel and Arick, it was like they were on either side of him, yelling into his ear.

They made it to a leveled out surface, close to the top. The higher they climbed, the stronger the wind blew. Canaan was soaked from head to toe and half-frozen.

"Break!" Canaan yelled above the thunder. Azazel reached up to start climbing but paused at Canaan's voice.

"Please," Canaan panted. "I need a break."

Azazel watched his hunched over form while bickering inside.

*"I told you to take it easy," Arick scolded Azazel. "But no one listens to me for whatever reason."*

*"Because you run your mouth too much, kid."*

*"You don't talk enough! Look at poor…Cain? Canaam? Can?"*

"It's Canaan," he huffed. He slumped underneath a large boulder sticking out of the mountainside. Canaan sighed with relief as his aching muscles relaxed. The rain no longer pelted at him, which gave him a moment to breathe.

*"Canaan!"* Arick continued. *"I told you other angels don't have the same stamina as us."*

*"Next time I'm definitely gonna get a different body,"* Azazel grumbled.

*"Oh, come on. I think you like sharing a body with me."*

*"It took me hours! Hours! To walk off how drunk you got us!"*

*"And that random boner we got."* Arick chuckled. Azazel groaned.

*"Don't remind me, kid."*

*"It could've been worse. I mean, it's been centuries since you've had a boner, so I'm sure it was a nice change."*

"Sorry but," Canaan grimaced. "Could you stop thinking, please? I beg of you to please stop." He pleaded as he rubbed his temples.

*"I wish,"* Azazel and Arick thought at the same time.

"Anything to shut this kid up," Azazel mumbled outwardly.

*"What? I can't think thoughts inside my own head now?"* Arick whined. "*Besides, how is that even possible? To stop thinking?"*

"It's not that you stop thinking." Canaan leaned his head back against the rock. His eyes closed. "It's quieting your thoughts to focus. Right now your thoughts are running around in every direction. Like a child that never sits still because you have too much anxious energy." Canaan peered at Azazel/Arick. "Learn to sit and relax those thoughts."

*"Fun fact about Michael angels,"* Arick replied. *"We're never relaxed...ever really. It goes against every principle we've been taught. There is always something we could be doing to getting better, getting stronger, or getting—"*

*"What, more perfect?"* Azazel interrupted. *"The Selaphiel is onto something, kid. You need more focus in your life."*

*"How would you know?"*

*"I've been in your life for only a few days, kid, and it's no wonder your dad was turning gray with you!"*

Suddenly, the thoughts turned from words to pure sound. Loud, off-beat and off-key sounds of a piano screeched in Canaan's mind. He winced as the noise continued. Like a child slamming their hands on a keyboard randomly. He clutched the side of his head and groaned.

"Please, Arick," Canaan pleaded.

It had been years since the last time he had felt affected by his own ability. Canaan retreated within himself to find shelter. A memory of his mother floated through his mind. Years ago, when he was a little boy, his mother rescued him from the voices and sounds of the people in the city. Scared, he hid as far away from others as he could, seeking silence. He hid in the basement of their villa.

His mother had found him though. He thought back to when she had crouched before him and placed her hands over his ears. The memory served as a blanket that wrapped around him, turning down the noise. Enough to make life bearable. A blanket of safety from covering his ears.

*That's right.*

He reached into his small satchel and pulled out his emergency headphones. Amos had given him the headphones in case he got overwhelmed. Canaan had laughed him off at the time, but now he'd never felt more grateful for his brother's caution. He pulled the headphones over his ears and sighed.

The headphones weren't fool proof. Designed by one of his ancestors, the headphones helped the Selaphiel heirs control and hone in on their powers. They didn't block out all of the thoughts but made the room quieter. Canaan chuckled. He hadn't used these headphones in years; now look at him. Back to the training wheels.

Canaan glanced back at Azazel/Arick, who were both staring back at him curiously.

*"S...are...th...e..."* The thought sounded so faint, Canaan couldn't hear the full sentence.

Canaan removed the right headphone.

"What was that?" Canaan asked.

*"Sorry about that,"* Arick replied. *"My father is a touchy subject."*

"Mine too." Canaan frowned. Dark thoughts whirled in the back of his head, which he pushed down. Now was not the time for those to play through his mind.

"Right." Canaan stood up and stepped back out into the rain. "I can keep going now."

Azazel eyed him from head to toe for a moment before nodding. He grunted and jerked his head toward the cliffside.

"That's the way," Azazel said. Canaan nodded before scaling the rock wall.

*Peace and quiet at last,* Canaan thought.

*"Perfect."* Azazel thought. He watched the Selaphiel heir climb high before allowing his real thoughts to the surface.

*"Allowing your real thoughts?"* Arick chimed in. His voice dripped with cynicism. *"What kind of sick, twisted person hides in their thoughts?"*

*"The Selaphiel Arch was right, kid,"* Azazel thought as he climbed the rock. He wanted to keep a good distance from the mind reader just in case. *"You need to focus your thoughts more. It will help you in every aspect of your life. Battle, sleep, less stress on the body."*

*"I don't understand what you mean by 'focus' your thoughts,"* Arick argued back. *"It makes no sense."*

*"Right now, you just let any little thought pop into your head, don't you?"*

*"Doesn't everyone?"*

*"No, kid,"* he grunted, nearly falling off the cliff. Canaan glanced down at him. Azazel gave a wave, to signal he was all right. He waited until Canaan continued upward before responding to Arick.

*"Your mind is similar to your body in that it needs rest and structure."* Azazel explained. *"Get a grip on your mind and...well I believe you could do anything you want in this life."*

*"Oh, so what are you some kind of expert or something?"* Arick jeered. Azazel raised an eyebrow.

*"I ONLY had my mind to deal with for the past few centuries. So yes, I AM an expert on this, kid."* Azazel shook his head while he climbed. *"The quietest your mind gets is when you're shitting your pants or getting stone-cold drunk."*

*"Shitting my pants, huh?"* Arick chuckled. *"I don't get scared."*

*"Kid, I know all of your thoughts. The only time you weren't scared was when you were fighting that crazy assimilate leader named Matthew. Every single second outside of that, you've been scared."*

*"I—"*

*"Don't bother denying it, kid. You can't bullshit me,"* Azazel said. *"I know that's why you volunteered to let me take over your body*

*and why death seems like relief to you. You're scared of living."* Azazel sighed. *"But that stops now because I need you and your shit straight if we're gonna get out of this alive. Now, I have a plan to shake the Selaphiel heir, grab a Gabriel body, and get the hell out of here."*

*"Shake Canaan? Why? He's helping us out."*

*"Rule number one, kid. Don't trust a mind reader. They look out for themselves,"* Azazel replied, watching the Selaphiel climb to the top. *"Rule number two is to always have a plan."*

*"What is this plan of yours then?"*

*"When we get to the prison, we'll find a Gabriel body and then ditch that place as soon as possible! We are not sticking around to do anything else!"*

*"Or..."*

*"No, kid."*

*"Hear me out,"* Arick said with a lighter tone. *"We could—"*

*"No funny ideas, kid,"* Azazel said firmly. *"We get in and get out. End of discussion. No hero business like last time. Look where that put us!"*

Arick sighed. *"No one ever listens to me."*

"Get used to that, kid," Azazel said out loud as he made it to the top.

At the top of the mountain's peak, they rose above the clouds. No more rain, but thunder and lightning raged further down. From here, they would have to fly the rest of the way to be undetected. The storm provided coverage for them to sneak in. With the prison being underground, few of the guards paid attention to the skies. They had to be fast and quiet for this to work. Azazel dreaded everything about this 'mission' of theirs, but it was his way out.

He'd never expected Arick to have a target on his back when he agreed to their deal. He planned to find a body and lay low for centuries to come. Create a life of peace and quiet for himself. Azazel sighed. He craved such simple yet luxurious goals.

Canaan removed his headphones before speaking to him.

"Which way now, Azazel?" Canaan asked. His eyes searched the mountain skyline.

"That way." Azazel jerked his chin westward. *"Odd."* He frowned.

Very few dared to call him by his real name aloud, and if they did it was with disgust.

*"Why's that?"* Arick's annoying voice echoed. Azazel opened their sore wings wide and launched into the air. Azazel winced as their back burned with exhaustion. With less gravitational pull in the demon realm, flying was easier, but it was at a cost. Everything had a cost in this realm.

*"You don't need to know, kid."*

*"Hmmmm,"* Arick mused. *"Another secret, I see. Oh well."*

Azazel shook his head in disbelief.

*"You should be more interested in who you shared your body with, kid!"*

*"It doesn't matter anyway."*

Irritation pricked its way through him. The audacity of this idiot! This young Arch had everything. His own body, power, wealth, and a family who loved him. It was almost like he didn't care about what happened to him.

*"That is correct, old timer."* Arick sighed. *"Whatever happens to me, I don't care."*

*"What is wrong with you, kid?!"* Azazel roared. *"Do you have any idea of how great you have it?! I would—"*

Azazel stopped his train of thought. He shouldn't let this kid get under his skin but…He groaned.

*"Kid, whatever pain you're going through, work it out or else you'll end up like me, and trust me you don't want what I got."*

*"Another fun fact about Michael angels, we don't address pain,"* Arick said in a flat tone.

No, Azazel determined, not a flat tone but a bitter one. He knew where Arick was coming from.

*"There is no way you know where I am coming from."* Arick snorted. Harshness presented that time. *"No one does and no one ever will."*

A tightness in their chest formed, like in the prison. A knot in their stomach drew his attention with a frown. Their wings shook but not because of the cold winds.

Azazel flew through the mountains in silence for a moment, weighing his options. Canaan followed him with his headphones still covering his ears. Azazel reflected upon Arick's thoughts and actions since he met him.

*"I was a Michael angel, kid. A long time ago,"* Azazel said quietly. He sensed Arick stirring in their mind.

*"Oh?"* Arick said with mild interest. *"You expect a standing ovation because you opened up a little?"* Sarcasm dripped with each word. Azazel's lips twitched.

*"I do, kid,"* Azazel chuckled. *"It's hard for us Michael angels to share anything about ourselves."*

*"Eh, I expected more."*

Azazel grinned.

*"You're a good one, Arick. I can feel it."*

*"Ew, I preferred it when you were a grumpy old-timer. Stop with all this...fuzzy stuff."*

*"Before I was punished, I was a principality. A high standing general for the Michael clan who fought side by side with the Original Michael angel. Your ancestor, kid."*

*"You went from old-timer to ancient now."* Arick's consciousness focused more on Azazel. *"Why are you telling me this now?"*

*"You remind me of Michael, kid."*

Curiosity burned throughout their mind instantly. He had Arick's full attention now.

*"What was he like?"* Arick whispered.

Azazel gave a small smile as he remembered.

*"He was nothing like any of the Michael angels now,"* Azazel began. *"My nickname for him was cry-baby because he wore his heart on his sleeve. He was the epitome of a gentle giant. Incredibly strong Arch who could destroy mountains with his bare hands and then burst out into tears at the sight of a butterfly accidentally getting crushed by one of those rocks."* Azazel paused. *"He once said he wanted to use his strength to protect the ones he loved. He hated fighting, especially if his opponent got hurt."*

*"He sounds like a pacifist,"* Arick murmured.

*"He pretty much was,"* Azazel agreed. *"It was the other Archs who pushed and manipulated him into fighting. The first time he killed a demon, he spent the whole day crying. Crying the entire time as he dug the grave, prepared the body, and notified the demon lord of the death. The demon had an illness of the mind and was seeing things that were not really there. The demon attacking thought some angels were humans and tried to eat them. Normally, Raphael would have helped Michael but*

*the other Archs ensured Raphael was occupied. Forcing Michael to fight the demon until he had no other option but to kill the demon."* Azazel sighed. *"When you held Matthew down to let your friends and family escape, it was like back then when Michael fought the demon."*

Azazel veered west.

*"I've tried to make a home in many bodies, kid. Over many centuries. And I can tell you with complete honesty you're one of the good ones."*

Azazel descended toward their destination. The prison in front of them was slightly north of the city. Ianua was underground and connected with tunnels. The mountain allowed a small swirl of black smoke to escape from the side. Unless one looked for the black smoke from above, it would never be known that there was an underground prison. Azazel landed behind some large boulders across from one possible entrance. He crouched low and indicated for Canaan to follow. Canaan removed his headphones as he landed beside him.

"Which way is inside?" Canaan whispered. "Do you know anything about the guards? About the prisoners?" The Selaphiel fired off question after question. Azazel tempered his thoughts while Arick's whirled with a newfound curiosity.

"Follow exactly what I do from now on," Azazel said, as he searched their surroundings again. "Only speak when I do this signal." He moved his finger across his mouth. "This means it is safe to speak. The guards vary based on whoever they can hire. So we might encounter a tiefling, a golem, or worse."

"Worse?" Canaan raised an eyebrow. Azazel glanced at him.

"You don't want to know," he whispered. "Follow me."

He stayed low as he quickly walked around the boulders. They made a large curve around the prison, careful to keep their steps quiet. Once the smell of smoke reached his nose, he slowed down. He peeked around the bend to see the shuffling of the tiefling guards. There were two of them. One stomped its foot over a cigarette, unaware of their presence. The other one hadn't finished their cigarette yet. No doubt trying to drag out their smoke break for as long as possible. For this plan to work though, they had to be patient.

He sat on the ground and indicated for Canaan to do the same. The tieflings complained to each other. They spoke the common demon tongue. The demon's language sounded fluid and light. Words blended into one another easily, making it a difficult language to learn. Unless you had an endless amount of time to kill like Azazel did. He had learned the demon's speech a few centuries back. Hoping to possess a demon's body and integrate into their realm, he grasped it quickly.

The guards spoke in anger at how they were reprimanded. Their boss was angry that a few prisoners had died under their watch. They complained that it was not their job to make sure prisoners didn't die. It was their job to make sure no one escaped. The other guard murmured that if more prisoners were dying, that meant the more they would be blamed for their deaths.

A dull bell ringing drew the guards' attention. One sighed before stomping out his cigarette. The bell signaled the end of their break. With their feet dragging, the guards went back inside. Moving on his tiptoes, Azazel followed. The guards grunted as they moved a large boulder, exposing the entrance. Within minutes, the darkness swallowed up the guards as they descended down the tunnel. Azazel waited for a few more minutes before approaching the door. All doors were infused with magic. He never knew whose powers they drew from, but he knew the doors would automatically close after ten minutes. If the guards lingered along the path, they were screwed.

Azazel tiptoed to the door, wings flared in case he needed to fly off. This body's advantage of heightened senses helped. He smelled the air for any signs of the tieflings while he listened for shuffling feet. No signs of guards. He waved Canaan over and stepped inside the tunnel. The sandy path quieted their steps as they ventured further underground.

Darkness encased them quickly as the door closed. The lack of light was nothing new to him, but he felt Canaan's hand on his back. Grabbing a handful of his tunic, Canaan shuffled along as Azazel led the way. Azazel drew from his memory of these tunnels to navigate, the ones that led to the guards' stations, as well as the ones that led to the torture chamber. If any guards were in a particularly foul mood, they dragged any prisoner out of their cell, into the torture chamber and mauled the poor prisoner for hours. The only rule enforced: No prisoner was allowed to die. The prison hired a few demonic healers to ensure that death was not easy to come by.

Azazel moved down the tunnel that would lead further west. The air grew stale the deeper they went, signaling that he was going in the right direction. He placed a sore hand along the wall to feel two dividing paths. A few times, they were lucky. Loud guards alerted them from far away, giving them enough time to hide around the bend.

While he had no doubt of Arick's strength, this body was still healing from injuries. His shoulders and wings ached fiercely while his ribs created sharp pains if he moved the wrong way. If this body wasn't the product of an Arch Michael and a Raphael child, chances were they wouldn't have made it out of the prison in the first place.

*"I think we should go down that way,"* Arick whispered in their mind. The path he referred to led south instead of west. In the other direction of the torture chamber.

*"Why are you whispering? It's not like anyone can hear you,"* Azazel chided Arick. A soft grunt from behind reminded him that they were in the presence of a Selaphiel angel.

*"Oh, right,"* he thought bluntly. He sensed Arick's smugness, though no words came forward.

*"I think we should go that way," Arick repeated.*

*"No,"* Azazel responded. *"The most likely place of where the Gabriel angels are being held is the torture chamber."*

*"How would you know?"*

*"Remember what I said about it being easier to jump into someone's body when their spirit has been beaten to a pulp."*

*"Oh..."*

*"Exactly, kid."*

*"But still!"* Arick implored. *"I don't know why but I get the feeling that we're supposed to go down that path instead."*

*"So I'm supposed to trust your intuition?"*

*"It hasn't led me astray so far."*

*"Your body is beaten and possessed at the moment kid."* Azazel scoffed. *"We go west."*

Azazel moved to take a step and froze. Every muscle locked up and tightened painfully.

*"No, we should go south,"* Arick argued. Azazel bit his lip to keep from groaning in pain.

*"Kid, now is not the time to play fight over the body."* Azazel pushed against Arick's consciousness. *"We could be spotted at any minute!"*

He forced Arick further back into their mind. Several muscles loosened and were back in his control.

*"Not quite!"* Arick yelled. The young heir yanked back control, causing their body to tumble forward. Muscles cramped as they each fought for control. Within minutes their body crumbled to the ground, twitching randomly as they fought.

*"Come on! Now is NOT the time, Arick!"* Azazel roared.

"Shut it!" Canaan whispered while they thrashed around.

Canaan slammed on top of them, knocking the wind out of their lungs. The Selaphiel heir then pinned both of their arms behind him, driving a knee into their back.

*"I might kill this angel,"* Azazel groaned.

*"I won't oppose,"* Arick grunted.

*"You wouldn't feel anything if you had stayed further into the subconscious,"* he reprimanded.

"Get off!" he whispered harshly aloud to Canaan. "I'm back in control now, so get off!"

After a long pause, the Selaphiel heir released them.

"It's like dealing with children," Canaan murmured under his breath. Azazel shot him a glare as he stood up.

*"Fine, kid,"* he said begrudgingly. *"Have it your way. We'll go south."*

*"Finally someone listens to me!"*

*"But remember!"* Azazel gave a mental glare to Arick. *"I'll haunt you for the rest of eternity if we both die in this body."*

He moved down the tunnel Arick had insisted on. The air down this path reeked of death and despair.

*"Oh boy."*

In the distance the sound of music could be heard. A fiddle played at a tempo that increased with each step they took.

Noah gasped as he emerged from the water. Warm air spread to his burning lungs as he gulped it down. He slumped onto the ground as the vines loosened their hold on his limbs and torso. Blood rushed throughout his body as the circulation opened back up. Chains would be looser than those vines the strange demon had used.

Behind him, he heard splashes of water. Groaning, he turned his head. His father broke the surface next, dragging the Azrael heirs up to breathe, followed up by Mikael. Noah released a long exhale as everyone sputtered. Everyone was safe for the time being.

Noah summoned what little strength he possessed to look around. The vines brought them to a strange rain-forested area. The trees and bushes were so dense and congested not a single ray of sunlight reached them from the canopy. Large mangroves reached down into the water they floated on. Lights sparkled in the air, as huge fireflies buzzed. Croaks and crickets blasted all around them, like an orchestra. Or a court hall.

In front of him, a throne carved out of a mangrove tree sat empty, for now. Along the sides, lay large banana leaves serving as curtains. Noah glanced down to see that he clung to an enormous lily pad. It appeared he was on a stage, about to stand before the king. Or in this case, the demon lord.

His stomach clenched as the noise of the courtroom crescendoed. He sank back into a lunge position, as he searched for an exit. Thick vines and leaves surrounded them.

There was no escape.

A high-pitch laugh echoed around the chamber. His father, Zewal, and Tariel huddled together on a lily pad to his left, while Mikael settled on the pad to his right. Mikael warned them that standing in front of the demon lord was the worst possible outcome of this mission. Yet here they stood. About to see one of the most powerful beings in existence.

*This would be a great time for a Seraphim to join us,* Noah thought grimly.

He heard the clicking and clattering of large insects gathering. A few eyeballs broke the surface of the pool to stare at them. A low croak told him large frogs sat underneath the surface of the water. A slithering motion in the water drew his attention. He inched closer to the lily pad with his father.

If they were to fight, they stood a better chance together. Mikael widened his stance as an enormous creature shot from the water and onto the throne. Water splashed as the rest of the body followed. Big, bigger than Mikael, the half-snake, half-humanoid demon slid onto the throne seat. A long, slender face, shimmering with blue and green scales down its body. The creature possessed bright, golden eyes with narrow slits as pupils. A wide mouth displayed rows of razor sharp teeth when it grinned.

"My, my, my," the creature's voice purred. "What do we have here?"

A frog-like creature hopped forward, offering up a large cape.

"Our oh-so-righteous, benevolent, charming, good-looking demon lord, Leviathan, Ruler of the river basin and spontaneity, one of the guards—"

Leviathan coughed loudly, cutting off the frog's response.

"You forgot to include Supreme Emperor of alcohol, drugs, and sexual pleasures." Leviathan narrowed his eyes at the kneeling servant. Snatching up the cape, the demon lord gave an exasperated sigh.

"Honestly," Leviathan hissed. "How hard is it to introduce the Lord you love and adore so much?" He paused. "Unless you don't love and adore me as much as I thought you did."

The little frog demon shook his head urgently.

"No! No, my Lord!" the servant pleaded. "Forgive my own stupidity. Please give me the honor of your punishment, so that I may serve you better in the future." The frog demon put his forehead to the ground and hands out to the side.

Leviathan peered down at him with a sneer.

"Ahhh," he hummed. "Very well. Since I am in a good mood at the moment, I will banish you to Mirage for a mere fifty years."

Gasps echoed through the audience at Leviathan's ruling. A few demons in the trees and shrubs whispered amongst themselves.

"Silence!" Leviathan yelled. He donned the shimmering golden cape before turning back to the servant. "Should you live past the fifty years, you will be welcomed back at my court but," He stared down his nose at the servant. "At the bottom of the rung, cleaning and serving those at the lowest level." He waved a glittery blue and green arm to the side. "Now go. Your face is making me sick."

The servant bowed deeply.

"Thank you, my Lord! Thank you for your mercy! We're so lucky to have you and your kindness!" the demon cried out as it hopped away. The frog disappeared into the dense brush just as a new servant appeared.

This servant was a gecko, nearly the size of Noah. Its tan body scurried across the mangrove branches within a blink of an eye.

"Our oh-so-righteous, benevolent, charming, good-looking

demon lord Leviathan, Ruler of the river basin and spontaneity, and Supreme Emperor of alcohol, drugs, and sexual pleasures!" The gecko announced, kneeling in front of Leviathan. "Please regard these intruders found by one of the patrol guards!"

For the first time since Leviathan arrived, he turned to regard them. Or really he twirled around, flaring his cape in the wind, to address them.

The yellow eyes landed on Mikael and widened. A forked tongue slid in and out of his mouth quickly once then twice. Leviathan tilted his head at Mikael as if confused. He crossed his arms and placed one hand on his chin.

"This guard actually caught that slippery assimilate bastard in my territory of all places?" Leviathan hissed. His lips curled upward in a slight snarl. Disgust coated every word he uttered. His scales darkened and shimmered as he regarded Mikael with disdain.

"They attacked a unicorn just along the edge of the mountain range, my Lord," the gecko answered. "We think they were heading to the Decimate mountains which is the assimilate, Matthew's, stronghold."

"DON'T speak the name of that scum in MY court!" Leviathan roared. He slithered with lightning speed to Mikael, grabbing him by the throat. "How dare you desecrate my glamorous and sophisticated throne room!"

Noah heard Mikael groan as Leviathan squeezed.

"He's not Matthew!" Elijah called out. Without looking away from Mikael, Leviathan whipped his tail around. Leviathan's tail struck his father so hard, he almost catapulted off the lily pad. Noah moved before his father landed. He leaped onto the next pad and knelt down to help his father up.

"Don't speak unless spoken to, Arch." Leviathan hissed the word as if it was the worst thing to be called.

Zewal and Tariel jerked up with their wings flared. Zewal's eyes somehow appeared darker than ever before. Zewal scoffed, his face scrunched into a leer.

"How unsophisticated," Zewal sneered. "Brought down to a hissy fit by an Arch."

Leviathan loosened his hold on Mikael as he whirled to face Zewal. The demon lord snarled. Zewal tilted his head back and gave the cruelest laugh Noah had ever heard from him.

"You want to die today, don't you?" Leviathan jeered. He dropped Mikael to the ground, forgotten, as he slithered to Zewal.

"I'm an Azrael Arch." Zewal's voice dropped several degrees. "Death is nothing to me."

Leviathan's tongue glided in and out again as he stopped in front of Zewal. Tariel's wings opened wide, ready to take off at any time. Her face scrunched in concentration. The harsh lines on their faces stood out as they stared down the Demon Lord.

"Azrael Archs?" Leviathan asked with less bite in his tone. He moved his head up and down as inspected. "It has been so long since I've seen your kind." Leviathan brought a claw to his chin. He sniffed the air "Are you the offspring of *the* Azrael Adjutor?"

Zewal's jaw tightened. "Yes, what do you know of our great ancestor?"

"Oh!" Leviathan squealed. He clasped his hands together. If a snake could blush, this was how Noah imagined it would look like.

"I have sooooo many wonderful memories with your great-great-great-great-great-great-great-great grandfather!" Leviathan cooed. "He gave me that same exact sexy look of disapproval! You even have the same smell! Awwwww!" Leviathan curled around Zewal and Tariel, forcing them back to back.

"I am in a much better mood now. Oh! Such fond memories." Leviathan coiled around them tighter. "Tell me then, what brings you all the way out here? In my domain?"

"We came here looking for Matthew," Mikael called out from behind. Leviathan grinned, displaying rows of sharp teeth.

"You're joking ,yes?" Leviathan chuckled, but his eyes narrowed.

"No," Zewal said, frowning.

"Ah!" Leviathan giggled. "You all are just so adorable to me now!"

Zewal and Tariel grunted as Leviathan's body constricted tighter. Noah attempted to creep closer to Leviathan, hoping to draw attention away from the Azrael siblings, but his father stopped him. In fact his father pushed back.

"Don't draw his attention," Elijah whispered.

"We need to help Zewal and Tariel!" Noah whispered back fiercely.

"If we get him too excited the demon lord may crush them by accident," Elijah said in a low voice. He dragged Noah up with him to stand.

"Will you hear us out please, demon lord?" Elijah called out.

"Hmmmmm." Leviathan relaxed his torso down to the lily pad, propping his head up with one hand. "This is all sooooo amusing now." Leviathan turned to Mikael, ignoring Elijah. "Who are you then if not the assimilate bastard?"

"I am Mikael Viribus, Head Arch of the Michael Clan."

Leviathan raised an eyebrow and tilted his head. "And?" he probed.

Mikael sighed. "And I am Matthew's younger brother."

Leviathan laughed out loud. After a few seconds, the entire throne room filled with demons joined in. All laughed hysterically.

In his laughter, Leviathan released Zewal and Tariel, curling in on himself as he cackled. He hooted and hollered as he rolled along the pad.

"Stop it! Stop it!" Leviathan cried out. "It's all too funny!"

Noah and his father glanced at each other before silently moving to Zewal and Tariel's side. The siblings were knelt down, clutching their sides when they approached. Mikael leapt over as well, landing in front of them. Mikael crouched low into a defensive position, ready to move at the slightest indication.

"Are you both ok?" Noah knelt down to Zewal. Both he and his father extended their hands to them, pushing their power forward. A light glow illuminated his hands as he pushed his healing powers into Zewal's side. Zewal grunted as his cool touch worked.

"We'll live," Zewal mumbled. "It's the hiking that'll kill us probably, not him." He indicated to Leviathan, who settled down.

"How does he know our ancestor?" Tariel asked, as she stood, healed by Elijah. "And what happened when we were captured? That was the most intense migraine I've ever had."

"Ahhh, that." Leviathan chuckled from the ground. "You must not know all of your history to be asking that question." He slid up to a seated position. "Every Archangel 'clan,'" Leviathan did air quotes with his hand, "their power is derived from our realm. And since our realm is ruled by three demon lord domains, your power really is derived from our power."

“What?” Zewal whispered. His eyes widened. “No, that’s impossible!”

Leviathan giggled. “Nothing is impossible, little cutie.” He clapped his hands together. “I just had a brilliant idea!” Leviathan called out. “Let’s take this party to my brother! He would be just as delighted as I am with this little group!”

Cheers from the audience rang out. While the demons in the room applauded Leviathan’s idea, he struck a pose, shimmering his scales. A faint glow grew all along his body.

“Oh no,” Mikael said as he paled. For the first time ever, Noah saw fear enter into Mikael’s eyes. “Not the demon lord Beelzebub.”

Leviathan laughed. “Of course, Beelzebub! Satan’s too much of a party-pooper!”

Light swirled around his body, and the temperature in the room lowered. Wind picked up around them like a tornado. Leviathan’s laughter could be heard above the wind, but Noah no longer saw him, as a bright light consumed him. Vines wrapped tightly around their hands and feet once more, causing them to crash to the ground.

“What?!” A growl emanated from the light.

“Come on, brother,” Leviathan purred. “That’s no way to greet me.”

Another vicious growl echoed around them.

“You are so…grumpy today, brother,” Leviathan whined. “Did I disturb another one of your…games?”

“Never mind that!” the voice roared. “What is it you want?”

Another chuckle from Leviathan.

“Oh, brother, I think you’ll be interested in what I have to say.” A pause. “But…I want to see your face when I say it.”

“NO—” The voice cut off as the wind around them picked up.

“Hold onto your feathers, Archs!” was all Noah heard before he was dragged to the center of the lily pad. The croaks and crickets from the shadows cheered around them as they descended into the bright, white light.

# Chapter 6

The tall grass provided little shelter against the rushing winds, as Ben and his party walked. The microscopic red bugs, repelled by the lotion Barmen provided, faded to a memory. Though Isabella and Gabriel repeatedly checked their arms and legs throughout their journey.

They passed by some strange-looking animals that Barmen said were harmless demon antelope. The Raziel heir explained how many demons lived non-violent and peaceful lives.

Intrigued, Ben decided to get as much information out of Barmen as he could about this strange realm.

"How exactly does this realm work?" Ben asked. The grass grazed against his skin as he moved closer to Barmen.

Barmen slowed his pace as he struggled to word his answer. His thoughts weighed on his mind with how much knowledge he possessed of the demon realm.

"First, I should begin with telling you the biggest fundamental lie you've been told," Barmen started. "Everything you've been taught about the realms has been a lie."

Ben stumbled forward. He heard how true this was in Barmen's mind.

"In what ways?" Clarissa asked with a furrowed brow. She walked on the other side of Barmen.

"For one, you and I were taught how the realms are stacked on top of one another. First the demon realm, then our realm and then the human realm is at the bottom. Creating an upside down pyramid look," Barmen replied.

"Yeah, because that's to showcase our hierarchy, right?" Gabriel asked from the right.

"That's what the Original Archs wanted us to believe as a way to limit interaction with one another," Barmen explained. "The *real* structure of how our realms work is more cyclical in nature. One realm is not 'above' another."

"I don't…understand," Isabella murmured beside Clarissa, pulling at the tall grass as they walked.

"Hmmm, let's see. How can I explain?" Barmen paused for a moment. "You understand how our powers work, yes?"

"Uhh," Isabella stuttered, and Gabriel gave a sheepish shrug.

"Our power is an accumulation and expression of energy particles. The amount of energy particles an angel is born with is determined by their rank. Those of higher standing, like Archs, are born with more energy than those of lower rank. Also the clan you were born into determines how you can express those energy particles," Clarissa rattled off. "Since Isabella and I were born of the Uriel clan, we can express those energy particles only as fire and wind manipulation. Whereas Gabriel can express his only through opening portals between places."

Everyone paused in their walk with agape mouths at Clarissa.

"What?" Clarissa shrugged. "I paid attention to those boring lecture classes."

"Yes, but…" Gabriel started. "I…you're not as air-headed as I thought you were," he finished.

Clarissa narrowed her eyes at him. "What's that supposed to mean?" she said threateningly. Sparks flickered along her fingers.

"Yikes! Don't do that! We're in a grassy field. Everything will set ablaze." Gabriel leaped back.

"It doesn't matter because Clarissa is correct," Barmen said as he turned to her. "You explained it better than I could have. Thank you."

Clarissa blushed, and the sparks on her hands extinguished.

Barmen continued on their path before going on with his lesson.

"So with that explained, every living creature in all three realms releases energy particles. The type of energy and the amount vary based on what that creature is and where they are, but nonetheless energy is released," Barmen described. "Humans release their spiritual energy usually through emotions. Most of the time they aren't aware of it, which is why they barely notice when a demon is feeding off them."

"Demons feed off their spiritual energy and not their emotions?"

Isabella asked.

"Well, humans release their spiritual energy when they're feeling certain strong emotions is the more technically correct answer," Barmen corrected. "That abundance of energy, all those billions of particles humans express, flows into the demon realm. Feeding and fueling their entire world." Barmen waved his hand around them. "Once that energy flows into the demon realm, the demon lords have the ability to manipulate all of this widespread energy however they please. That is what makes them so powerful. Whereas us Archs can have only two or three abilities at the most with our spiritual energy, the demon lords can nearly do anything they imagine. With a few exceptions of course." Barmen sighed. "There are always exceptions."

Ben caught a flash of thought through Barmen. *Staffs...Satan... Power...*

"Such as?" Ben asked.

"For one, the demon lords are able to power their large dominions because of how spread out their energy is. If they wish to do something incredibly powerful, they'd have to call all that energy back to them. Each demon lord possesses a powerful staff that acts like a magnet to call all their spiritual energy to them."

"Powerful staff?!" Gabriel asked with flared wings. "I thought that was just part of the scary stories parents told their kids to get them to behave."

"I'm afraid they are very much real." Barmen grimaced. "The staff pulls an insane amount of spiritual energy to the user. If any of us are around one of the demon lords when they wield one, it will drain us completely, not just of our power but possibly our life too."

Ben shuddered at the thought of such immense power. *What if...?* He shook his head to clear his thoughts. One task at a time.

"So the energy humans express flows into the demon's realm. Then does that mean the energy expressed in the demon realm flows into our realm. And our energy flows into the humans'?" Ben asked.

"Exactly." Barmen nodded. "Instead of our realms being stacked on top of one another, we all feed into the next realm, like a constant cycle. When I first learned of this, I imagined the cycle of rain. How the rain changes to another state to serve its purpose and then moves onto the next."

Clarissa hummed in approval. "That makes perfect sense to me.

But…" She glanced at Barmen. "How do we know you are telling the truth? Why would our ancestors teach us something false?"

Barmen gave a humorless laugh. "Our ancestors…" Barmen sighed. "The politest way I can put this is that our ancestors tried their best to do what *they thought* was best for all of the realms. And that included lying about how all of our worlds worked." Barmen paused in his stride to glance back at them. They stopped short. "None of you have to believe me. I am a Raziel angel after all. But I have nothing to gain by lying to you. In fact, telling all of you this fundamental truth would be a bigger disgrace upon our ancestors than my black market trade. It has been every Raziel Head's duty to bear this secret of how the realms work." Barmen rubbed his tired face. "I am probably the least honorable Raziel Arch in this line. So take what I tell you with caution." Barmen faced forward. "We're getting closer to the city."

Ben turned his head to see they were indeed closer. No more than a mile out stood a cluster of grass huts with smoke coming out of the top. Closer to the mountains, at the base, appeared to be pyramid shaped structures.

"Gabriel," Barmen called out.

"Yes?" Gabriel murmured, his eyes glued on the buildings in the distance.

"Transport to that first pyramid building. On the right side of the building, there should be clothes hanging out to dry at this time of day. Grab as many cloaks as you can. We will wait for you here."

"Why the cloaks?" Gabriel asked.

With a pointed glance to Clarissa and Isabella, Barmen replied.

"The less attention the girls attract the better," he scoffed. Clarissa bristled.

"We are adults, need I remind you?" she retorted.

"You don't need to remind me, darling," Barmen responded. "It's the demons I don't want to remind."

"All right," Gabriel said before opening a portal with his hand. The light from the portal was momentary, disappearing as soon as Gabriel passed through.

"Why is it the Raziel Head's duty to keep such a secret?" Clarissa asked after a moment of silence.

Barmen inclined his head toward Clarissa.

"My father, and my father's father, and his father before him,"

Barmen started. "believed—no saw with their own eyes how…chaotic angels became with this knowledge. Like a child who knows where the cookie jar is." Barmen paused. "My father upholds my ancestor's belief of not allowing the child to know what a cookie is, so that the child will never go looking for something he or she doesn't know exists."

"Who gave your ancestors the right to decide that?!" Isabella asked, outraged. Barmen gave a sad grin.

"All of the other original Archangels of the clans," Barmen answered. "They all believed in the philosophy that ignorance is bliss for our people."

Ben heard the truth in every word Barmen spoke. In his thoughts, Barmen didn't care what they did with this information. A memory of Barmen's flashed through his mind. One of his father giving him that harshest thrashing of his life for sharing family secrets with an outsider.

*"Never betray this family again!"* Another snap from the sheath his father used to beat him. Anger burned within Barmen's mind at the memory. Not just anger, but a defiant kind of anger. Ben blinked, shocked at Barmen's cool expression.

He never knew Joshua Scio treated Barmen with severity.

"Ben," Barmen called out. His eyes remained on the city in the distance. "Stay out of business that's not your own."

Ben paused.

A mental wall came down hard in Barmen's mind. A dull ache stretched across his head at the sudden impact. Ben rubbed his eyes as his head throbbed. The Raziel Arch's power allowed them the special ability not only to create illusions but to distort the mind of whomever they wished. Thus creating a great defense against any Selaphiel angel wanting to know more.

Ben scoffed. "That's rich, coming from an Arch who wants to know everyone's business."

A flash of light announced Gabriel's return. The strip of white light expanded then contracted as soon as Gabriel leapt out, carrying a large bundle of clothing."

"I was able to grab cloaks for all of us!" Gabriel exclaimed with a wide smile.

"Good, everyone put these on and cover up," Barmen said. "Angels, let alone Archangels, are an unusual sighting in the demon realm."

"What about our wings?" Isabella asked, reaching for a cloak.

Everyone grabbed a cloak from Gabriel. "Gabriel and Ben took a serum in the human world, but we didn't"

"I have a rough plan for that," Barmen said, donning his own cloak. "The business associate of mine that I mentioned earlier lives on the outskirts of the city. We will stop there first before going into the big city."

"Without our wings won't we stand out more as humans?" Clarissa asked. Barmen shook his head.

"Not necessarily," Barmen replied. "Some humans live in the demon realm, as pets or companions. In a major city, everyone expects some diversity. We will stand out more with our wings."

"Very well," Ben said as he pulled the hood up on his cloak. "We better get moving, then."

Clarissa helped Isabella adjust her cloak to ensure her wings were hidden.

"Allow me," Barmen said to Clarissa. A light blush spread across her face as she turned around to allow him to adjust her cloak. Gabriel and Ben exchanged a pointed glance.

*I can't wait to get back home to Charlotte.* Gabriel sighed.

Ben nodded in sympathy. The farther he moved away from Atarah, the tighter his chest constricted. Urgency thrummed through his veins as his thoughts turned to her. As water was essential for fish, she represented his home and his ability to live. He needed to do something and fast. Too many times, he had been useless in defending the ones he loved. This was the way he could do better.

"All right," Barmen called out. "Let's move out."

They followed after Barmen. The tall grass shrunk the closer they traveled to the city. In less than an hour, they were within the outskirts. The city of Umbra spread further apart than Ben anticipated. Most of the buildings on the outskirts were low, no more than three stories high and built in a pyramid shape. The strange looking homes attached to one another with Arch-covered stone walkways that moved. Off in the distance, a tall building erected in the middle of the city stood out.

Barmen whispered as he walked how the magic from the demon lord powered and fueled every city within their domain. The movement of the stairs, the electric lanterns that turned on at night, everything was from the ruler of this domain. Strange vehicles moved around them, powered by electromagnetism. Clarissa asked what would happen if the demon lord should ever die. Barmen gave a grimace before stating he never wanted to find out.

The cloaks that Gabriel managed to steal for them made for a great deterrent. A few glances their way but no outright stares. Covered up, they moved with care to not draw any attention. Not long after they traveled past the first few buildings, Barmen indicated for them to stop.

"Wait here," Barmen whispered. "Try not to draw any attention."

The building he walked into was another pyramid-shaped structure with a large wooden door and no handle. The planks of the wooden door split apart as he whispered a word in a language Ben didn't recognize. Once Barmen walked through the threshold, the planks sealed back together.

Now, along the edge of the city, they stood waiting for Barmen to get the serum they needed from a run-down looking building. Ben tapped his finger on his crossed arms as he stood by. The closer they ventured into the city, the more urgency built up within him. As if his body knew what dangers lay ahead. The others fidgeted as well.

Gabriel's wings twitched every now and then. His eyes surveyed their surroundings without pause. Isabella's hands trembled, creating miniature tornadoes on her fingertips. Clarissa grabbed onto her sister's hand to stop any wind from picking up.

Ben closed his eyes to focus on the thoughts around them. There were a few demons on this side of town. Mercifully, no one paid attention to four strange, cloaked beings hovering outside of a building. According to Barmen, creatures loitering outside was not a strange occurrence in the demon realm. Demons came in many strange sizes, shapes, and cultural backgrounds.

However, that didn't stop one city guard from eyeing Clarissa. The police officer was a salamander demon. Large, standing at nearly seven feet tall, and with yellow irises that narrowed in on Clarissa's smaller form. Ben stepped in front of Clarissa a little bit, to block her from the demon's sight. He forced his face to remain impassive and bored, as if he hadn't meant to move in front of her.

Ben heard the salamander's thoughts become intrigued by the two females and their strange hunched form. Ben groaned. Clarissa shot him a confused look. She opened her mouth to speak but sounds of pained grunts emanated from the closed door Barmen walked through.

Her expression changed from one of confusion to hard focus.

She moved fast. Before Ben could stop her, Clarissa banged on the door with her fist.

"Hey!" she yelled. "Open this door!"

Ben snatched both of her wrists to stop her, but it was too late. Heads and minds turned their way at the commotion. The salamander gleamed. The guard now had a reason to interrogate them.

"Let me go!" Clarissa growled at him. When he refused to let her go, she gave a huff as his only warning before her hands turned blazing hot. Ben jerked his hands away and cursed quietly.

*Let that...teach you...not touch...* Clarissa's thoughts faded in and out, but Ben's eyes were on the guard.

The others noticed the salamander when he appeared right in front of them. Moving swiftly, Clarissa jumped back to Isabella when the guard stood to his full height, towering above them.

"Well," it drawled out. "What have we here?" Its yellow eyes scanned each of them but lingered on Clarissa.

"We are merely passing through here." Ben stepped forward to the guard, holding his hands out. "We don't want trouble."

"What was *she* doing banging on dear old Geager's door then?" The salamander tilted his head.

"Our friend—" Clarissa started.

"A mere misunderstanding," Ben interrupted. His head throbbed as he switched back and forth between reading everyone's thoughts. Geager, from the salamander's memory, was an alchemist who dealt out some illegal potions from time to time. Harmless, for the most part but drew interest when females were involved. Another guard approached from the side. This one was shorter, barely coming up to Ben's waist.

"What's the problem here, Zamut?" The second guard's voice sounded deep and smoky. He possessed an abnormally large mouth, with a long braided beard stretching down to his knees. A ridiculously large axe dragged behind him. Ben's heart sped up at the sight of the weapon.

"These..." Zamut paused. He lifted his nose and sniffed at them. *Strange smell...* Ben caught the thought too late. Zamut reached out with lightning speed and grabbed Clarissa by the throat. She gave a short yell of outrage as she struggled against his hold. "Females? At Geager?" Zamut leered at Clarissa.

Panic grabbed a hold of him as the second guard drew his axe forward. Ben scrambled to think of a way out of this situation when a hand clamped on his shoulder. Ben jerked his head to the side to see Barmen. Ben nearly sighed in relief.

"Yes," Barmen said in a cold voice. "What seems to be the problem here, officers?"

Zamut's eyes twitched to Barmen's shoulder and flinched. Zamut immediately released Clarissa and backed away from them, from Barmen. The gleam from a silver pen attached to the upper left corner of Barmen's tunic caught his eye. That hadn't been there earlier.

"Apologies, trader," Zamut bowed his head slightly. His tail curled inward as if protectively "We mistook your company for…miscreants."

"Yes, sir," the other guard mumbled. Both backed away as if Barmen would pounce on them at any time. Fear permeated their minds as their arms shook.

"Hmmmm," Barmen hummed as he watched Clarissa rub her neck. "I trust," Barmen lifted his hand up, pointing three fingers at the salamander, "that this misunderstanding won't happen again."

Both of their mouths opened as if to scream, but no sound emanated. Their bodies stiffened and eyes rolled to the back of their head. The guards' minds blurred as terror overtook them. Frozen, they had no choice but to endure whatever illusion Barmen set upon them. Ben's eyes widened at the cruelty in their minds. Sporadic images flashed his mind as he read the guard's tortured illusion.

He never wanted to get stuck on Barmen's bad side.

Barmen strolled to Clarissa and Isabella; his eyes never left Clarissa's throat.

"Here, take this." Barmen handed over two small vials of a black liquid. "This serum is a little different from the one back at home. Your wings will disappear painlessly. You can call forth your wings back at any time, but it will hurt."

They both quickly swallowed the contents of the vials. The faster they drank, the easier the serum went down. Their wings faded, like sunlight over the horizon, gradually.

"What happened to your eye?" Clarissa asked softly while they waited.

They all looked up to Barmen's face to see the other side of his face was indeed bruised. His right eye was blackened, and swelling ran along the brow.

"Nothing but a little misunderstanding," Barmen said with a wave of his hand.

He turned to walk up to the guards, snapping two fingers beside their heads. The two demon guards crumbled to the ground, gasping for air. A hard expression overcame his face.

"You two came at the perfect time." He sneered down at them. "Both of you are to take us before Lord Beelzebub immediately." Barmen's command was curt and unyielding. The guards trembled as they scrambled to their feet. Too frightened to speak, they both nodded their heads in agreement.

"Also," Barmen held up a finger and his voice dropped low. "If either of you, so much as look at these two females, you'll never know a day of peace for the rest of your existence." His blue eyes turned to ice. "Do I make myself clear?"

The guards nodded in unison, still too scared to speak.

"Then get moving." Barmen shooed them away. They scurried ahead, limbs shook as they directed them.

"Subtle," Ben said, coming to stand beside Barmen. "I was about to crap my pants until you came along."

"You'll need to hide that if you are to stand before Beelzebub," Barmen replied as he walked down the street, following the demon guards. "Demons have no respect for those who can't hold in their shit."

Ben's lips twitched in amusement as he followed after him. Clarissa, Isabella, and Gabriel all fell in behind them. Each of them eyed the surrounding buildings and demons with caution and skepticism. Traveling deeper and deeper into the city, the buildings shrank in size and stacked on top of one another, creating higher skyrises. In the distance, mountains towered above them with buildings peppered along the ridges. Demons of all shapes and sizes walked around them, giving them a wide berth when they passed by. A few curious glances were shot their way, but dismissed within seconds. Demons ignored them, to Ben's relief.

Soon, the city of Umbra towered over them. Under less stressful circumstances, he might admire the beauty of the city. Somehow, light illuminated underneath them as they walked down the street, and it faded behind them. The industrialized architecture, the advanced technology, and diverse culture of Beelzebub's domain was fascinating. Ben guessed this was why Barmen approached Beelzebub first to strike a deal instead of the other demon lords. Innovation and expansion described Umbra

City to the utmost degree.

Asking Barmen to bring them to Beelzebub proved to be a wise decision. The shock of this new world would have overwhelmed him, and especially the others. Behind him, Isabella clutched her sister's cloak as she looked around in wonder and fear. Clarissa's and Gabriel's faces grew paler with each step they took. From the low hum of their minds, he read their fear and nervousness as plainly as their faces showed. Ben wondered if he would have time to warn them to mask their faces before they stood in front of the demon lord.

Barmen had done a good job of warning them of what the demon cities were like, but little could have prepared them from walking the streets. As they approached the steps of a ridiculously tall building he had seen earlier, more demons lined the streets to enter various buildings.

They stopped before large, white marble steps.

"This is it," Barmen said softly. "Hide your fear. The fact that no one has accosted us means that Beelzebub already knows we are here and is expecting us."

"Accosted us?!" Gabriel said, outraged. "Those guards from earlier were going to attack us!"

"Does the fear ever go away?" Isabella asked. Her hands trembled by her side, her eyes on the building. Barmen peeked at her hands before turning back to the stairs.

"The fear never leaves." Barmen sighed. "But we don't let that stop us now, do we?"

"No." Clarissa declared with narrowed eyes. She grabbed her sister's hand, and faced the tall building with determination. A ghost of a smile appeared on Barmen's face, but was gone in a matter of seconds.

"This is more than fear, guys!" Gabriel whispered through gritted teeth. His eyes twitched as the crowd drew closer. "This is pure insanity!"

"Let's get on with it," Ben said. His own hands shook for a different reason. Excitement hummed through his body. From here, he sensed the power thrumming through the demon lord. Raw power that he wanted to possess.

He climbed up the steps with enthusiasm. The others trailed, a little more reluctant, behind him. Now, was his chance. The opportunity to play with the key players in this grand game between the realms. He clenched his fists as he went over his prepared speech in his head. All the possibilities of how the conversation would go and what actions to take. His headache grew from a dull ache to stabbing pain as he attempted to read the demon lord's mind at this distance. Nothing but silence greeted him.

*No matter*, he thought. *I just need to get closer.*

At the top of the steps, large red doors creaked as they opened. Inside, a long metal shaft at the opposite end ascended to the top floor, leaving them to see the ceiling. The floors themselves curved along the building. On every floor, Ben could see workers moving quickly from office to office. Demons, dressed in black and white suits, walked by them talking on small devices. A few gave a quick curious glance before getting drawn back into business. During Ben's few brief times in the human realm, a place called 'Wall Street' appeared eerily similar to this building.

"What is this place called?" Ben breathed in amazement. Barmen grimaced as a demon hurried by him, talking quickly into a strange-looking item.

"This is one of Beelzebub's favorite cities because it's his center of operation. It's where he conducts most of his business. The capital, if you will." Barmen tilted his head upward to the top floor. "This place is called The Bull."

"The Bull?" Clarissa echoed as she glanced up. "Why is it called that?"

"You'll see soon enough," Barmen mumbled. "This way," he called out. Barmen turned his heel and started toward the long shaft at the end of the building. Their heels clicked as they walked; no one stopped them.

"This is called an elevator," Barmen explained. The word rang a distant memory from Ben's time in the human realm. "It'll take us directly up to see him." Barmen paused. "Only those allowed up can take the elevator. So if I press this button and the light doesn't turn on, he will refuse to see us."

"He already knows we're here," Ben said back to Barmen. "Five Archangel heirs to say the least. There is no way he is not at least curious as to why we are here."

Barmen frowned at him. "You're right, but I still feel the need to explain to you how it works." He pressed the button. They all watched with anticipation, leaning in close, as he lifted his hand away. A light appeared on the button, and they all released a sigh. A short bell rang, and the metal doors opened to a small rectangular box. Enough room for them all.

At Barmen's urging, they quickly filed in, right before the metal doors closed. The metal box shifted and moved upward at a high speed. Ben's lips twitched as he struggled to keep his excited grin off of his face. The others didn't share his sentiment. He smelled the nervous stench of Gabriel permeating this enclosed space, while Clarissa and Isabella sent out involuntary sparks of flames or small gusts of wind as they climbed to the highest floor. Their shoulders tensed as the elevator slowed to the top.

A bell's single ding rang out.

Ben leaned forward as the metal door opened. His headache spiked as he focused his power, ready to latch onto the demon lord's mind. The room was not what he expected. He had pictured a dark, dungeon-like room with cries of pain and anguish but saw none of that. The room, carved out of the same white marble from downstairs, was open. Large, floor length windows extended to the far wall, displaying the entire city. He saw snow capped mountains in the distance and a single desk.

Gazing out the windows, stood Beelzebub. Ben froze and Clarissa's and Isabella's mouths dropped open as the demon lord turned to greet them. Again, nothing of what Ben expected.

Beelzebub, dressed in an all-black suit, looked human in body only. He stood tall and muscular with jet black hair and a deep set of ruby red eyes. Two large horns sat on top of his head. His face gave Ben the impression of what a bull would look like in human form, with a wide nose and square jaw line. The facial features created an odd dichotomy of a disturbing yet attractive face.

Beelzebub cleared his throat.

"Welcome." A deep, rich voice came out of Beelzebub's mouth. "To formally introduce myself… " He lifted a gloved hand to his chest. "I am Beelzebub, demon lord of this domain."

Power rippled off of Beelzebub in waves. Despite the lord's casual movements, everything in Ben's body told him to turn tail and run as far away as possible. The hairs on the back of his neck stood up at the sound of the demon lord's voice. He locked out his joints to keep from shaking, refusing to show any kind of weakness.

Barmen stepped forward and knelt.

"Lord Beelzebub," Barmen's voice sounded strained. "Benjamin Doctrina, heir of the Selaphiel Clan, requested to meet with you, my lord."

Beelzebub inclined his head toward him. His red eyes gleamed with interest.

"Benjamin Doctrina," Beelzebub rumbled. "I have heard…interesting things about you."

"Oh," Ben said, relieved his voice was even and cool. "You've heard of me? Lord Beelzebub, I'm honored." He gave a small bow. Bile rose up in his mouth at his own words. To bow before the demon lord, his enemy, burned his pride down to his core. Shame threatened to consume him until he reminded himself that this groveling was necessary. Soon everyone, including the demon lords, would be nothing more than bugs beneath his feet.

Beelzebub grinned. It was anything but friendly.

"I have come here to offer a proposal," Ben said before he lost his nerve. "If you would be so inclined to hear it, my lord."

Beelzebub opened his mouth to speak when a blue light flashed from his desk. Everyone's attention moved to the light. The demon lord glared at the flashing light and sighed.

"My apologies, please give me one moment." Beelzebub said as he approached his desk. He tapped a flat looking, white plate, where the blue light flashed from.

"What?" he growled at the plate. Ripples of fear crawled through Ben's body at the sound. His body urged him to run but his mind refused. Now was his chance and he wasn't going to waste it. Not after how far they had come.

"Come on, brother," a silky voice purred from the plate. "That's no way to greet me."

A savage growl emanated from Beelzebub and nearly caused Ben's knees to buckle from terror. More power rippled around them as Beelzebub grew irritated. Ants crawling on him would have felt better than the feeling of the demon lord's power. He wanted to take a shower now. Meanwhile the voice from earlier didn't sound deterred. Instead the voice laughed from the other end. The sound echoed around Beelzebub's office.

"You are so…grumpy today, brother," the voice said breathlessly.

"Did I disturb another one of your…games?"

"Never mind that!" Beelzebub roared. "What is it you want?"

Another chuckle. "Oh brother, I think you will be interested in what I have to say." A pause. "But…I want to see your face when I say it."

"No!" Beelzebub said, but it was too late. A flash of light blasted in front of them, blinding them all. Ben heard screams behind him as a gust of wind pushed them backward. Once the light faded, Ben checked on his group.

Clarissa and Isabella cowered by the closed elevator door. Sparks sprouted in Clarissa's hands, Isabella clutched her sister's cloak, and Gabriel reached out his hand and grunted with effort. Alarm shone in his eyes.

"I can't open a portal," Gabriel whispered in shock. "We can't escape! We're trapped!"

Ben whipped his head around to Barmen, who hadn't moved from his knelt position.

"What the hell Barmen?!" Ben yelled. Barmen flinched but another laugh drew his attention. The same laugh from before. Ben turned back to see an irritated Beelzebub and another, more terrifying creature.

On top of the desk sat a half snake, half humanoid creature with a long, slender face that bore glittery blue and green scales down its entire body. The slithering body contracted and relaxed along the desk as if doing a leisurely stretch. The creature had bright, golden eyes with narrow slits for pupils. A wide mouth showed rows of razor sharp teeth when it chuckled once again.

"I told you NOT to show up unannounced, Leviathan! " Beelzebub rumbled.

"But, big brother," Leviathan purred as he stretched out along the desk. "I've brought gifts for you." He lifted his tail and pointed to the far side of the room. Ben almost fell to the floor.

In the corner, knelt Mikael, Elijah, Noah, Zewal, and Tariel wrapped up in vines. Two Archangel Heads and three heirs of different clans. Ben's heart dropped. How was this possible? Mikael possessed the most strength out of any Archangel. Zewal and Tariel had the best abilities to drain any of their enemies. With Noah and Elijah, they should be unstoppable. Yet here they were on their knees, looking exhausted. Why were they here?

Ben's mind went numb for a moment as shock stunned him. All of the moving pieces moved in different positions than he had anticipated. Why? Why!?

Another laugh echoed. Leviathan cackled as he slithered off of the desk.

"The look on your face, brother! Priceless!" Leviathan's scales shimmered as he moved to Beelzebub's side. Beelzebub's look of surprise appeared genuine. Ben scrambled to focus on his mind. Why was Beelzebub surprised by the Archangel Heads but was not surprised when they arrived? Silence greeted him again as Ben strained to read his mind. Sharp pains stabbed Ben's head immediately. Ben cried out and fell to his knees as he clutched his head. The pain continued for a few minutes more before lessening. Trembles wracked his body as he attempted to stand.

"Ahhhh, it's just so cute when they try," Leviathan cooed. "It's too bad they must remain so ignorant. They would make amusing pets."

"Leviathan, let's get back to business now that you've made your…theatrical entrance." Beelzebub said gruffly.

He stepped around his desk and toward Mikael. Ben noticed for the first time his feet were made up of hooves. Beelzebub's feet clicked as he made his way over. Mikael remained silent and stoic as Beelzebub crouched down to examine him. Beelzebub reached into his suit and pulled out a double edged dagger with a red handle in the middle.

Ben held his breath as Beelzebub lowered the dagger to Mikael and cut him loose. Ben released his breath. He needed Mikael alive if he and Atarah were to create the future he wanted. Mikael shook free of his binds as he stood to his full height. He was the only one at eye level with the demon lords.

"What a splendid gathering this is," Mikael said with sarcasm as he rubbed his wrist. Leviathan cackled again.

"I know, right!" Leviathan jeered. "Brother! Imagine my surprise when one of my sentinels arrived at my house of pleasure and dropped these five Archangels at my feet." Leviathan pointed to Mikael. "I nearly killed him on the spot because I thought him to be the Matthew fellow."

Ben froze.

"That's not what concerns me, brother," Beelzebub said as he eyed the rest of them. "What concerns me is how they traveled to our realm undetected?" He looked at Leviathan with narrowed eyes. "You especially should have sensed their arrival."

While Beelzebub's glare made Ben want to hide under a rock, Leviathan gave a disinterested shrug.

"You and big sister always get so tied up about such small things. I was busy getting high when they probably stumbled into my domain." Leviathan yawned. "Ugh, already I'm getting bored of this interaction. I thought you would give me a better, enraged reaction."

"What do you know of my brother?" Mikael asked. He stepped forward to Leviathan.

"Quiet!" Beelzebub roared. He backhanded Mikael, sending him flying across the room and smashing into the wall. "Don't speak unless spoken to," Beelzebub hissed.

Mikael slumped to the ground, bleeding from his mouth. He lifted his head up to Beelzebub, glaring as he spat blood onto the floor. *Only he could have handled such a powerful blow,* Ben thought.

"Ahhh!" Leviathan grinned. "There's that angry reaction I was wanting to see." Leviathan coiled himself on top of the desk. "My only guess as to why so many Archangels are here is because of that pain in the ass, Matthew Arch."

"That piece of shit," Beelzebub growled, glaring back at Mikael. "You must be related to him to bear such a resemblance." Beelzebub stomped his way to Mikael. His eyes shone with the promise of violence and death.

Ben scrambled to think of a new strategy. How could he turn this to their favor? His powers didn't work; neither did Gabriel's. Did anyone's powers work? Ben glanced at Barmen's still kneeling form. He hadn't moved an inch despite all that had happened. Barmen refused to look up. *Come on!* Ben thought, *think!* How was he going to bullshit his way out of this? He glanced back at Clarissa and Isabella, both struggling to bring forth their elemental abilities, and an idea came to him.

He didn't give himself time to think through his actions. He forced his body to move before he changed his mind. He scrambled to his feet and leapt in front of Mikael, facing Beelzebub, arms outstretched.

"You said you wanted to discuss business, yes?" Ben's words tumbled out of his mouth. His voice and his arms shook now. Beelzebub paused. Behind him Leviathan groaned.

"Ugh! Business, business, business," Leviathan sneered. "Why be obsessed with something so boring!"

"Shut it!" Beelzebub roared. "What is it you want?" He sneered down at Ben. Ben could have sworn his eyes glowed.

Ben swallowed thickly. "As I said earlier, we have a proposal."

At the word proposal, Leviathan and Beelzebub tilted their heads at him.

"Go on," Beelzebub growled.

"We…" Ben stuttered. "We want Matthew gone as well…" He paused. "Uh, so we have a plan to get rid of him but…" He struggled to grasp an angle they would accept.

"But you need more power," Leviathan purred from where he perched. "It's what everyone wants from us. More power. Same story, different players." Leviathan sighed. "Here I thought you were going to be interesting."

"No," Ben breathed as Beelzebub took one step. "Hear me out!" Ben cried out as Beelzebub took another step. The demon lord paused.

"Well what is it, then?" Beelzebub growled.

"We have a plan to get rid of him but…" Ben glanced at Leviathan. "You're in the way actually."

Leviathan eyes shot toward him. Beelzebub growled, but a huff from Leviathan stopped him.

"We're in the way?" Leviathan hissed. His slitted pupils narrowed in on Ben.

"Y-yes," Ben stuttered again. "You see, Matthew is obviously evading you. So I've devised a trap we can lay for him. We're not as much of a threat to him compared to either of you." Ben glanced back and forth between the demon lords.

"Hmmm, it's true. We are the bigger threat," Leviathan purred.

"And he is a slippery bastard," Beelzebub said. He straightened his suit as if his temper had cooled off. Ben slowly lowered his arms.

"So help us—" he indicated to himself, "—help you." He indicated to Beelzebub. "I felt your power from the moment we stepped into the city, and I am sure he can too. So we need to lay the trap for him when he least expects it."

"How do you plan on doing such a thing?" Leviathan purred. "Our powers stretch across our domains, save for the pesky Decimate Mountains that the little cockroach loves to hide within. Along with his traitorous assimilate followers."

Assimilates? What did that mean?

"Well," Ben looked around to think of any answer. He landed on the dagger. "We don't need your powers, but we would appreciate it if we could use your tools and resources to catch him." Ben peeked at Beelzebub.

"Our resources?" Leviathan sat up from his coiled form. "What do you know of our resources, Arch?"

"I know that you have a rich trading business," Ben waved to Beelzebub. "And I've heard of rumors of powerful weapons and items produced by the demon lords that are second to none."

Leviathan grinned. "We *are* second to none after all."

Ben chuckled nervously as Beelzebub took another step closer.

"What items did you have in mind, young Arch?" Beelzebub growled. His red eyes narrowed as Ben's gaze flickered to the dagger.

"The dagger?" Beelzebub grunted.

Ben shook his head.

"Then what?!" Beelzebub roared.

"I want Satan's staff!" Ben said hurriedly.

Silence stretched across the room. Leviathan and Beelzebub regarded him with shock, with some glee on Leviathan's side. Beelzebub's eyes widened at his serious expression.

"You want Satan's most powerful magical item? You heard that too, brother?" Leviathan asked with a wicked smile.

"I heard," Beelzebub murmured, before turning back to him. "You have to be either the dumbest or bravest Arch to have ever existed."

Ben let out a humorless laugh. "Neither. I'm desperate."

Beelzebub eyed him as if truly seeing him for the first time.

He resisted the urge to squirm under his gaze. He had spoken true. He was desperate. Desperate to claw his way up to true strength and power. Desperate to keep his loved ones safe. To be untouchable! Growing up weaker than his brothers, many Archs bullied and harassed him. He'd lost count of how many times his face was shoved into the dirt. Or how the Arch aristocrats whispered wondering if he had been born a bastard because his mind reading abilities were not as good as the others in his family. Or that he was just the 'spare to the spare' of a son. The 'disposable son' was what a few bullies named him. Ben locked his eyes back with the demon lord in front of him. Fire burned in his heart for the life he wanted to create. So many times, throughout his life, Archs had looked down upon him. Disregarded him. Disrespected him.

Seeing Atarah and his family abused as punching bags as well broke something within him. Seeing his parents die, then almost Atarah, right before his eyes changed him. The way Matthew destroyed his homeland. Manipulated Atarah like a puppet in the human realm and then beat her to near death! He needed strength now more than ever.

Those memories fueled his need to gain more power. Desperate might've not been the right word after all. He was done with those he loved being a punching bag.

"You got balls, little Arch." Beelzebub spoke after a long silence. "No one has ever dared to ask for something so powerful." Beelzebub hunched down to his eye level. "Offer a trade with me and I'll offer up all of our staffs to help your group."

"Wait just a minute!" Leviathan jerked up. "Don't go offering up *my* staff just because this youngling gives you the excited tingles." Leviathan slithered from the desk and toward them.

Side by side, the two demon lords towered over the rest of them. Beelzebub placed a gloved hand on Leviathan's shoulder.

"It will be fine, little brother," Beelzebub said. "He will not last long with all of the staffs anyway."

The information Barmen had given him earlier proved to be invaluable. The staffs were powerful magical items that condensed most of their power and strength. As he learned from peeking through Barmen's mind during his explanation, a demon lord's power stretched across their domain. They could call back their power but not all of it *unless* they used their staff. This was the exception Barmen had mentioned earlier but never explained. Interesting that demon lords had limitations to their powers. Their staffs contained the ability to draw massive amounts of energy to either power or to destroy whole realms.

Little did anyone else know that Matthew wanted the staffs. In the brief glimpse that he read from Matthew, the crazy bastard thought of the powerful item. He planned to use the staffs to combine the realms together. Causing the ultimate amount of chaos to every realm in existence. However, Matthew had kept this plan a secret. If Ben could stop him from attaining one staff, he could stop Matthew's plan from happening, protect Atarah and his family, and gain some of the greatest magical power in all of the realms. They would be untouchable! This was his plan from the start, and he needed to make sure no one else screwed it up. Not his brother, not Mikael, no one!

"I can handle it," Ben refuted. Beelzebub nodded while Leviathan appeared horrified.

"You cannot be serious, Beelzebub!" Leviathan cried out as he grabbed his brother's shoulder. "Satan will be PISSED if she knows what you're agreeing to here! Also it's reckless!"

Beelzebub grunted. "I thought you were the Lord of Spontaneity?"

"I thought you were the brooding, serious one!" Leviathan argued. "I didn't bring them—" he pointed to Mikael's group "—here so you could cut a deal with all these Archs. I brought them here so we could have a good laugh!"

"These Archs will *all* have to remain unharmed," Ben quickly interjected.

"And have our powers back *without* consequences," Zewal called out from across the room.

*Our powers back?* Ben wondered. He glanced back up at Beelzebub.

"When you have the staffs, we won't be able to manipulate your ability as much," Beelzebub explained.

"Manipulate our abilities?" Ben asked.

He remembered his headache from earlier and Gabriel's inability to teleport out of here. Clarissa and Isabella attempting to call upon fire and wind to no avail. His stomach clenched at how much of a vulnerable position he put them in. He glanced down at Barmen, kneeling. He must have tried to warn Ben of the dangers in his own way.

Beelzebub followed his line of sight and grunted.

"Oh, except him. Illusions and distortion of reality falls more under Satan's power," Beelzebub explained.

Leviathan scoffed. "All she needs is one."

"Leviathan is the originator of elemental magic, death magic, and healing magic. Whereas I am the originator of strength, teleportation, and mind reading magic," Beelzebub continued. He strolled to his desk and opened a drawer.

"Why does Satan only have one type of magic?" Ben asked, as he stared at Barmen. Barmen hadn't moved this entire time. Could he…?

Ben moved to where Barmen was and reached for him. Barmen's image fluttered before his hand could touch him: an illusion. Shock rocked his body as he realized, Barmen could use his powers this entire time and *knew* it. Clarissa, Gabriel, and Isabella's mouths dropped open as the illusion wafted again. His heart dropped as he wondered when and where Barmen slipped from them. Clarissa walked forward, away from Isabella to kneel by Barmen's illusion. She reached out to touch his face. Her hand moved right through, the illusion drifted apart, like smoke, disappearing and leaving nothing behind. A grimace came across her face as she pulled her hand to her chest.

*Such a good liar.*

Her thought came through to him as loudly as if she had spoken it.

"Because the power to contort reality is the strongest type of power any being could have." Beelzebub explained once he found what he was looking for in his desk. "Satan is our younger sister and the strongest."

Leviathan rolled his eyes. "And the bossiest, bitchiest, and ugliest of them all."

"You're just jealous, Leviathan," Beelzebub pulled out an old, dull-looking stick out of the drawer.

"Ew!" Leviathan gagged at the stick. "How come you never take care of your things?" he accused. "My staff is *clean* and glammed out at all times."

Beelzebub gave him an exasperated look. "Respect that we choose to live different lives, brother," he growled.

"Not if you choose to live unglamorously," Leviathan retorted as he waved his hand in the air. A light flashed in his hand. A similar sized stick appeared in his hand but completely different than his brother's ragged staff. Leviathan's staff gleamed and shined. Covered in shining stones, glitter and sparkles, the staff looked in better condition than Beelzebub's.

"I even added a little jingle sound button to it." Leviathan clicked a button on the side of the staff. A small tune of twinkling chimes blasted from the staff. "So when I want to use it, I can wave it around like this with the sound." Leviathan waved the staff in the air like a wand.

Beelzebub released a long exhale as Leviathan twirled around with his staff.

"I expected my brother, who barges in unannounced, to respect my space. How dumb of me," Beelzebub murmured, shaking his head.

"No one changes for the sake of others, brother," Leviathan said as he came to a stop. "That's a universal rule. People only change for themselves."

Beelzebub nodded with a frown. "I didn't need that reminder when your actions are so loud."

The demon lord lifted a gloved hand in the air. A brief flash, then another staff appeared in his hand. This staff was painted red and wrapped with a black thread down its length. Leviathan, frowning, handed over his staff. Beelzebub then held out all three staffs in front of them.

Mikael coughed, drawing attention.

"What comes next?" Mikael asked from his position. Beelzebub grunted and snapped his fingers. Immediately everyone's bonds and injuries disappeared. Everyone scrambled to their feet and moved closer to the desk, where the demon lords stood.

"Now comes the tricky part for *you.*" Beelzebub indicated to Ben. "Here are our staffs. It will take some time for Satan to notice that her staff is missing. Use that time wisely to trap this annoying pest. Once Satan notices her staff is gone, she will come for you. Once she does, our deal is off, and it will be time for me to cash in what you will owe me."

"What do I owe you?" Ben asked with shaking hands. Beelzebub brought a hand to his chin.

"For three powerful staffs, every single one of you here will owe a demon lord one favor in the future. A favor of our choosing."

"That's not fair!" Clarissa called out. A hiss from Leviathan silenced her.

"You *all* walked in here willingly, sweetheart," Leviathan sneered. "What did you expect to happen?"

Clarissa and Isabella paled. Noah and the Azrael siblings shook their heads vehemently. The others shouted their protest.

"Ben!" Elijah yelled. "Don't take that deal! It will affect everyone, not just you! It's all of us!"

Everyone looked at him with panic in their eyes, pleading against the proposal. Ben wavered for a moment. His plan to be out of danger lay right there! Within his grasp! Everyone shouted their protest, but Mikael remained silent. Ben peeked at Mikael, who watched Ben with pity in his eyes.

Ben sighed. No one would understand.

Ben reached forward for his staff. Beelzebub lifted the staff away and grasped onto his hand. "I did not say I would give all *three* staffs to you." A sharp sting burned his hand where Beelzebub held on. A pungent smell of burning flesh flared in the air. Everyone screamed as a symbol burned into their right hands. Beelzebub turned to Mikael and Elijah, as they examined the new burn marks, with a grin.

"You two have a lot of youngsters to look after."

The sun beamed through the curtains, blasting a wave of heat. At high noon, the hot weather peaked. Sweat coated Gabriel Sr.'s body as he sat in the large, private library of Joshua's home, a lounge area with several velvet chairs facing each other in a semicircle. The bookshelves reached the ceilings and stretched along every wall in the room. All of the books were given the same brown, leather cover, making them indistinguishable for each other. In true Raziel fashion, knowledge was revered yet guarded. However, it mattered little to him what Joshua did with his books and knowledge.

Gabriel tapped his fingers against each other to calm his nerves. His thoughts moved once again to his son. Twenty, as the family called Gabriel Jr., for the number he was in the line of succession, had disappeared by the time he'd returned to the room back in Malachi's coastal villa.

He had just finished reading the letter from Amos, asking him to bring Ben to Quaesitor, when he walked back into the room. His stomach dropped as he searched the empty room. He opened a portal to Joshua's estate to look for his son and the other heirs, only to find nothing.

In fact upon his arrival, he'd interrupted one of Joshua's council meetings on adding improvements to their city's buildings. Joshua, Farah, and two other generals he didn't know as well all conversed, seated in the library.

Joshua's eyes widened when he recounted Ben's request to be brought to Barmen. The Head Arch didn't ask why or when the encounter happened either. Once Gabriel finished his story, Joshua stood up and dismissed the meeting. Everyone seated faded away, like smoke in the wind. Illusions.

"Please wait here a moment while I search for Barmen." Joshua's voice sounded hoarse. His silvery wings flared as he exited out of the room. Gabriel's own wings twitched endlessly while he waited. His urge to roam around the lands to search for his son was driving him to insanity. He clasped his hands together and squeezed. He focused on maintaining a calm composure—and failed.

His right leg bounced in the chair as his agitation grew. He ordered his people into lockdown until every missing Gabriel angel was accounted for, and that included his son. He knew the itch and irritation his citizens had with the lockdown orders, but he had little choice. None were safe until Matthew's experiments were stopped.

His hands pulled at the hair on the back of his head. He had thought it odd when so many soldiers came up missing or gone from their posts. He never thought to question whether they were being held prisoners as lab rats!

He jumped to his feet. He paced in circles around the library, the urge to move building within him. His people must be struggling too. Under lockdown, none were allowed to leave their homes. Designated angels and principalities were allowed to roam within the city, to deliver food and services to those in need but it was not enough.

Gabriel angels were not meant to stay in one place. They needed freedom, the ability to roam as they pleased. He understood that just as much as any other. He sighed as he continued his aimless walking. He flapped his wings for extra exertion. The movement helped fight against the anxiety a little.

*Enough of this,* he thought.

He widened his hands to make a portal when a knock at the door stopped him.

"Yes?" He dropped his hands to his sides. The heat gathering in his palms dissipated.

"Thank you for waiting so long." The door opened wide to reveal Amos, the new Head Arch of the Selaphiel clan. His dark brown eyes zeroed in on his twitching wings and picked-at nail beds.

"I came as soon as I could," Amos finished. The young Arch's eyes were sunken in and his posture slouched forward. His jaw almost dropped when he saw how Amos's wings dragged along the floor.

Gabriel froze his face to hide his shock at such disgraceful display. If that were him, Gabriel wouldn't bother showing up at all, if he knew how undignified he looked. Amos glanced down at his wrinkled, wheat-colored tunic. The sand dune insignia outlined with green thread sat on the upper portion of the right arm. While appearing clean, Gabriel didn't doubt Amos had probably slept in it the night before.

Amos released a humorless chuckle.

"I am afraid I don't get much sleep nowadays." Amos' voice deepened. Disdain dripped with every word. "Nor do I have the luxury of worrying about appearances anymore."

Gabriel stiffened. His wings seized their twitching.

"I am sure you have a lot on your shoulders," he replied through gritted teeth. He'd forgotten momentarily that Amos heard his thoughts.

*"At what point could you hear my thoughts?"* Gabriel thought his question. Amos' narrowed his eyes further at Gabriel.

"It's rude to ask us questions through your mind."

"I thought you discuss things all the time through thought," Gabriel countered.

He remembered back when Aesop ruled, he'd converse with his wife all of the time, privately. There were times at dinners the prior Selaphiel leader mixed up the conversations and gave an unrelated reply.

Amos pursed his lip at the memory in Gabriel's head.

"Only to those who you are very close with," Amos answered. "We don't have such a relationship, so it is rude to ask in such a manner. Plus, it will leave everyone else out of the conversation."

"We are the only ones here," Gabriel huffed. His wings twitched again as his anxiety crept back up.

"Not for long." Amos took a seat in one of the chairs. He stared at a door on the other side of the room, waiting. A minute went by before the door opened, revealing Joshua. His hair was slicked back and his clothes changed. He wore a more traditional blood red tunic, with his clan insignia of a book on the right shoulder.

"Apologies for the wait." Joshua closed the door behind him and joined them. "I'm having a difficult time hunting down my son."

"Me as well," he replied with a raised eyebrow.

"And to have the words spoken out loud," Amos sighed, "it was my younger brother who requested you take him to Barmen, Joshua's heir, Gabriel?"

It had been spoken as a question, but Gabriel knew Amos heard the answer in his head. Amos' wings flared slightly.

"Again, let's include everyone in the conversation." Amos

clasped his hands together while his elbows rested on the armrests.

"Very well," Gabriel turned to Joshua. "Amos is correct. Ben asked me to take him directly to Barmen." He gritted his teeth at the memory. "While I read Amos' latest message, the youngster coerced my son to take him instead! Escaping like a thief in the night." Little concealed the venom in his voice. "I came straight here to find my son then thrash that sneaky, conniving—"

"Be careful, Gabriel." Amos' eyes narrowed on him. "That's my brother you're talking about."

"Is that supposed to be a threat?" Gabriel scoffed. "I've been around longer than anyone else in this room." His wings flared. "You would do well to remember that, youngling."

Amos stood in his chair, wings flared wide. Gabriel's hands glowed as he prepared for a fight until Joshua stepped between them. His silver wings stretched the space between them as a barrier.

"Hold steady." Joshua's voice turned to steel. Immovable and firm in his command. His eyes pierced Gabriel first then Amos. "Gabriel is right, young Head." Amos's wings puffed. He opened his mouth to protest but Joshua stopped him. "You don't want to mess with the Arch that can transport your insides to another realm while the rest of you stays here." Joshua turned back to Gabriel with a frown. "Gabriel, we both know this behavior is beneath you."

Gabriel straightened his tunic and forced his wings to relax. His behavior was childish; he needed to remain calm and controlled. If he remained composed, he would get his son back sooner rather than later.

When his wings continued to twitch, despite his best efforts, he stiffly sat in one of the lounge chairs. He scrunched his wings behind him, before facing the other two Arch heads with a stone face. He wiped all emotion from his eyes and jaw. Joshua grunted as he took the last available chair.

"Now then." Joshua clapped his hands together. "Amos, you sent out letters asking to meet us here. I know each of us are busy, so let's get on with it."

"Are you truly here with us or are you just an illusion?" Amos asked. Joshua's lips twitched.

"Does it matter?" Joshua fired back.

"How I envy your ability," Amos replied, rubbing two fingers against his temple.

"I ordered all of the servants in the building to vacate while you are here. Yet you still hear everyone?" Joshua frowned. "The transition must be difficult."

Gabriel bit his tongue. When the Head Arch died and the heir acceded to power, all of the prior Head's power transferred to the next ruler. The change from heir to leader created a painful kind of growth spurt. The body had little preparation. The heir, in-fluxed with more energy than he was used to, must feel the growing pains. Gabriel remembered his first year as Head of his clan with some embarrassment. He sneezed one time in the library of Mortem and accidentally transported himself to one of the mountains in Belli Causa. Controlling his new strength took time.

He glanced at Amos. He wondered how long it would take the new Head to manage his newfound strength. Amos continued to rub his temples.

"The transition has been difficult, but I am not here to discuss that," Amos replied. "I have a plan to help secure each of our borders against Matthew and his ability to open portals wherever he likes."

Fire erupted in his belly at the spoken words. Each of the portals Matthew opened represented the sacrificed lives of his people. He clenched his fists together to keep his fingers from twitching. He wanted to hear the young leader's plan.

"I have sent my younger brother Canaan to spy for me in the demon realm," Amos continued. "He is due to come back soon, and the intel he has secured will be vital."

"I've wondered how Matthew has been able to survive in the demon realm for so long. Also how he was able to amass such an army in the first place," Amos explained. "To wage a sizable enough war against us would mean he's gained money and power. Those two items are vital. The power he's gained has come from the new religion he created in the demon realm. Many of his followers believe Matthew will create a better life for them by combining the realms together."

Joshua and Gabriel scoffed.

"If by a better life, you mean killing everyone within all of the realms, sure. That's one definition," Gabriel sneered.

"Well, it is the definition that he has sold to many of the general population," Amos countered. "Many demons see him and his plan as a way of salvation from their current lives and are willing to die for it."

"That is how he has gained influence over the subjects," Joshua jumped in. "But what about the money? Where is the money coming from to arm his followers?"

Amos leaned forward.

"The money, I suspect, is a combination of his followers and—one of the demon lords."

Gabriel's eyes widened. One of the demon lords? His stomach dropped and his leg bounced. None of the Arch heads, with all of their powers combined, could take on the demon lords.

"We don't need to take on all three of the demon lords," Amos continued. "We just need to take on the one that's funding Matthew."

"Which one is it?" Joshua's eyes, normally cool, were aflame.

Amos rested his chin on top of his clasped hands.

"We aren't sure," he answered. "I was hoping to venture into the demon realm myself to find out. My range and concentration is better than my brother's but—"

"You need at least one heir to remain behind to ensure the line of succession," Joshua finished.

Amos frowned as he nodded.

"Canaan is my current named heir with Ben as the second," Amos explained.

"That is why you were so insistent for Ben to return home," Gabriel realized. "I could have transported you anywhere in the demon realm and you could've heard their thoughts from a safe distance."

Amos nodded.

"The distance is key," Joshua chimed in with gritted teeth. "The closer you are to the demon lords, the more they can influence your ability to use your powers."

"But we can't dwell on old plans," Amos said. "For now, we focus on what we can do. Joshua." Amos turned to him. "Gabriel. With both of you, I want to plan a counter attack on Matthew and the demon lords."

The blood in his veins turned to ice. Only centuries of training allowed Gabriel to keep the shock from his face, but Amos talked further.

"With both of you, I want to create a large portal and an illusion," Amos started, but Gabriel shook his head.

"Whatever you are planning, I promise you it won't work," Gabriel replied. His stomach clenched at the thought of going up against the demon lords. They were like children trying to out fly full grown adults in a race. It simply wasn't physically possible.

"We're going to outsmart them," Amos insisted.

"It cannot be done," Gabriel emphasized.

"Hold on," Joshua spoke up. "Let us hear the young Head out." Joshua's eyes regarded Amos with intrigue. Gabriel frowned at Joshua. Both of them were considered young to Gabriel, but he had hoped Joshua would show more hesitancy. Gabriel, though young, had been around during the last attack from the demon lords.

He shuddered against the memory. The battle of the Archs from the sixteenth century. The demon lords sent Arch demons to fight for more control over their lands. The chaos and death from those battles haunted him to this day. The Archangels fought for five long years just to keep their lands and they'd almost lost. If it weren't for the Michael heirs at that time, they would've been doomed.

He had been so young during that time, but the memory of seeing an Arch demon remained vivid. Their ruby colored eyes with their ethereal beauty and sculpted face. Arch demons were the offspring from the demon lords. They ranked lower than their parents and were weaker in strength. They possessed long, slender bodies covered in black coal. With rubies for eyes and expressionless faces, it was easy to mistake them for mindless, strong dolls. Their faces and body type could change, but their eyes stayed the same.

He had thought them beautiful, until one Arch demon tried to eat him.

"What is this plan of yours?" Gabriel asked with reluctance. His body threatened to tremble from the chill running down his spine, but he forced his body still.

"I want Joshua to create a powerful illusion over me and you as we venture into the demon realm. I want him to mask me as Matthew while you remain invisible. With me as Matthew, I will rally as many demons to me as possible. Once all together, I want you to open the largest portal you can make, taking every demon within the vicinity."

"A portal to where?" The ice continued to spread throughout his limbs from his spine. His leg thrummed faster.

"A portal to Cherub Island."

Joshua's eyebrows raised to his forehead, while Gabriel's jaw dropped open. Did Amos go mad from all of the voices in his head? The young Head in question turned to him with narrowed eyes. Cherub Island lay within their realm off of Arena's coastal line. The cherubim stayed on their island and occasionally roamed along the western coastal line. It was estimated by Raziel angels over the years that the cherubim gathered around no more than one thousand in population. He had seen a handful of cherubim throughout his years since his region was along the western coastal line. He shared a look with Joshua. *All* of their region's coast bordered the Cherub Island, putting their citizens in the first line of danger.

The cherubim were only dangerous if provoked, and he didn't want to provoke them.

"I know this seems like an extreme plan—" he started.

"It *is* an extreme plan!" Gabriel struggled to keep his voice level. "Do you have any idea of what—" he sputtered. "H-h-how angry the—" the words tangled themselves within his mouth as his emotions came to the surface.

"Gabriel is right," Joshua chimed in. "What we are doing is kicking an angry hornets nest and then throwing that nest into a hibernating bear's den. It is a dangerous plan with dire consequences should we fail."

Gabriel swirled on Joshua.

"Fail?" he asked with wide eyes. "We aren't going to entertain such a reckless plan! We would anger the demon lords *and* the cherubim at the same time. The cherubim don't have to cross a realm to get to us when they live miles from our shores!"

"So what if we anger the demon lords!" Amos fired back. "They're a plague we've endured for too long!"

"It's a sickness that can get much worse if we let it! And the cherubim are just as big of a threat to our people."

"It is *my* shores they border the closest, so I do not need reminders of the dangers they pose," Amos sneered.

"Apparently you do!" Gabriel countered. "You were not alive during the last cherub altercation, so how could you possibly understand the full danger—no, the pure destruction they could inflict."

"We can't continue to sit on our asses and do nothing either!" Amos stood to his feet. "Hiding behind our borders does nothing. We need to strike back!"

"He has a point," Joshua rose from his chair. "My people and I took shelter behind our shields for too long. There comes a point where we have to fight back."

"Think of the chaos!" Gabriel Sr. implored, but Joshua flared his wings.

"No! Gabriel," Joshua boomed. "We are already in the mix of chaos. Think of your son! Do you wish for him or your people to always run scared of being captured?" He paused. "It is time for us to attack."

The ice in his veins cracked and splintered as he thought of his son. He never would have thought his son to have a large target on his back. In raising his son, he'd played it safe. He made political alliances with precautions and deals with other leaders for his son's benefit. The muscles in his back squirmed.

Rachael and he tried so hard for many years to have children. Their son was their miracle baby. When she gave birth to him, they both vowed to provide the best they could for him. The best he provided was a cage. He winced at the thought.

Amos turned to him. "You are either with us or against us. Now what will it be? Will you fight for your son and people?"

Gabriel glanced between them. Their eyes were hard and set on their resolve. He stood to his feet with his wings tucked in tight. His leg finally ceased its thumping.

"I am with you on this," he replied in a low tone. "If I cannot fight for my people's freedom, then I don't deserve to lead them." His heart weighed heavy in his chest at the truth and doom in his words. He knew the horrors of war and famine from his youth. As Head, he needed to do what he could to prevent such calamities.

Amos' jaw loosened from hearing his thoughts. The Selaphiel's wings relaxed by his sides while Joshua rang a bell for a servant.

"I will be joining you all soon," Joshua announced as his image faded like smoke.

Energy flowed through his hands as he readied for traveling.

"Did you know if he was an illusion this whole time?" Gabriel asked Amos, while his power thrummed through his body, like a thousand bees buzzed in his veins.

"I know it's an illusion when I can't hear thoughts," Amos answered as the sound of feet walking down the hallway echoed. "When I can't hear the person's thoughts, that means their body is outside of my range."

The servant, called earlier, entered the room with an array of weapons, food, and travel packs. The servant placed everything along the table in front of them. He raised an eyebrow at Amos, who picked up a vicious-looking dagger.

"Out of range?" Gabriel said with some surprise. "If he's within your range, then how do you know if it's an illusion?"

Amos frowned. His eye continued to inspect the dagger.

"There is a saying in Chrysi, 'step on a cat's tail and a sound of pain comes from its mouth, not the tail.'" Amos put the dagger on his belt. "I need to find the tail."

# Chapter 7

The light beamed in through the sheer curtains as the ocean breeze came into the room. Muffled voices surrounded her, but Atarah couldn't lift her heavy eyelids. Awareness crept into her mind as she struggled to wake.

Her limbs ached as she attempted to sit up. Everything was heavy. Her arms, legs, lifting her chest up to breathe took effort. A cramp along her lower abdomen made her pause in her efforts to move. She groaned as the pain stretched along her back and down her legs.

"Here you go." A soft voice spoke.

A cooling touch spread from her stomach to the rest of her body. She unclenched her fist as the soothing sensation reached her limbs. She sighed as her wings relaxed. She peeked through her eyelids, using all of her new strength.

Charlotte stood beside the bed with both hands glowing above her. Her face scrunched in concentration as her power flowed. Atarah opened her eyes fully to search the room.

What happened to her? Where was she? Why did Charlotte look so haggard?

She tasted the salty breeze that drifted through the open balcony. The sound of crashing waves reached her ears. It was nighttime, which limited her vision outside. However the room she slept in was well-lit with lanterns. The flames flickered along the wall as another shadow startled her.

Atarah turned to see her mother, Ava, coming to a stop at the door. Mother gasped at her gaze, nearly dropping the vase in her hands.

"You're awake," she whispered. Ava's hands shook as she hurried to the bed. "You're finally awake!" Mother said louder.

Charlotte jumped in alarm when their eyes met.

"Ah!" Charlotte screamed. "You are awake!"

Atarah snorted. "Why wouldn't I wake up?" She paused. "Unless I'm…dead?" She glanced between Charlotte and Mother curiously. "We're all dead?"

Charlotte laughed while Ava encircled her in a large hug. Pain once again erupted across her chest and stomach. Atarah groaned but she didn't dare pull away from her mother's embrace.

"Of course you're not dead, dumbass!" Charlotte chuckled. She rubbed her eyes, as tears swelled. "I've worked too hard to keep you alive!"

"The best damn healer in all of the realms, you are, little jewel!" Ava cheered as she pulled back. "Charlotte worked night and day, bringing you back together piece by piece."

Tears flowed down her mother's face freely. Puffy, tired hazel eyes greeted Atarah. Her wings trembled as she clutched her mother's hands. Ava wore an empire waist, forest green dress that flowed to the floor. Her disheveled hair curled in every direction within a messy bun, but she still looked stunning.

Atarah's vision blurred with her own tears. Her lips trembled as she reached for her mom.

"I've missed you so much," she wheezed out.

Atarah took her time to look around the room. While the room was not massive, it wasn't small either. The bed she lay in took up much of the room with a small table beside her. To her left, the room expanded to a balcony with outdoor seating. The chairs consisted of woven fabric and wool that sunk when sat on.

*We must be near the coast*, she thought as the sound of crashing waves reached her.

"What happened?" she whispered to no one in particular. Charlotte exchanged a glance with her mother.

"Do you not remember anything, Atarah?" Charlotte asked, grabbing a hold of her free hand.

Atarah furrowed her brow as she struggled to remember. Her mind drew a blank. What was the last thing she remembered? When she and Arick were…

"Arick!" Atarah gasped. She leaped from the bed. Or tried to.

Pain shot throughout her body. Everything ached and groaned in agony and soreness. Charlotte and her mother moved her quickly back into the bed. Atarah's body protested any and all movements.

"Arick's in trouble!" Atarah yelled at her mom and Charlotte as she attempted again to stand. Both frowned at her before exchanging another glance between each other.

"Easy there, love," Mother soothed. "Do you know how long you've been asleep for?"

Atarah whirled her head back and forth between Charlotte and her mother.

"What?" Atarah asked. Her heart hollowed out at their pained expressions. "A few days…" Her voice drifted off as sorrow pulled in her mother's eyes.

"It's been nine days since Ben pulled everyone back from the human realm," Charlotte whispered dispraisingly.

Nine days.

The world tilted as the words ricocheted in her mind. She'd never had to recover for that long! Ever! Why? Why did this have to happen to her?

*It's because you're not good enough,* a whisper echoed through the dark corners of her mind. *This whole time you've been pretending to be a Michael angel, but in the end, you couldn't cut it.*

Atarah slumped in her bed as her insecurities festered at her own failures. Tears swelled in her eyes as the image of Arick, battered and broken, filled her mind.

Tears fell down her face. She saw her mother and Charlotte speaking to her but heard nothing they said. All she heard was the cracking of Arick's bones as he fought until the very end to save her…

A sob ripped out of her. Her mother and Charlotte pulled her into a bug hug as she sobbed. She couldn't save herself let alone those she loved! Never had she ever felt so defeated by her own weaknesses.

Father would never see her as someone capable of leading. Mother would be more fearful for her now! And Arick… Another sob racked through her. She didn't know how long she sobbed on her mom's shoulder or how long Charlotte rubbed her head. She allowed herself to not dwell on how long she cried. Not to dwell on how much of a burden she'd been to Charlotte and her mother.

How foolish she was at the summit meeting to hope she could

be different than what she was. She was and always will be the pathetic loser who never fit in. She was the same small and scared little angel who got picked on and beaten up by the other Michael angels. The angel who could never win a fight or be seen as a leader. She cried as she thought she really was just another female sitting in a waiting room to be married off, never to lead.

She allowed herself to break down. Mourning for Arick, who was probably lying dead somewhere and for her own failures. She cried so much her mother's pretty dress became damp with her tears. Several minutes ticked by before Atarah noticed her mother's soothing voice.

"There, there, my love," her mother murmured. Her arms tightened around Atarah. "Shush, I know it hurts. I'm right here for you." Atarah sniffled.

"Arick might be dead, Mom," Atarah said between sobs. "I-I couldn't do anything to help him! I failed. I failed at everything!"

"Atarah," Mother said softly, pulling away just enough to look in her eyes. "Do you remember what Arick told you on your first day in Silva?"

Atarah shook her head as he wiped away tears.

"He said 'There's nothing bleaker than a woman who doesn't know her own strength.'"

"How do you know he said that?" Atarah asked, surprised. Mother turned to look at Charlotte, who blushed.

"It…well, what he said really struck a chord in me because I see how strong you are, Atarah, and it's what inspires me," Charlotte murmured. "You inspire me. To work harder, to be the best version of myself that I can be." She paused as she fidgeted with the green tunic. "I was always anxious and awkward growing up and…never very certain of anything about myself." She peeked at her mother. "I was always compared to you, Ava, on anything I did. It was a huge blow to my confidence." Charlotte turned back to her. "But since you came into my life, Atarah, I've pushed myself more than I ever have before. I am confident now and stronger in who I am as a person." She paused as tears welled in her eyes. "Don't say you're a failure. Because you're not. Everyone falls down, but you've always gotten back up again. That's what gives you true strength."

Tears fell down all of their faces, and they pulled together in another embrace. They stayed there for several more minutes, letting tears flow. A weight lifted off Atarah's heart at Charlotte's words. Her chest loosened as she took in their love. She was safe and loved.

A slow clap echoed across the room.

They froze.

Atarah was the first to see him. Her stomach hollowed out at their newest arrival. She tightened her hold on her mother and Charlotte, tempted to prevent them from turning their heads. Another clap drew their attention. Atarah protested as they pulled away to see who was at the door. Mother's face paled so much Atarah worried she would faint. A gasp escaped Charlotte's lips as her wings trembled.

"My, my my, what a touching moment you all shared," a deep voice said. That voice sent chills down her spine.

Matthew leaned causally against the door frame entering into her room. Most of his markings were covered by the long, black tunic he wore but a few peeked out along the neck. The strange markings appeared darker in color than the last time she saw him. His face was drawn in, and his eyes looked red from lack of sleep. Despite his casual appearance, Atarah was terrified of him.

From the shaking of her mother's limbs, she wasn't the only one afraid.

"What are you doing here?" Atarah said in a low voice.

Matthew's eyes pivoted away from her mother to her. He gave a fake grin as if he was their friend and not the tormentor of their lives.

"I've come to take all of you home," Matthew spoke as if it was good news he shared.

A strange tingling sensation spread all over her body as she pulled away from her mother. A strange out of body experience overtook her. A strange thrumming circulated through her limbs, like bees were in her blood.

"You will not touch any of us." Her voice sounded different. This should have alarmed her, but she was too detached to care.

Matthew frowned. "I thought I taught you how to respect your elders." He gave a half shrug. "I guess you have to learn another lesson."

Lights glowed on both sides of her. From the corner of her eyes she saw her mother and Charlotte's hands glow so bright it nearly looked like they held stars in their hands.

"Oh, look at this," Matthew jeered at her mother. "The scared little birdie of mine has finally learned to peck."

"I-I d-d-don't belong t-t-to you," Mother stuttered. Matthew quirked his head to the side. His eyes narrowed in on her mom.

"I'll never let you go." His voice turned threatening. "I'll make sure you're nothing without me."

Atarah tensed. Her body, still in the weird, trance-like state readied itself. He moved as fast as she remembered but…somehow he looked slow to her.

Power coursed throughout her body. This time, the Michael Armor came forward with ease. The armor slid over and across her body as she moved. Matching the same speed as Matthew, she was there in front of Mother before she blinked.

Matthew widened his eyes for a split second before Atarah slammed her fist into his face. The armor enclosed her whole body just before she made contact. The full force of her power honed in, like a laser, on her blow.

A loud boom echoed across the room as he flew backward, slamming into the far wall. Hunched over, he steadied himself. He spat out some blood and teeth before fully righting himself.

"It looks like someone got stronger," Matthew said as he narrowed his eyes at her. "It's too bad you'll never be strong enough."

He smashed his hands into the ground, breaking through concrete and tile. The marks all along his body glowed red and pulsed. A strange humming sound reverberated around them before pulling toward Matthew. Atarah's body lurched forward as if a magnetic force was drawing her closer to him. She'd rather die than let that happen. She knelt down onto the ground and punched her fist into the ground to create a hold.

Charlotte and her mother leapt from the bed behind her and now aided her. The power flowing into her from her mother and aunt, two advanced healers, may be how she kept Matthew at bay. Mother and Charlotte extended their hands out toward her, sending her not just healing but additional strength. However, as more seconds ticked by, the more the power drew over to Matthew instead of her. Atarah's eyes widened as she realized Matthew must have some sort of special ability to draw the power of others to him. Like the Abaddon.

"No matter how hard you try, I'll always be stronger," Matthew called out. "Whether you like it or not, you all are coming with me."

The villa shook from the force of his power. In the distance, she heard the screams of those working in the villa. Alarm bells rang, alerting everyone that an enemy was here. Maybe help would be on the way?

"Don't get your hopes up, sweetheart," Matthew taunted. Right as he spoke, Atarah noticed his plan. The markings he bore around his body moved onto the floor around them creating a large circle that stretched all the way out to the balcony. The symbols glowed and pulsed faster. Atarah gasped as she realized they were trapped.

"Hold on, ladies," Matthew called out.

The humming noise grew so loud Atarah covered her ears. Wind gathered and spun around them. A tornado swirled with them in the middle. She crawled to her mother and Charlotte, fighting against the wind. Her mother clung to Charlotte as they crouched down low. Charlotte's mouth was agape with a scream, but Atarah only heard the roaring wind. Charlotte reached ahead. Atarah clasped onto her, desperate to hold onto each other.

A white light shined within the circle. The floor burned where they knelt. Chaos ensued all around her and the villa rumbled. Loud cracks echoed as the floor split around them. Atarah tried to see where Matthew was but only saw the blinding light from the ground.

Suddenly, she fell. The light forced her eyes shut as she descended. Weightless, yet a magnetic pulling forced her to move. She thrashed around, hoping to grab a hold of something. She flared her wings out wide to fly but to no avail. She called out for her mom and Charlotte but heard nothing.

It was over in a matter of seconds. Atarah landed on her back with an *oomph.* Pain shot through her wings as she scrambled to her feet. The armor she wore disappeared along with the strange pins and needles sensation. Her body felt lighter as she moved. Groans sounded off beside her. Whirling around, Atarah sighed in relief.

Charlotte and her mother lay beside her, moving stiffly off the ground. Atarah rushed to them.

"Are you all right?" Atarah asked frantically. Her eyes scanned her mother's body for any broken bones.

"We're fine, love," her mother grunted. "Nothing is broken, sprained, or strained."

"Where are we?" Charlotte asked with quivering limbs.

Atarah turned around, taking in her surroundings.

They landed in a large poorly lit room with lanterns. Clinks of metal drew her attention to the walls. She saw metal chains hanging along the walls. At the far end of the wall, a body swayed and groaned.

Atarah gasped.

At the far end of the walls hung Gabriel angels. Blood dripped from their bodies and into waiting buckets on the ground. Their uniforms were in tatters; their bodies appeared malnourished and dehydrated. Bruises marked all over their bodies from repeated beatings; a few of them had body parts missing. One had a missing nose. Another had his eyes gouged out. Several others had missing feet and hands.

Atarah gagged as the stench registered. To the far left, a bucket of flesh rotted in the corner. Most likely it was *their* flesh in that bucket. A few groans turned their attention.

They all scrambled to their feet. Atarah grabbed a hanging lantern, while Charlotte and her mother went to the nearest prisoners. Upon bringing the light closer, the angels looked worse than she expected.

"Water," one angel pleaded. He was hanging closest to them. Chunks of his legs and wings were missing.

"Charlotte, check the internal organs first while I start on the wings," her mother commanded.

Charlotte extended her hands quickly. Within minutes, the angel revitalized. Not to full health, but at least further away from death's door.

A single eye peered at them while the other eye remained swollen shut.

"You need to leave," the angel rasped. "Leave before the red cloaks come back."

"Tell us your name," Atarah commanded.

"Makoto," he answered. The swelling in his face lessened.

She spied a long rusty nail on the floor, and an idea came to her. She leapt into the air, where the lock on the chains sealed on the ceiling. Jamming the nail into the lock, she picked around until the chains broke loose.

A thud on the ground followed by another groan told her the angel was free.

"Try the others, Atarah," her mother said as she crouched down to help him up.

"No!" The angel heaved. "Please listen to me. Run as far away as you can before the red cloaks come back."

"What are you talking about?" Atarah asked as she landed. From above, she counted at least another dozen or so Gabriel angels chained up. There was a lumpy pile in the far corner of the room, too dimly lit for her to tell, but she suspected it was a pile of dead bodies.

"The red cloaks are his followers!" Makoto implored. "Please leave while you can!"

"I am afraid that is not possible." A dark chuckle followed.

They whirled around to see Matthew standing a few feet away. The marks appeared back on his skin but smaller than before. The symbols no longer glowed either.

"Ah," Matthew said as he followed her gaze. "I had to use a lot of Gabriel blood to transport all three of you here. That's why I am not glowing as much."

"Blood?" Charlotte paled.

"Yes." Matthew frowned. "I thought I already explained this to you. How we have discovered a way to utilize Gabriel blood to our benefit."

"What is it you want, Matthew?" Atarah asked, stepping in front of her mother and Charlotte. She tried to call upon the power she wielded before but felt nothing. In fact, her body felt disturbingly numb. No power thrumming through here like before, pure nothingness.

"What I want?" Matthew scoffed. "In the end, what I want is what everyone wants. Whether they realize it or not, everyone wants the same thing. Peace."

"What happened to you?" Ava whispered. Matthew moved his gaze up and down her whole body before answering.

"Just experienced the enlightenment that I needed," Matthew replied. "Now with you and Arick back at my side, you will join me as I combine all three realms together. Once together, there will be no more hierarchy, no more prejudice or discrimination against any beings. We will all live as one as we should."

"You're insane," Atarah murmured with wide eyes.

"Arick is living proof of how ridiculous our socially contrasted society is!" Matthew smirked.

"Arick is alive?" Atarah gasped.

Matthew nodded. "With Arick I intend for him to rule over the combined realms in my stead. I want him to witness our kingdom come together and unite. I will call it: the confluence! I want him to rule over those that thought of him as less than because of his birth."

"Arick will never agree to that!" Atarah argued. "Arick is nothing like you!"

Matthew's eyes trailed back to her mother. "He will for you two."

She opened her mouth to protest but stopped. The memory of Arick throwing himself over Matthew so she could escape flashed across her mind. Her stomach dropped as those words rang true.

"Over time, he will realize that this convergence is what is best overall for all societies."

"If you combine all of the realms, Matthew, it wouldn't bring the worlds together," her mother spoke up from behind her. "The force of it *will* end up destroying all of the realms. It won't end the way you imagine."

"Oh, Ava." Matthew shook his head. "You were never as much of a dreamer as I was. But that is ok, for now." He took a step closer. They stepped back in response. "When my dream does come to fruition, I will rule the new world of angels, demons, and humans alike. I will be a fair ruler and outlaw all forms of hierarchy."

Atarah scoffed. "Except for yourself!"

"Well, I know what is best for everyone," Matthew replied. "I will remain uncorrupted and so will Arick."

"You are sick in the head if you think this will work. You will destroy all of the realms with this plan you have," Charlotte murmured, horror coated her words.

"Everyone is so pessimistic when I explain the possibilities of our new world!" Matthew sneered. "You all will be thanking me soon enough in the years to come."

"So you will just keep us prisoners until then?" Ava asked with wide eyes.

"Well as ruler, I need an heir and a spare," Matthew replied smoothly. Ava paled. Her breathing turned erratic. "I'll need a spare eventually." Matthew waved a hand. "So that will be your other purpose instead of just…motivation for Arick to do as he's told."

"You are a monster," Atarah breathed.

"Monsters are relative," Matthew fired back as he snapped his fingers. A creak of a door opening alerted them to the other side of the room.

"Elders," Matthew commanded, "put these females in separate cell blocks in the southern corridor." He narrowed his eyes. "None of the guards are to touch them without my permission." His voice dropped to an icy tone.

"Yes, master," a choir of voices answered.

When they stepped into the light, Atarah saw four figures approach them. Tall figures dressed in deep red cloaks drew closer. Each was a different type of demon but Atarah couldn't discern what kind. They moved fast. Within a blink of an eye, a red cloak pounced on her. She screamed in pain as a talon dug into her right arm. This creature weighed a ton, or felt like it. Using its body weight, the cloaked follower shoved her to the back door. She flailed about trying to break free. The harder she thrashed about, the more the talons dug into her.

Screams from behind turned her head. She saw Charlotte and her mother grabbed in the same manner by two other hooded figures and ushered to the door.

"Come now, Arch!" the creature spat with disgust. He shoved her out the door as a new scream erupted.

"As for *you,*" she heard Matthew say.

She threw back her head to get one more glance at what was happening. Makoto knelt before Matthew, withering in pain as the last cloaked figure clawed into his back.

"You will fuel my next trip. We are very close to the convergence." Matthew's smile sent chills down her spine. "Bleed him dry."

The red cloak pushed her through the door just as Makoto's pained cries turned into screams of terror. She thrashed and fought the whole way down, screaming as she went. Fire burned in her chest as she vowed to destroy Matthew.

She saw the other two figures in front, carrying her mom and Charlotte down the hall. Doors with bars lined the hallway with only one lantern lighting the way. At the end, one cloaked figure kicked a door ajar before unceremoniously dumping Charlotte inside the cell.

"Get in!" the cloak said as he delivered a kick to her chest. Atarah thrashed around, seeing red as he kicked her friend.

"Damn!" the cloak holding her grunted. "This one fights like a hellcat."

Another cloak chuckled. "Well, put her in the next cell." The cloak peered down at her struggling mother. "You'll go into the cell next door."

A hard shove catapulted her into a dark cell. The door slammed behind her the instant she passed the threshold. Atarah scrambled to the door and started punching it.

"You'll be sorry to ever mess with us!" she yelled out. Another chuckle followed.

A cry of distress followed by a door slam signaled her mother being placed in her own cell. She punched the metal door over and over again. The numbness of her body slowly dissipated as her knuckles throbbed. She didn't relent. On and on she pounded on the door as rage coursed through her. Rage at Matthew and their own helpless situation. Dents peppered the door. She occasionally heard the guards' jeers at Charlotte and her mother, but they stayed away from her cell.

Eventually she slumped against the wall of her small cell. For as small she was, this space closed in around her, leaving her little to no room to walk around. She stood to her full height but if she stretched out her arms, both of her hands would touch the walls. She sat down on the cold, hard ground to think. She pulled her knees into her chest and closed her eyes. Somewhere in here, Arick was alive. She took solace in knowing her brother was alive. For the moment, her mother and Charlotte stayed out of harm's way.

How could she get them out of here? Where were they exactly? What did Matthew mean by 'home?' The minutes ticked by as she sat with her thoughts. She wondered what condition Arick was in and where her father was. As her thoughts swirled, it was then she noticed that she didn't know where any of the others were. Gabriel Jr., Arick's rag-tag team, and Ben.

A sharp pain pierced her heart as she thought of his name. The panic in his face and the kiss they shared before everything happened. Regret soured her tongue and she wished to change their last moments together. Ben said he loved her. Tears threatened to spill over as she feared the worst case scenario. How stupid she must be? To be too stubborn to love someone! Atarah's lips twitched at the thought.

She thought back to all the times Ben fought for her, nearly died for her. Her heart constricted. This cell shrunk more in her mind. The walls closed in as despair wrapped itself around her chest. This time, tears spilled over her face. Images of everyone she loved flashed through her mind. She *had* to do something! Her mother's words of doom echoed in her mind. If Matthew's plan went through, everyone and everything she loved would be destroyed.

*You inspire me, Atarah.*

Charlotte's words whispered to her heart. She rubbed her eyes. She couldn't give up. She was a Michael angel; she had to fight until the end. As she shifted on the ground, a prick at her thigh called her attention. She patted along her leg and froze. The rusty nail she used to free the prisoner earlier! In the struggle to grab a hold of her, they didn't bother to check whether she grabbed anything. Atarah released a long breath.

*This rusty nail is a start!* she thought.

She needed a plan. She crouched low and peered underneath the door. Vaguely, she saw the red cloaks of two of the three captors. The third captor's robe shuffled passed her door and back through the door they came through.

*That's where all the Gabriel angels are being held,* she thought.

She saw no doors further down the hallway where their cells were located, but that could've been due to poor lighting. She peeked back toward the other two guards. She'd have to take them out fast, but how? They both possessed claws or talons of some kind. She could pick the lock on the door and catch them by surprise, but the third guard could attack at any moment.

She sat back and put her hand to her chin. What would her father do? After a few minutes, a reckless plan formed in her head. She had a plan of attack and an idea for a trap to lay for the guards. This would be her one shot to rescue everyone and herself. She crept to the door and picked at the lock. She had to be quick and efficient if she was going to save anyone. She moved as quietly as possible, pausing every time the lock clicked. Her heart thundered in her chest as she waited for the guards to grow suspicious. They never did, so she continued.

Sweat dripped down her brow as she worked the lock. She slowed down her breath to stay quiet. Her palms trembled while she pushed the nail side to side. Another click. Pause. Then silence and she continued. This pattern repeated for some of the longest minutes of her life.

*Come on,* she thought. *Almost there.*

As the last part of the lock clicked, a large boom echoed from the first room they landed in. She jumped as her cell trembled as if a small earthquake occurred. She dove down to peer underneath the door again. The guard's feet shifted uncertainly until one of them moved toward the loud sound.

*Great, that only leaves one guard for me to deal with,* she cheered. The last guard shuffled halfway down the hall before returning back to their doors. The feet pointed to the door as if he wanted to follow his partner. Another boom echoed from somewhere. This time the last guard sprinted down the hall, leaving their doors unguarded.

Atarah released a breath. *Finally some luck on our side!* she thought.

She pushed the door open, freezing as it screeched open. She paused as she waited for a guard to come running in to attack her, but nothing happened. Keeping her eyes to the door, she immediately started to work on Charlotte's locked door.

"Stay quiet, Charlotte!" Atarah whispered in a harsh tone.

"Atarah?!" Charlotte whispered back. "What happened? Was that loud sound you?"

"I don't know what it was, but I thank the Trinity for whatever happened."

No longer worried about catching the guards attention, she worked faster. The lock unlatched within minutes of her working on it. She swung the door open as Charlotte came flying out, tackling her in a tight embrace.

"You truly are amazing!" she rasped. Atarah hugged her back. Fear and urgency forced her to move onto her mother's lock.

"Mom!" Atarah whispered. "Are you ok?"

Silence greeted her.

Atarah patted on the door. "Mom?!"

A stifled sob reached her ears. Panicked, Atarah jammed the nail into the lock. She twirled the nail around as if that would unlock the door faster. After a few harrowing minutes, the lock clicked open. She jerked the door open as her heart roared in her chest.

Her mother lay curled up in the corner of her small cell, suppressing her sobs. Atarah lurched for her.

"I'm here!" Atarah said, grabbing onto her mom's hands. Her mom's hands were ice cold. Her eyes swam with tears at her mother's trembling form.

"He really isn't going to stop," her mother murmured. She put her hands on her mom's shoulder, forcing Ava to look into her eyes.

"*We,*" she said with a tight jaw, "will stop him! We just need to think of a good plan."

"First," Charlotte whispered. "We need to get to safety."

Atarah nodded. "That too. Let's go!"

She helped her mother up from the floor. Atarah took the lead down the hall with Charlotte and her mother taking the rear. She peered through the small crack of the door that the guards left ajar. In the room they had been in, no less than an hour ago, Gabriel angels still hung from the ceiling but no red cloaks or Matthew could be seen. She gently pushed the door and stepped in.

She ventured closer to see if any of the angels were still alive. She froze. In the center, Makoto hung, upside down, with slashes all across his neck and chest. Blood drained from his body into a waiting bucket at the bottom. She paled.

"Mom! Charlotte!" Atarah whispered. Neither hesitated.

"Atarah, cut them all down as fast as you can." Her mother's voice still trembled. "I think we can save them all."

Atarah winced. Saving them all would cost them time. Precious time to escape. She looked around for a greater weapon than a rusty nail. The cloaks had to have used something to cut up poor Makoto. Out of the corner of her eye, the gleam of a blade caught her attention.

She rushed over. The blade was short and curved. She pulled it out of the bucket. It was covered in entrails and blood, Atarah gagged. It was a dagger with two sharp points. Disgusted yet intrigued, she took a closer look. She covered her mouth to keep from breathing in the stench. The blade had an attachable compartment. With slight pressure from the handle, a piece of the blade fell. A detachable dagger, she realized.

She scrambled to where her mother and Charlotte worked on Makoto. She flew high to where the chain was anchored and swung with all her might. The dagger shattered the chain and cut through the ceiling. Atarah startled at how easily the chain had broken. Maybe she really did get stronger?

Makoto remained silent as his body fell to the ground. Atarah wondered if he was alive before moving on to the other chained prisoners. She sliced through the restraints with ease. One by one, Charlotte eased the descent of the prisoners. On the last one, she used her hands instead and ripped the chain out of the stone wall.

Once the last prisoner sunk to the ground, Charlotte extended her arms out. Her hand glowed as her power flowed into the angels. Atarah worked on removing the binds around their wrists. With their combined efforts, each prisoner was freed and recovering. As their alertness increased, Atarah asked all of them questions.

"Are there any others?" she asked as she released the last restraint. A few moans and groans answered her. She glanced at her mother and Charlotte. Her mother continued to help Makoto, who was in bad shape, while Charlotte scrunched her brow in concentration. She would have to wait and let them work.

She drew her dagger and crept toward the only other door that didn't lead to a cell block. A dark hallway greeted her; no guards and only a few lanterns lit the way. The hall curved, preventing her from seeing further down. If she had to guess, they were underground somewhere. All of the walls were made out of hard stone. She touched along the walls and stepped forward. Was she back in Belli Causa? The walls were warm. The walls of her home remained cold all-year round.

She placed both hands back on her hilt. She wasn't home, but they were somewhere underground. Possibly the Coal Mountains? She knelt down and dug her fingers into the dirt. She expanded her senses to take a look around this strange place. She closed her eyes as the sensation of running feet vibrated across her palm. She sensed guards running further down into the tunnels.

*So many tunnels,* she nearly groaned out loud. She heard many other prisoners as well. Based on their growls and grunts, they didn't sound as if they were angels. Atarah flinched as the horror of where they might be reached her. She begged the Trinity that it was all in her mind. She pleaded for everything before her to not be true.

From the snarls and slashing she sensed not too far away, she knew demons patrolled these tunnels. The strange cloaked guards from before, the 'followers' of Matthew were demons. She opened her eyes. The most likely scenario of when Matthew mentioned his 'home,' was bringing them to the demon realm.

Atarah's heart stopped at the thought. They were screwed if that was the case. How were they supposed to get back home? Atarah jerked her head up as she remembered her brother. Arick was still somewhere down in these tunnels. Could she locate him? She closed her eyes again and focused. She tried to find any scent or shuffling feet pattern that resembled Arick. There were so many sounds and scents all throughout the tunnels, she couldn't distinguish anything! The only hint of anything happening was the thundering footprints heading further south.

Whatever the big boom was, it wasn't something the guards had planned. She crept back into the room and closed the door.

"How is everyone doing now?" Atarah asked Charlotte.

"A few of them were in better condition," Charlotte explained. Sweat dripped from her face and her voice sounded strained, but she didn't let up for a single moment. "Did you see anything out there?"

Atarah shook her head. "There are no guards out in the next few hallways. They are all moving further underground. Whatever that bang was must've been bad news for them."

"Let's pray it keeps them occupied because these angels need serious help," her mother called over her shoulder. "Makoto's barely hanging on. He's lost so much blood."

"I may have some bad news too," Atarah said with a grimace. Charlotte gave a humorless chuckle.

"Worse than being attacked by Matthew and dragged into a dungeon?" Charlotte said with sarcasm. Atarah's lips twitched.

"Kind of."

"Uh-oh," Charlotte and her mother said at the same time.

"I think Matthew brought us to the demon realm." The words spilled out of her in a rush. Her mother's wings twitched once in response while Charlotte's slumped to the ground. "This may mean we're trapped."

Silence stretched between all of them. As the gravity of their situation crashed down on them, Atarah placed a comforting hand on both of their shoulders. The glow from their hands faltered for a few seconds.

"We may be of some help," a voice rasped to her right. All their eyes went to Makoto. He lay limp in Ava's arms, but being awake and alert was a very good sign.

"Makoto!" Atarah exhaled. "You're gonna make it!"

A ghost of a smile danced on his lips.

"So far, it appears that way," he murmured. "Individually, all of us are too weak to transport a way out of here. But—" A dry cough racked through his body. Ava patted his chest as he heaved.

"But?" Atarah pressed, leaning in closer.

"But," Makoto wheezed, "together and with both of their help," He indicated to Charlotte and Ava. "We may be able to pull enough spiritual energy to get back to our own realm."

"That's great!" Atarah exclaimed.

"And if we can't generate enough energy? What then?" Charlotte asked, her brow furrowed. Another round of coughing claimed Makoto. They waited until he gathered enough breath.

"If we don't gather enough, we may just transport somewhere different in the demon realm. I don't know." He gasped another breath. "For all I know we will only gather enough energy for transport a few feet."

"Oh no," Charlotte moaned.

"But!" Atarah argued, "it's still possible we could gather enough to get back home!"

Makoto coughed again. "It's still a possibility," he rasped.

"That's better than nothing!" Atarah stood to her feet. "All we need to do is get Arick, come back here, and then transport back to the spirit realm and warn the others that Matthew is about to start his crazy convergence plot."

"Atarah," Charlotte called out, alarmed. "What do you mean get Arick? We don't know where he is. Nor do we know where the guards went."

"Are you saying we leave him then?" Atarah asked, shocked at her protest. Charlotte shook her head.

"I am not saying that," she started. "All I am saying is that there are a lot of variables, and we need weapons to defend ourselves. If you go off to search for him, Ava and I will be defenseless against anyone who shows up."

Atarah paused. Charlotte made a valid point, but frustration boiled within her at her protest. Atarah glanced down at the Gabriel angels and then back at the door. The angels needed more time to recuperate under Charlotte and Ava's hands. Atarah turned back to Charlotte.

"What if you bolt the door shut?" Atarah suggested. "Even I had a hard time making a dent in these doors, let alone whatever guards may come by."

"That is a good idea," Ava chimed in.

"And weapons?" Charlotte asked. Her wings trembled just as Atarah realized how terrified Charlotte was.

"Here." Atarah clicked the detachable dagger out of its place. "Take this and stab anyone who tries to hurt you."

"But what if you don't come back?" Charlotte whispered in desperation. Atarah knelt down beside her and pulled her into a hug. "I already healed you from the brink of death," Charlotte murmured. "I can't bear that again."

"You can," Atarah whispered. "Because we are all stronger than we think we are."

"My love," Ava said with tears in her eyes. Atarah turned away only to be embraced again by her mother. "Charlotte's right. You really do inspire others." Ava sniffled. "I am so proud of you."

Atarah hugged her mom tightly.

"I'll be back as soon as I can."

*Help!*
*Dear all the realms make this end!*
*I can't take this anymore. I just wanna die!*
*It's been so long since I've seen the sun...*
*I wonder how long until I can go on my lunch break?*
*Do you think anyone will notice my tattoo?*
*WHY?!*
*I could go for a beer right now.*

Thoughts flooded in all at once for Canaan. He thanked his lucky stars that Azazel/Arick quieted as they scurried through the tunnels. The sound of the fiddle continued to play along the halls; however, it wasn't the loudest. For him, the sounds of mixed thoughts from guards, tortured prisoners and Arick/Azazel created the most noise. Canaan gritted his teeth to bear the insufferable ruckus.

*This will all be worth it soon enough,* Canaan thought.

If he could return home with the valuable intel he'd gathered so far, he might be able to save more regions than his own. Azazel/Arick paused at the end of the pathway. The tunnel split. One way going left, the other way going right.

*"I say left,"* Azazel thought.

*"I say right,"* Arick replied.

*"All right, now you're just being difficult,"* Azazel scoffed.

*"I don't know why I feel this way, but I REALLY think we should go right,"* Arick implored.

*"Well, if I don't do it, you'll just throw another hissy fit right?"*

Azazel replied.

*"Correct!"*

"Well then to the right we go," Azazel whispered out loud to Canaan.

"I…" Canaan began while he concentrated. He focused on the voices individually. "I think Arick is right. There are guards approaching from the left, about half a dozen. Going to the right we'll avoid them."

*"Ha!"* Arick cheered. *"I got good instincts! You should listen to me more."*

*"Don't get too cocky, kid."*

"Let's go!" Canaan whispered.

He dashed down the corridor to the right, taking the lead. With his hand lightly touching the wall, he paid more attention to the minds around him than moving. Fewer guards patrolled over here, and he wondered why. Most of those on patrol duty were thinking about how to pass the time.

*Have 'fun' with the prisoners, or to take a smoke break instead?* one guard pondered further down the tunnel. *It's not like they care about what happens to them anyway…but Reif got in a lot of trouble last week when the prisoner from 05215 died. Maybe I'll just take a smoke break then. Best not to stir the pot with this job.*

Canaan slowed as they drew closer to the guard. This particular guard was not alone either. Canaan peeked around the corner quickly to see a golem standing beside the guard. As still as the stone it was made from, the golem was inactive at the moment. Its light gray stone face displayed two empty eye sockets, no nose, and a single long slit for a mouth. Two holes along the side of its face served as ears. Golems were built tall and large. At eight feet tall, golems towered over most. With their long arms stretching down to their knees, they'd been used for construction or security jobs due to their durable build. Golems made great slave labor. They were mindless dolls that did whatever their master commanded without question. That explained why Canaan didn't hear another voice. Golems didn't have thoughts. Only the mission assigned to them by their master. Canaan huffed.

Golems, while dense, possessed incredible strength and were tough to beat in a fight. Canaan peeked around again. The guard who he heard from was another tiefling. On the smaller size, the tiefling fiddled with the key rings on his belt.

*I'll need to leave this behind while I'm on break,* the tiefling thought. He gave a hard kick to the golem's leg.

"Oi!" the guard yelled as he rubbed his own leg. "Get up. I am going to take a break."

The golem didn't stir. Like a statue, it remained still and lifeless.

*Ah, well. Not trying that again. My damn leg hurts*, the tiefling pondered for a moment. *I'll just leave the keys right on its arm, that way I can't be blamed for not handing them over.*

The second guard tucked the key rings into one of the elbows the golem had crossed. Satisfied that the ring wouldn't fall, the tiefling guard took off down one of the other two hallways.

*"At least we know that way leads out now,"* Arick whispered. *"Lucky us,"*

*"We have a golem to get past. I would not count us so lucky,"* Azazel said grimly.

*"I think we can take it,"* Arick mumbled. Canaan turned to Azazel/Arick, shaking his head furiously.

*"The Selaphiel's right, kid,"* Azazel thought, while nodding in agreement.

*"What's so scary about golems anyway?"* Arick asked.

*"Did you not see that tiefling's kick?"* Azazel replied. *"It did absolutely nothing! Also golems follow only the command of their creator. They cannot be reasoned with, manipulated, distracted, or anything else. Once it knows an intruder is there, it will stop at nothing to eliminate us."*

Canaan nodded.

He had heard about golems through the minds of other demons. They were very difficult to destroy since they were made from hard stone. Relentless stone dolls described them best. How would they get past this one? Also where did that key lead? Canaan peered around. No door or cell appeared to be anywhere.

*Why can't we teleport out of here? Please someone help us...* a faint whisper of a voice echoed.

His eyes widened. There were prisoners somewhere around here! Gabriel angel prisoners! Where could they be?

He turned and beckoned Azazel/Arick forward. Once he leaned down, Canaan whispered what he'd heard.

"Arick was right," he said softly. "I hear the thoughts of the Gabriel angels close by."

*"That's great!"* Arick thought.

*"Hmmmm, they must have a concealment spell around the cell,"* Azazel pondered. *"They really do not want these prisoners getting away."*

"Do you know how to get rid of it?" he whispered, glancing back to the golem to make sure it hadn't moved.

*"It's more of an illusion I guess. Once you are aware that it's there and break through it, the illusion dissipates."* Azazel peeked around the corner with him. *"If I had to guess I would feel along the wall the golem is leaning against. Once you touch the door, it'll break up the illusion."*

*"Sounds like a plan,"* Arick chimed in, sounding closer somehow.

*"Hold on kid! Don't take over just yet,"* Azazel grunted. *"The best plan of action for now would be for us to take on the golem and have Canaan slip around us to free the prisoners. Now, these creatures are strong, so we're gonna need to use either a gogoplata or omoplata hold."*

A pause echoed in their shared mind.

*"How do you know such advanced fighting moves?"* Arick asked with some amazement.

*"I've been around a long time, kid,"* Azazel thought dryly. He looked down at Canaan. *"You ready, Selaphiel?"*

Canaan listened to the hidden Gabriel angels. Many of them bore injuries of lacerations and missing digits. He waded through the images of what they were seeing. They hung above the ground in chains, each blindfolded. They could hear and talk to one another but were afraid to. Too much noise alerted the guards, which led to a beating. Outside of the beatings, one of the only times their blindfolds were removed was when these strangers covered in deep red hooded cloaks came into their cells. The cloaked figures would drag one of them out at a time to an adjacent room and bleed them. Sometimes the cloaked figures ripped off clumps of feathers or cut off a hand or foot.

Whatever they were, the Gabriel angels feared the red cloaks more than the golem outside their cell door. *Interesting,* Canaan thought. *Red cloaks?*

*"Ahem! You ready, Selaphiel?"* Azazel yelled mentally at him.

# Chapter 8

Arick waited impatiently as Canaan snapped out of whatever mind trance he'd escaped to. Canaan dipped his chin.

"I hear them all in there." Canaan whispered. "There are three rooms behind that door and they're in one. Many of them aren't in good shape."

Arick pushed his consciousness forward as Azazel relented control. Switching was growing easier and smoother.

*"Don't mess around on this one, kid,"* Azazel chastised. *"I'll take over if it gets too hard."*

*"Yeah, yeah,"* Arick replied, waving a mental hand in dismissal.

From Canaan's signal, Arick stepped around the corner to face the golem. He gave a sharp whistle.

"Hey buddy!" Arick called out. "I'm gonna need you to take a step outside for a minute or two."

Silence.

The golem remained still as stone. Arick glanced side to side, to see if any other guards lingered around. Nothing and no one moved.

*"Are both of you sure this thing will be a problem?"* Arick thought to Azazel and Canaan.

*"Don't let your guard down,"* Azazel replied while Canaan nodded his head in agreement. *"Get closer and touch the wall behind it. The sooner we can see the door, the better."* Azazel encouraged.

Arick approached with light feet. The golem matched him in height as he stepped closer. If Azazel and Canaan weren't here, Arick would have thought it to be a simple statue. He reached up to pat the wall beside the golem. As soon as his hand made contact with the wall, the golem's head snapped to Arick.

Its empty eye sockets glowed blue with life. The golem activated. Without giving it too much time to maneuver, Arick delivered a strong blow to the head. The sound of crackling rock rebounded along the walls. Pain shot up his arm from the impact. He gritted his teeth while blood dripped from his knuckles.

*"That wasn't smart,"* Arick thought as his hand throbbed. The golem stumbled one step backward before righting itself. He watched the key to the door fall behind the golem.

*"Watch its feet, kid, and attack at the joints,"* Azazel coached. *"Otherwise good job, the door's there."*

The illusion lifted, revealing the iron-made door. Chains spanned across the door in a crisscross pattern, sending the extra message of no escape. Arick peered behind the golem to analyze the door, but those few seconds cost him. The golem returned his punch with the same ferocity and speed as he gave.

Arick narrowly dodged his attack, taking a step back. The golem moved forward with him, following up with another swing. Completely ignoring the key. Arick stepped further back.

*"That's it, kid,"* Azazel said. *"Let's give Canaan some space to work with the door."*

Canaan wasted no time. Once the golem cleared the door, he dashed forward. Canaan crouched to examine the lock. He frowned after a minute.

"Try to keep the golem occupied for as long as you can, Arick," Canaan called over.

"That's the plan," Arick grunted as he avoided another punch.

Canaan picked up the key and wiggled it into the lock. The chains on the door rattled with the motion, echoing in the hall. The golem paused in its attack on Arick. With a loud snap, its head, arms, and legs all pivoted around, facing Canaan.

"Watch out!" Arick yelled out.

He leapt onto its back, wrapping his arms around its neck. He used his weight to throw the golem off balance, sending them crashing to the floor. He maneuvered fast to bind the shoulder, restricting any more movement. Other guards' voices shouted down the halls. Their time was nearly up.

"Looks like we made too much noise," Arick grunted as he tightened his hold.

The golem's limbs cracked and groaned as it fought to get out from under him. Arick squeezed hard, using all of his strength. The stomping of feet pounded closer and closer, as more guards were alerted.

"It doesn't matter, I opened it!" Canaan called out. "Get over here now!"

Canaan waved him over as he stood within the threshold. Arick released the golem and sprinted to the door, while the shouts drew near.

"Help me close and lock up the door! It'll buy us a little bit of time." Canaan yelled over the guards. Arick slammed his body into the door to close it. The door nudged an inch or two. Canaan threw his body into the door as well. They both groaned as they strained to close the door. The sound of stone cracking alerted them to the golem's movements.

"Come on!" Canaan cried out. "Push!"

*"Yeah, kid! Use that Michael strength!"* Azazel shouted in their mind.

He took a deep breath and pushed with all of his might. The door creaked as it slowly shut. The golem's hand reached the door as Arick forced it shut.

Canaan locked the door with lighting speed. Arick slumped to the ground, panting. A relieved chuckle escaped him as he glanced at Canaan.

"Holy trinity, we actually did it!" Arick exclaimed. Canaan gave a small smile as they basked in this small success. Arick stood up and reached a hand out for Canaan.

"Now we—"

A huge slam against the door cut him off. The impact shook the door and the entire tunnel. Arick and Canaan jumped back.

"I think we need a different exit plan," Arick murmured. The growing voices of guards reenforced the urgency to escape.

"I agree," Canaan said, pulling on his arm. "Let's get moving!"

They ran from the door just as another large bang reverberated down the tunnel. The door rattled again and groaned. The door wouldn't hold for long.

"The plan still the same?" Arick asked as they jogged.

"Yes! Top priorities are to find a different exit and then escape with the Gabriel angels through that exit," Canaan panted. "Wait, I hear something up…" Pant. "Up ahead." Another pant.

A few seconds ticked by, and three figures approached them. The figures were clothed in red robes and their faces obscured by the hoods. From the way the figures ran at them, Arick guessed they weren't friendly.

No point in wasting momentum, Arick picked up his speed and tackled right into them. The collision knocked all three of them into the walls with a loud snap. Skidding to a stop, he delivered blows to the head and neck on each one to ensure no one would get up any time soon.

Canaan placed his hands on his knees, attempting to catch his breath. Arick removed one of the red-hoods to see a gray half-goat demon. He took off the others to see they were all different demons. One appeared to be another tiefling, while the third was a cenobite, a tall, pale faced demon with pierced flesh all around its body. Cenobites possessed no hair but often had loose skin around the head and neck. This cenobite bore piercing along its brows, nose, and lips.

*"Interesting,"* Azazel mumbled.

*"Why's that?"*

*"These demons don't usually hang around each other since they're from different domains,"* Azazel explained. *"Matthew must be working hard to recruit everyone."*

*"Yeah, well they can all stay together,"* Arick replied back. He ripped parts of their robes to bind them all together. Satisfied that they were bound tight, he backed away.

"Let's keep going," Arick said as Canaan straightened up.

Another loud bang shook the tunnel they were in. This time the sounds of chains clashing followed. The door was about to come down. They took off without another thought. They ran down to the end of the hall, coming to a forked end. Both opposing tunnels were poorly lit and offered no clue as to where the angels were located.

*"Left or right, Canaan?"* Arick thought as he flexed his jaw.

"I think we should go left. That way could be our new exit route," Canaan said after a moment.

They ran down the left corridor. This one was not long at all. Within a few seconds, they made it to another door. The *only* door with one lantern nailed to the stone wall above it. Arick put his ear to the door.

Silence. He heard nothing on the other side. Canaan frowned as he stepped up to the door. He shook his head.

*"Can't hear anything?"* Arick thought to him. Canaan shook his head again.

*"Still wanna go through this door?"* Arick asked. Canaan nodded.

*"Let me go first, then,"* Arick replied as he reached for the knob. He twisted with care. His brows shot up in surprise as the door opened. No lock or resistance. He pushed the door open and braced for any attacks.

Darkness. Pure pitch black greeted them. They both peered their heads into the room. He saw nothing from how dark it was.

*"The lantern, kid!"* Azazel's voice made Arick jump. *"Use the lantern to look around."*

Lifting one hand, he ripped the lantern from the stone wall. He raised the lantern up to see if there were other lanterns along the wall.

*"Look for any switch of some kind too, kid,"* Azazel instructed. *"They have electricity here, kinda like the humans do."*

*"Oh."*

Arick felt along the wall and found it. He clicked on the lights. As the room came to light, music of a fiddle played in a merry tune. Canaan's gasp served as his only warning. Arick looked up and almost dropped the lantern. His stomach hollowed out at the sight before him.

Hundreds of bodies stacked up against the walls of the room, all the way to the ceiling. Bodies of Gabriel angels lay, drained and discarded without a care. Their mouths agape in a silent scream as their bodies decomposed. *Many* bodies presented different states of decomposition, creating the foulest stench Arick had ever endured. His knees shook. He doubled over and gagged at the smell.

*"Damn,"* Azazel murmured.

Canaan covered his nose and mouth before entering the room. The floor squelched as he walked across; Arick didn't want to know why. From the sight of blood and guts, he could take an educated guess.

In the center of the room, a huge container, nearly as high as the ceiling, stood with blood filled to the brim. A machine flashed on as Canaan approached, jingling a tune of activation.

"Is this how he plans to converge all of the realms together?" Canaan asked with wide eyes. "By the blood of all of these angels?"

"He must've killed thousands of angels," Arick said, covering his nose and mouth.

"Possibly tens of thousands if he experimented on them," Canaan countered.

"I thought…all of this was recent," Arick said as he moved closer to a pile of bodies.

*"What?"* Azazel called out. *"No, Matthew's been busy for at least fifteen years in the demon realm quote, unquote 'working' on his craft."*

"What?!" Canaan whirled around to face him. "What do you mean working on his craft?" Canaan's jaw tightened. His eyes darkened with suppressed rage.

*"By the time I heard the demons or his followers talking about him, that was about fifteen or so years ago, possibly longer,"* Azazel explained.

"And you let him do this!? THIS to our people?!" Canaan stomped over to Arick and grabbed him by the collar. "What kind of monster sits back and lets thousands of innocent angels die like this!" Canaan roared.

*"There's no point directing your anger at me, Selaphiel,"* Azazel's tone turned cold. *"You angels aren't my problem."*

Canaan jerked Arick away in disgust before storming back to the machine at the base of the container.

"How do we destroy this?" Canaan slammed his fist on the tank.

*"Beats me."* Azazel gave a mental shrug.

*"Come on!"* Arick thought angrily. *"You said you were going to help us!"*

*"And I did!"* Azazel countered. *"Who got you this far AND undetected? Me! Who told you about the guards and this place? Me! I've been helping you this whole time, kid. It's not my fault you found something you didn't like."*

"Enough." Canaan hunched over the buttons and display on the machine. "Our squabbling now doesn't bring back their lives." He rubbed a hand through his hair.

"No," Arick mumbled as he glanced up at the tank full of blood. "But we can make sure their spilled blood doesn't hurt others."

Canaan tilted his head at him.

"What?" Canaan asked. Arick walked along the side of the tank.

"Let's destroy this now," Arick said, tightening his jaw. "Before he tries to use this for that crazy convergence idea."

*"Is that...a smart idea?"* Azazel sounded apprehensive. However, Arick hadn't merely suggested the idea to anyone. He clenched his fist as he stared at the dark red liquid, his mind made up on his next course of action.

He peered back to Canaan, his jaw set. Canaan gave a grim nod back.

"Let's do this."

Ben gritted his teeth against another icy blast of air. His limbs trembled, desperate to stay warm. His suffering was met with no sympathy. Noah and Zewal sneered every time he stepped too close to them while the females, Clarissa, Isabella, and Tariel ignored his entire existence. Mikael and Elijah were the only ones casting concerning glances his way as they climbed.

They ascended up the Decimate Mountains with little tools or equipment, including warm clothing. The mountains were the only place Matthew remained hidden. Since the mountains served as the natural 'border' between all of the demon lords for domains, no one ruled over the area. The mountains created an odd neutral zone for any and all demons to seek refuge. Part of the demon lords' frustration in capturing Matthew was due to him sheltering within the mountains.

Beelzebub explained that neither he nor his siblings could step inside the mountains, for it would cause further territory disputes. To solve this problem, Beelzebub called forth a horse-like creature named Middle Hippus. He was a three-toed miniature horse that navigated with ease in the mountains.

"Hippus here will lead you to where we suspect Matthew to be," Beelzebub said back in his office. "Hippus won't be able to take you the whole way but try to get you as close as he can to the city of Ianua. That has been his favorite hideout so far."

"Ianua?" Ben echoed back.

Beelzebub moved and handed his staff to Mikael and Leviathan's staff to Elijah. They both winced as the staffs touched their skin.

"Use these well," Beelzebub grunted. The demon lord turned to him last. “Here,” he said as he extended Satan’s staff out to him.

Ben used both hands to grab onto the staff. The staff was heavier than it looked and stung his fingers. Within a few seconds, energy swirled around him, as if drawn to him.

“Call upon your power as you normally do, and the staff will activate. Spiritual energy will gather around you so fast, you won’t know what to do,” Beelzebub said with a sly grin.

“Why not give me all of the staffs?” Ben asked, furrowing his brow. Beelzebub’s grin grew wide.

“You will see why in time,” Beelzebub answered. “I wouldn’t recommend using the staffs until you are in the mountains. The sooner you use them, the sooner Satan will find you and our bargain will be finished.”

Ben grimaced as the memory faded away. He shook his head to stay present. He needed to make sure he did this so that Atarah would be safe. A hard bump into his shoulder caused him to stumble on the rocky path.

*Bastard...*

The simmering thought whispered across his mind, as Noah glared down at him, not remorseful in the slightest. *Bastard...doomed... us all...* Zewal walked beside Noah. The Azrael siblings dripped in sweat and exhaustion. Even so, Zewal managed to shoot him a scathing scoff before continuing on. They pulsed with the color red around them.

Noah’s thoughts burned with anger at him, for the deal he made with the demon lords. Ben sighed as he picked himself up. He wiped all emotion off his face and stared back at Noah. He’d thought of Noah as a spoiled brat, and this was his tantrum because he didn’t get his way. In the end, he couldn’t care less.

All that mattered was that he held power. Not all of it yet, but he would soon enough. He glanced down at the red staff in his hand. He sensed the energy gathering where he gripped the staff. He struggled hard to *not* use his powers. It was one thing when thoughts were blasted his way, it was another if he went searching through Noah’s mind.

After a moment, Noah continued on the upward path after sending one more glare his way. Clarissa, Isabella, and Tariel hiked by him, not giving him a single glance. Mikael picked up the rear end of their hiking line and stopped. His aura shined a soft green, like the new growth of spring.

"Why'd you do it?" Mikael asked. Before he could answer, Mikael put a hand on his shoulder and used the other to pat down his back. Dust and pebbles fell from him with each gentle smack. Ben raised an eyebrow up at Mikael.

"You don't hate me, then?" His voice sounded rough and foreign to his own ears. Mikael frowned.

"No, son." Mikael sighed. "Hate has never served me well," Mikael scratched his head. "So I try not to serve any hate out to anyone."

"Even to Matthew?" Ben prodded. They both moved on with their hike.

"Matthew," Mikael sighed, "I don't hate. I'm angry, disappointed, and disgusted with what my brother has become over the years. All of the lives he's damaged and hurt through his actions is like a dagger into my heart every time, but I still cannot find it in my heart to hate him."

"How?" Ben asked, marveled. He thought of his own brothers and irritation sprung up. He and his brothers fought growing up and recently. "You were best friends growing up? Is that the secret?" he asked.

Mikael grinned. "In a way, yes." He paused. "I was always getting in trouble growing up. I didn't have a single care in the world when I was young. It didn't matter to me if my actions effected others, so long as I could do what I wanted when I wanted." Mikael peered down at him. "This mindset ended up getting me into a lot of trouble with my parents and other Archs. I was 'the embodiment of selfishness and inconsideration' in my father's own words." Mikael grimaced. "My father wasn't wrong either. I was a difficult child in every way. Even worse teenager too. I listened to no one except Matthew." Mikael's gaze glazed over a bit. "Matthew saved my butt more times than I care to count growing up. He advocated for me when everyone was against me on the outside, but behind closed doors gave me harshest reprimand that surpassed my father." Mikael's lips twitched. "We fought in our own way. I always hated it when people compared me to my brother. Our own parents compared us every chance they got. Who was stronger? Who behaved better? Who looked bigger? Who could lead more or plan more wisely? You name it and we were pitted against each other. I would act out every time it happened as if to prove we were different people. My behavior, of course, annoyed my brother, and we would fight it out."

Ben climbed over some boulders as he listened to Mikael. His voice, oddly, soothed him.

"Everyone yelled at me most of the time growing up," Mikael continued. "The 'Why can't you be more like your brother?' they would yell. Always shouted something about how I needed to be different or how horrible of a child or heir I was back then."

"What changed?" Ben asked. They were nearing the top of the summit. The air grew thin with each step.

"In all the years and different fights we had, Matthew didn't raise his voice at me. He never needed to. Matthew never once asked me to change how I was as a person. My behaviors and actions he wanted me to change but never who I wanted to be." Mikael paused for a moment. "It took me many years in my life to realize that I just wanted one person in my life growing up to say it's ok to be whatever I wanted to be. It's ok to *not* be the Arch everyone expected me to be. Matthew was the closest one to say that, and it was right before he disappeared into the demon realm on the day we thought he died."

Mikael stopped on the path and turned to him. Ben halted too. A fiery yet soft look came into Mikael's eyes, a look of pure compassion, as he spoke.

"You are enough, Ben."

A shiver ran down his spine as the words rolled over him. Ben locked down his arms to keep them from trembling. His body no longer felt cold.

"You are enough, Ben," Mikael repeated. "You don't need power, magical staffs or more land to make yourself more of the 'man' you think you need to be. Everything you need to be a man is already inside of you." Mikael leaned in closer. "Atarah will love that man, not the outside stuff. That man, I would trust my daughter with. Until he shows up, don't expect my blessing." Mikael patted his shoulder before walking around the bend in the path, leaving him stunned. In a daze, he followed as his mind reeled.

At the top, their guide, Hippus, released a neighing sound, pointing his head at another mountain peak. After that, he turned back down the path they had come from. Ben surveyed the mountain Hippus indicated to spot a small rising line of smoke.

"The black smoke," Mikael called out to everyone, "means someone is burning something. That's where we will aim for." He pointed to the base of the mountain, opposite where the smoke rose.

"Everyone will stay here." Elijah extended his wings in front of

Noah. "All of you kids are in enough danger as it is."

"Kids?" Clarissa scoffed. "Danger? What kind of life do you think we lead?" Her eyes narrowed in on Elijah. "Don't underestimate us just because you are the one that's scared."

"And it is wise to be scared!" Elijah retorted back. "All of you are the future of our realm! Did any of you think this through?" Elijah's brown aura flickered. Panic flickered across his mind as Clarissa's determination strengthened the others' resolve.

"Gabriel." Elijah focused in on Gabriel. "I know for certain your father is worried sick about you." Gabriel flinched at the mention of his father.

"I know he is but…" Gabriel's voice drifted. Elijah whirled around to Zewal and Tariel.

"You two." Elijah pointed to their tired faces. "You have gone beyond your limit, physically and mentally! Can you imagine how terrified your father must be after only just getting your mother back."

"Don't!" Zewal panted. His face twisted into a sneer. "Mind your own business, Elijah."

Tariel, too exhausted to speak, sent out a withering glare to support her brother's sentiments. Elijah sighed as he raised his hands out in disbelief.

"Mikael, back me up here. They *all* need to go home where it is safe," Elijah implored. Mikael eyed everyone individually for a moment. Assessing them. He started with Clarissa then Isabella before making his way down the line. Gabriel held his head high, his brow furrowed, determined.

Mikael moved on to Zewal and Tariel, who promptly lifted up their middle finger to him from their perched rock. Mikael released a quiet chuckle before moving to Noah.

Something in Noah's gaze softened as Mikael stepped closer to him.

"Tell me something, young Archs," Mikael grunted as he sat on a rock. "Why is it you all are here?" He rested an elbow on his knee. "Now that we are alone, away from demons and as safe as we will be, tell us what has happened."

"Mikael!" Elijah protested.

"Let us hear them out, Elijah." Mikael raised a hand to him. "It has been a long time since you and I were young and reckless, but I remember the conviction I had with every mission I set out on, no matter how stupid."

Elijah sighed before lifting his arms in defeat.

"Very well, but let's be quick about this! We don't know when the next rogue demon will come by," Elijah conceded. Mikael nodded before turning to Noah.

"We will start with you, Noah. Inform everyone where your story starts and how we all ended up together," Mikael encouraged.

"Oh, thank the Trinity!" Tariel exclaimed, slumping further onto the rock. "We get a real break."

Noah frowned as relief overcame Tariel and Zewal's faces. Elijah's assessment had been correct. The Azrael siblings were past their limits. Noah waved everyone forward.

"Let's sit down and get this all out then," Noah said as his eyes lingered on Zewal and Tariel. One by one, they sat on rocks or leaned against a small tree trunk. Forming a circle, Ben sat next to Mikael, ignoring any glares shot his way. Once everyone settled, Noah cleared his throat. His red aura changed to a softer shade of pink.

"I am here for Arick, plain and simple," Noah called out. "Originally Zewal, Tariel, and I ventured into the Maze of Uncertainty to find a seraphim."

"A seraphim?!" Isabella exclaimed. Clarissa furrowed her brow.

"How stupid could you be?" Clarissa retorted. "Seraphim don't like to deal with us Archs. It's well documented that we need to *avoid* them at all costs."

Noah's jaw tightened at her tone, but his voice remained calm.

"It is…reckless, I'll admit," Noah started.

"Damn straight it is!" Elijah thundered next to him.

"Seraphim have immense knowledge about luciferians and halflings!" Noah defended. "If I can get an ounce of information from them in the hopes of helping Arick I will!"

"You will go nowhere near that *halfling,*" Elijah sneered. His face scrunched in fury. "He is a danger to you and our society. Nothing you do will ever change that, son."

Mikael's face tightened at Elijah's remarks. His eyes darkened as his aura turned from a light shade of green to a darker red.

"My son is not, nor ever was, a menace to society, Elijah." Mikael's voice deepened. "I'll remind you that he stayed at your house with no problems. Except for the ones you put on him."

Noah frowned. "I bear that shame and responsibility. I didn't welcome Arick as I should've, which is why I am trying my best to help him." Noah turned to his father. "I want others, including you, to see him as he truly is and not by title. A good Arch. He's a better one than me."

Elijah shook his head at his son. "I will not trust him ever again with my family."

Noah looked pleadingly at his father. "Please…just—"

"There are other stories to get to besides whatever family drama you're in now," Clarissa interrupted. Noah sighed as he continued with his story.

"Zewal and Tariel were kind enough to accompany me through the maze because I didn't know what I was doing. We traveled deep into the maze and ran into my father and Mikael while battling a kraken."

"A kraken?!" Isabella spoke out again in amazement. Clarissa nudged her to keep her silent. Every word rang true as Ben listened. He knew Noah was right. Arick was the better Arch compared to them. He thought back to when Arick sacrificed himself so that everyone could escape in the human realm. Arick's panicked thoughts swirled around making sure everyone, including Atarah, made it away from Matthew. That kind of selflessness couldn't be faked, but it didn't matter to many.

Ben heard the concealed disgust Clarissa and Isabella possessed when the topic of Arick came up. The Uriel sisters held the same belief as Elijah, that Arick was dangerous and not to be welcomed back. Zewal and Tariel's auras turned a darker gray. Sadness flowed around their minds, but Ben tried to keep their thoughts at a distance.

He glanced down at the red staff in his hand. He didn't want to activate the staff until they were right in front of Matthew himself. Then he'd get back to Atarah as fast as possible.

"Our story," Mikael spoke out. "Since it became intertwined with Noah, Zewal, and Tariel's started with reports about the Abaddon."

Clarissa paled, while Isabella shuddered. Ben repressed the urge to flinch at the memory of the Abaddon. The first time he almost lost Atarah, another moment where he didn't have enough control.

"I know you three were there when the Abaddon attacked my city." Mikael's voice sounded regretful. "I am forever grateful for each of you defending my city and its people. The Abaddon is no easy foe to defeat."

"We made it out," Isabella whispered. Mikael nodded.

"I'm glad you escaped. Unfortunately so did the Abaddon. So I asked Elijah for help in searching for the Abaddon."

"Why Elijah?" Ben asked in pure curiosity. Last time he had seen Elijah, the Head Arch had been full of vengeance and jealousy.

"Elijah's a powerful Head and healer. He would be instrumental in fighting the Abaddon."

"Why not any other heads?" Isabella asked from where she sat.

"Well, keep in mind, many of the Head Archs are busy with rebuilding their cities. Chrysi Poli, Aquam Caput, Quaesitor, and many other smaller cities in the surrounding areas," Tariel chimed in from beside her brother. The color in her face appeared better as she spoke. "'Elijah was a wise choice for a partner considering the circumstances."

Mikael gave a small grin and nodded.

"Clever observation, Tariel," Mikael said. Tariel blushed and averted her gaze.

"Tariel's right, but not all the way right," Mikael continued. "The last reason why was because it gave me a good opportunity to resolve 'family drama' as you put it, Clarissa."

"So you can stop dragging others into it, finally." Clarissa crossed her arms. Mikael chuckled.

"We're all royalty in a way, so all family drama is everyone's business, sadly," Mikael countered. Clarissa frowned but said nothing.

"After enlisting his help, we traveled all the way down from Chrysi Poli to track the Abaddon. The track led us to the Maze of Uncertainty where we found Noah, Zewal, and Tariel." Mikael paused. "Then we found a portal leading from our realm to the demon realm in the Maze."

"Oh!" Isabella said. "Clever spot to put a portal. Hardly anyone goes into the Maze, and it can lead straight out into the Coal mountains. No wonder so many demons gathered in the south."

Mikael and Elijah nodded.

"We connected the dots just as you did. Zewal, Tariel, and Noah were quite insistent upon coming along, much against Elijah's wishes of course. So we all ended up landing in Leviathan's domain, just outside of the city of Atlantis. We were trying to escape into the mountains, but one of his guards caught us and well here we are," Mikael finished.

"Atlantis?" Ben inquired. Barmen hadn't mentioned much of

Leviathan's domain other than it was known for wine, partying, mind-altering drugs, and overall debauchery.

"Atlantis is one of the three cities. We landed in the marsh just outside of the city. We trudged through wetlands and marsh for a long time before reaching the tropical rainforest. We nearly made it to the mountains, but a unicorn attacked us which drew more attention to us."

"Unicorn?!" Isabella exclaimed again.

"You can't keep sounding surprised at every little part in the story, Izzy." Clarissa elbowed her sister again. "We'll never get through all the stories in time."

"Oh," Isabella murmured. "Sorry. I just thought unicorns were mythical."

Laughter escaped them. Noah and Tariel laughed while Mikael, Elijah, and Zewal tried to contain their amusement.

"Trust me, there's nothing mythical about them," Zewal said as he scrunched his nose. The memory of the encounter returned to him, and Ben shuddered at the image. "They're disgusting creatures I could do without ever seeing again."

"I second that," Tariel said. "Very gross."

"What about you?" Noah spoke to Ben. His tone reflected suspicion. "Why are you in the demon realm with Barmen's illusion? Other than causing all of us trouble?"

Ben ignored the jab as he debated about how much to share. In the end, it was Clarissa who decided.

"Wait," Clarissa spoke up. "I don't think any of you know what happened to Ben and the others in the human realm."

Eyes moved across several faces, but Mikael's narrowed in on Clarissa.

"What do you mean, what happened?" Mikael's voice deepened. He sat up straighter as his wings flared. Clarissa swallowed at his hard gaze. She averted her eyes and nodded to Ben. Those golden eyes tracked everything.

*Great,* Ben thought. He'd be the one to break the news. He cleared his throat to speak, but as soon as he opened his mouth nothing came out. Mikael's gaze turned colder as the silence stretched.

"What happened, Ben?" A command. "I will not ask again."

Ben's heart thundered in his chest as tried to form the words. His body flashed hot and cold as he thought of how to say what needed to be said.

"When Atarah and I were in the human realm…" He paused as his heart twisted. He'd never imagined he would be the one to tell Mikael the bad news. "Atarah, Gabriel, Charlotte, and I met up with the rangers." He stopped again and his chest tightened.

"Yes?" Elijah urged. His eyes widened at the mention of his daughter. He sat up in the same tense position as Mikael, their eyes pinned to him.

"We were trying to get more information about Matthew," Ben continued. "So Luke decided to enlist the help of a watcher."

"A watcher?!" Elijah said, outraged. He whirled on Mikael. "You told me they would be safe in the human realm with the rangers!"

"Silence! Please, Elijah!" Mikael boomed with a raised hand. "Let him finish."

Ben tried to swallow, but his mouth dried out.

"Atarah and Arick found a watcher…and…made a deal with it," Ben finished. It felt as if worms crawled underneath his skin. Sharing information, like this, out loud was foreign to him. If it was really important he always just thought the information to his family or fellow Arch. He glanced at Elijah's face and cringed. What he was about to share next would be another discriminatory nail in Arick's coffin.

"What was the deal, Ben?" Mikael said softly. Ben shook his head.

"I don't know the full extent of what was said. I got to them after the bargain was made," Ben explained. "What I do know is that Atarah was not happy, and the watcher gained possession of Arick's body."

Mikael froze.

"My son," he breathed. "My son agreed to be possessed by a watcher for information on Matthew?"

Ben nodded. "Atarah was very mad at Arick, but that's how we knew about Matthew's experimentation on Gabriel angels."

"Experimentation?" Mikael paled.

"Gabriel angels?" Elijah exclaimed. "The ones that are going missing?"

Ben nodded again.

"Wait, wait, wait." Mikael held up a hand. "Tell us everything you know, Ben."

Ben flinched as he knew that would include the information of

Barmen.

Clarissa scoffed. “He’s a Selaphiel angel. You’ll never get all of the details out of him.”

“Quiet, Clarissa,” Elijah said. “What about Charlotte? What happened to my daughter?”

“What happened to Atarah?” Mikael pushed.

More and more, his stomach tightened at the pressure. He could tell them everything up to Barmen, he supposed.

“Right after the deal was struck. Matthew appeared.”

Elijah and Mikael shot up. Their fists clenched and faces enraged.

“Go on!” they both commanded, storming up to him. Ben scurried back from them, stopping when they ceased their advance. He scrambled to his feet.

“Matthew was there—”

“For me!”

They all turned to look at Gabriel.

“He was there to take me and maybe the others. But definitely me,” Gabriel Jr said, rushing to Ben’s side. “We never would have made it out if it weren’t for Arick.”

“Arick?” Mikael’s voice thickened. “Where is he? What happened to my son?” Fear and panic poured into his eyes.

Ben slumped his head as he continued.

“Atarah suffered severe injuries from Matthew. By the time Gabriel opened the portal, he was knocked unconscious.” He took a deep breath. “Arick held Matthew down while I dragged everyone out of there. We all made it except for Arick.” Ben peeked up at Mikael. “We haven’t seen or heard from him since.”

Mikael’s face shifted to one of devastation. The gravity of his words weighed Mikael down. Elijah put a hand on Mikael’s shoulder as his wings slumped.

“We landed by the coastal villa Clarissa and Isabella resided in. Atarah, Charlotte, Gabriel, myself, and all of the rangers we were with, all stumbled on their front door step. They took us in and helped us recover our strength.”

“My son,” Mikael murmured, his eyes downcast. “My daughter.”

“Atarah continues to recover in their villa. She hadn’t awoken at the time I left for Bar—I mean the demon realm.”

Mikael brought his gaze to Clarissa.

"That's why you joined them?" Mikael asked. Clarissa frowned.

"We joined because." She paused. She gave a quick glance to Ben, as he shook his head. "We thought we could use money from the demon realm to help rebuild our city" She continued carefully. "The rebuild of our beloved city has been very difficult for our father."

A moment of silence stretched between them. Mikael appeared shaken while everyone else looked on with curiosity.

"How did you all get to the demon realm?" Zewal asked as his black eyes tracked between Clarissa and Ben.

"Through me again." Gabriel raised his hand in the air. "I was the first one to recover after Matthew's attack. After father learned what Matthew was doing with Gabriel angels, this made him terrified."

"Rightfully so," Elijah scoffed. Gabriel Jr pursed his lips.

"Father wanted me to return home and remain…confined for 'my own safety' as he put it."

"Isn't it hard for Gabriel angels to stay in one place for any length of time?" Tariel chimed in.

Gabriel nodded with slumped wings.

"Father knows this, but he was too afraid to listen to me." Gabriel answered. "When I heard of Ben's plan, I didn't think of anything else other than staying free. Not being tied down to a bed somewhere."

"What about my Charlotte?" Elijah asked Gabriel.

"Charlotte's the reason we're all alive," Gabriel said with a smile. "She was amazing. She revived Ben and I within a few days. She's with Atarah now back in Malachi's villa just outside of Aquam Caput."

Elijah's shoulders slumped with relief as he sighed.

"So once you gathered strength," Mikael drew everyone's attention, "you all decided to venture into the demon realm, which is strictly forbidden," He said with a pointed glance to Gabriel Jr., who blushed a bright shade of red. "Without consulting any Head Archs. In fact, you deliberately hid your plans from anyone else and recklessly put your lives in danger!" Mikael finished with a condemning tone. "All of you!" Mikael walked around, looking each of them in the eye. "The future leaders of our realm left without any consideration to the consequences of your actions."

One by one, they lowered their gaze in shame. Blood rushed to Ben's face as he resisted the urge to defend himself. Only one person knew of what they were doing: Barmen. Ben wondered if Barmen could hold his illusions from the spirit realm or if he still roamed somewhere in the demon realm. It mattered little now.

"All of you need to understand," Mikael said standing in the middle of their circle. "There is heavy responsibility with your role as heirs."

"We do understand!" Clarissa protested.

"No, you do not." Mikael spoke in a low volume, but his tone dripped with disappointment. "If you understood your role, you wouldn't have left your cities defenseless. You wouldn't have brought your sister into this dangerous realm." Clarissa flinched, but Mikael was not done. "Gabriel, you are your father's *only* heir with a target on your back." He whirled to Zewal. "Same to you, Zewal. You put your sister in danger and left your people." Zewal's wings twitched before slumping to the ground. Mikael turned to Noah, who stuck his chin out defiantly.

"Noah," Mikael murmured. "There are many other ways to help Arick. While I am grateful for all that you've done for my son, I know Arick would not approve of you risking your life like this."

Noah's face crumbled. Lastly Mikael turned to him. His heart thundered in his chest as those golden eyes pinned him. Only a handful of times had he felt the kind of guilt Mikael invoked. The time his mother got hurt trying to break up the fight between him and his brothers. Or when Atarah looked at him with hurt and disgust in her eyes.

*"Ben,"* Mikael thought. He flinched as Mikael's voice echoed in his mind. *"The path you're on doesn't lead to where you think it does. Choose wisely."*

Mikael said not a single word aloud. He conveyed his inner feelings toward Ben through emotion. Ben read other people's moods and auras better than hearing specific thoughts and words. The aura Mikael projected was yellow and green. The colors of hope.

Ben winced. It would have been better if Mikael gave him a harsh reprimand out loud.

Mikael nodded before turning around to address everyone.

"We are all here now," Mikael called out enough for everyone to hear. "We must decide what we are going to do."

"We are going to stick with the plan!" Noah protested.

"Yes!" Clarissa agreed. "We need to trap Matthew now or else he'll keep coming for us! For our homes!"

Mikael nodded. "We will capture Matthew and have him answer for his many crimes, but we don't need all of you to do this." Elijah nodded in approval.

"The journey ends here for many of you. It's time for you to go home," Elijah said, joining Mikael.

"Not for me," Noah said.

"Nor me," Zewal stood, his wings flared.

"I agree," Ben stepped forward. "I need to do this for our realm."

"I need to do this for my home," Clarissa stepped forward next. Isabella moved to follow but a hand from Clarissa stopped her. "However, Mikael is right. We can't needlessly endanger others."

Zewal turned to his younger sister. "That I can agree with as well."

"Zewal!"

"Clarissa!"

The younger siblings objected together.

"You said we would always do these battles together!" Isabella yelled. The wind around them swirled as her agitation grew.

"This battle has to involve one of us being safe." Clarissa spoke in a softer tone. "Mikael is right. Our father needs one of us there with him."

"You will be stronger with me by your side!" Isabella persisted. Clarissa gave a sad smile.

"You're right, but that strength is what our father needs."

The wind picked up more as Isabella deliberated.

"Zewal, don't become just like father!" Tariel spoke out against Zewal.

"Tariel," Zewal started.

"I have just as much right to be here as you do, even more so! I'm not the next in line, so I should be the one to stay," Tariel argued. Her wings flared wide.

"Tariel!" Zewal's voice turned cold. "You cannot stay here." The finality in his voice offered no compromise or compassion.

"I still need your help deciphering that book only you can read," Noah said to gentle the blow. Her wings shook as she looked around for support. There was only grim agreement.

"Tariel, Isabella, and Gabriel should all return to the Spirit realm. You, each, should tell the Head Archs of what has transpired. They will need to know." Mikael paused. "Especially Joshua."

Ben jumped. The urge to read through his mind nearly overpowered him. He dug his fingernails into his palms to keep from using his powers, to avoid activating the staff. Mikael and Elijah had yet to ask why Barmen's illusion was there with them. Did they know about his black market? Did Joshua? Barmen's mind appeared panicked at the thought of Joshua finding out about his little deal with Beelzebub.

"We deserve to be here," Isabella continued. "All of us will be affected by the deal Ben made with Beelzebub."

Guilt pooled in his gut again. Ben furrowed his brow. He rarely felt this much guilt and shame. With Atarah, he understood his shame because he cared about her view of him. Why did he care about the others? Ben shook his head. No, he didn't care about the others. Only what they could do for him or how he could use them. That was why he cared.

"That's right," Noah said as he narrowed his eyes at Ben. "Because of the deal you struck, all of the demon lords will be after us!"

"What sort of repercussions will that have on all of us? Does anyone know?" Zewal said with venom.

Both Head Archs frowned.

"What I know of Beelzebub is that he is an ambitious, greedy lord. He will always twist the deal in his favor. Leviathan cares about having fun and being amused." Mikael shuddered. "It is Satan we want to avoid."

"Is she really that scary?" Isabella asked.

"She is feared for a reason," Mikael answered. "She is a solid leader, one of strategy and very intelligent, but you never want to get on her bad side." Mikael hesitated for a moment. "She is one of the few creatures who can go against a seraphim and possibly win."

Everyone gasped. A pit grew in Ben's stomach as he stared down at the staff in his hand.

"The seraphim are the keepers of all three realms. Satan attempted, many centuries ago, to conquer the Spirit and human realms. The seraphim were the ones to hold her back, not the original Archangels."

Shock rocked Ben. This little detail was omitted from their history books.

"Why did we not know this?" Clarissa asked, outraged. "Why were we told lies of how the realms really worked?"

"The original Archangels didn't want interaction between the realms. They wanted to maintain a homeostasis in a way of our worlds. There is relative peace compared to the time the Originals ruled. The ideology of ignorance was agreed upon unanimously. To their point, teaching the importance of separation and hierarchy has worked and continues to work in our realm," Mikael explained. "Only a few Head Archs know of this knowledge and pass this down between the generations."

"Joshua knows this…" Ben said in realization. Mikael nodded with a frown.

"The less people know, the fewer will ask questions. Like how the energy between the realms travels. How the energy from the demon realm is the energy we use in the spirit realm, which leads into a cycle. From the demon realm to our realm to the human realm, back into the demon realm. Like the circle of life, the flow of energy always transfers into the next realm."

"Very few know this real history," Elijah chimed in. "This is the most heirs who have been told this truth."

"You really think our people, angels, will riot if they know the real history?" Clarissa challenged.

"That is what the Originals thought," Mikael countered.

"But you must agree with them on some level to continue this secret," Zewal came in.

"This is but a small part with little consequence to us Head Archs. Since it has worked for the last few centuries, why disrupt the peace our people have?"

"Because it is built on lies," Noah argued. "Our people—"

"Will be chaotic," Elijah interrupted. "The Raziels were wise to withhold this information from the public."

"It creates a skewed bias that hurts others," Noah argued. "Look at Arick's situation!"

"Arick *needs* to be viewed lowly." Clarissa chimed in. "He is not the same as us." She scrunched her nose as if disgusted at the thought of Arick. Noah's jaw tightened at her tone, while Tariel flared her wings.

"We could look down on *you* for your weak conviction and lack of loyalty," Tariel sneered. "Someone like you would stoop so low as to cut a deal with a demon lord."

Fire sparked along Clarissa's fingers while the wind picked up. Isabella blew the wind around their formation.

"What's your problem, Azrael?" Clarissa said as she and Isabella took a menacing step forward. "Jealous because no one wants to make a deal with a creepy-looking creature like you."

The air gathered strength around them and pulled. Ben grabbed onto the rock he sat on for leverage. The others crouched low to avoid getting blown away. One solid ignition from Clarissa and they would all be encased in flames. Trapped by the air, the flames would burn in the tornado Isabella created.

Mikael stepped between them, with his wings flared wide.

"Enough," he boomed above the roaring wind.

The wind died down and the sparks fizzled out. Ben glanced between the two female heirs. In a fight, he was sure Tariel would win against Clarissa. However, against both Uriel sisters, Tariel would struggle.

Ben jumped at a sudden movement. Zewal moved so quietly, no one saw him coming.

A heaviness weighed on Ben, as if all the strength in his body drained away. His body ached as he struggled to stay upright and failed. His body fought for breath, for life. All around him, everyone fell to their knees or slumped against a rock. Only Mikael remained standing.

"I said that is enough, Zewal," Mikael said in a strained voice.

Ben sighed in relief as the awful feeling of sickness passed. Gabriel and Noah shuddered nearby as their life energy poured back into them.

"Ugh," Noah groaned. "I hate it when you do that, Zewal. I'd rather face the kraken or a j'ba fofi again."

"Apologizes," Zewal murmured. He stood over Clarissa and Isabella's crumpled forms. "Sometimes my emotions get the best of me."

"And everyone thinks *I'm* the scary one," Tariel mumbled. Zewal's lips twitched as he shifted closer to his sister.

"You're scary when you want to be." Zewal retorted.

Clarissa and Isabella flinched as their consciousness returned. While Noah and Gabriel helped them up, Clarissa glared at Zewal.

"Freaks," Clarissa hissed.

She leaned on Gabriel's shoulder for support, but the anger in her eyes held enough strength to say she was not one to give up. Elijah lifted his hands to heal everyone, but Ben jerked forward. He snatched Elijah's hands down before the Arch Head could do something stupid like use his powers.

"Don't!" Ben cried out. "Once you use your powers, Satan will be on our trail before we know it."

"And whose fault is that?" Noah said with narrowed eyes.

Mikael flared his wings wide. The force of his wings extending nearly knocked everyone back. The whoosh of air silenced everyone. His glare pinned everyone in place.

"I will not repeat myself," Mikael boomed. His voice deepened, making Ben feel like a child being scolded. "Tariel, Isabella, Zewal, Gabriel, Clarissa, *and* Noah will all return to the Spirit realm." Mikael whirled on Noah, his mouth opened to protest. "No!" Mikael thundered. "None of this is up for debate. You all are to return home, tell your parents what has happened and stay put until all of the Arch Heads can get together. All of you are part of a deal with a demon lord, which is *nothing* to take lightly. Gabriel, you are to take everyone home safely and that is an order," Mikael finished.

A direct order from a Head Arch. No one would dare defy an explicit command. Mikael wasn't their Head Arch, but his position and status remained above their own. The heirs had no choice but to return.

Gabriel nodded solemnly.

"But—" Noah started, but Elijah cut him off with a shake of his head.

"No," Clarissa groaned weakly. Neither she nor her sister had recovered from Zewal's attack.

"Gabriel, open the portal and be quick," Mikael commanded, his jaw tight and shoulders set. There was no winning this argument.

"Ben, the only reason you are still coming with us is because you still hold the staff. Once we deal with Matthew and get rid of these staffs, you are to go home as well."

Ben's heart constricted at his words. Home was wherever Atarah stayed. She flooded his mind as he wanted to return to her as soon as possible. Was Mikael helping him? Or was he another barrier between him and Atarah? He resisted the urge to peer into Mikael's mind. What was his real motive? Ben nodded. He would find out; he always did. For now, he would play along with Mikael and his game until Ben received his real goal.

Atarah and power.

Mikael narrowed his eyes at Ben for a second or two before nodding in return. A glow emanated from Gabriel's hands as he split the realm. The blazing portal opened before them in a matter of minutes. Gabriel gave a short, awkward wave before dragging Clarissa's limp body across. Zewal and Tariel were the next ones to go through. No goodbyes or waves. Just a fierce glare and a finger pointing to him from Zewal.

"Fail," Zewal said, "and you will suffer the consequences." His cold voice sent shivers down Ben's spine.

Without another word, they both exited out of the demon realm. Noah carried Isabella's limp body in his arms, conflict evident in his eyes.

"Go, my son," Elijah urged. "Go and check up on your mother, please. She needs your help too."

Noah tightened his hold on Isabella. His head hung low, and his eyes remained fixed on the ground.

"I leave the rest to you," Noah said finally. He walked through the portal last. Once they were both through, the portal shut within seconds, closing any other chance of escape.

In the distance, a boom echoed across the valley, like the sound of clashing rocks. Ben, Elijah, and Mikael jerked back toward the mountain the Hippus pointed to earlier.

Mikael's wings flared while his aura grew dark and fearful.

"Let's move out." A sharp command.

# Chapter 9

Atarah grunted from her opponent's impact. She blocked the cenobite's ax as it aimed for her heart. She tucked and rolled around the demon, giving herself access to its unprotected back. She swung her dagger upward with all her might.

Her dagger sliced through the demon like butter. She barely broke a sweat. She took the demon out so fast and easily. *Maybe I have gotten stronger?* she pondered. The cenobite donned a brown tunic and had needles piercing down its neck. One demon stood guard a few yards down from the room where they were brought. The room she left.

She continued down the hallway to find Arick. Her eyes widened at the sight before her. Three cloaked guards lay, tied up, on the ground. A tiefling, another cenobite, and half-goat demon. *Who tied them up?* she wondered.

The sounds of stomping steps drew her attention to the end of the hall. There were only three directions for her to go: the way she came, the long hallway with the tied up demons, or down the path to her right. Down the enclosed space, a large statue marched toward her in a slow and steady pace. Its glowing, blue eyes focused on her as it moved. It stood so tall, the golem shoulders scraped against the sides of the tunnel. The sound of crunching rocks was lost to the sounds of its feet.

She tilted her head at the golem while power rushed through her limbs once more. She lifted her sword to the stone figure. The demon guards came from the direction the golem now walked. If golems blocked these corridors, their chance of escape would be limited. The golem needed to be disassembled for everyone to get by.

When the stone puppet stood no more than a few feet away, she struck. She used her momentum to drive her dagger into the golem's neck. To assist her blow, she extended her leg and kicked the golem's head right off.

A resounding snap signaled the dislocation. The head rolled back down the corridor while the body froze. Taking advantage of its stillness, she swung against the shoulders next. She stabbed through the joint several times before the golem tried to counter. It flayed its arms in an attempt to fend her off. Within a few strikes the stone arms popped right off.

Atarah lifted her dagger to start chopping off the legs when angry shouts caught her attention. Perplexed, she stabbed the golem through the chest and pinned it to the side of the wall. That would keep it still for a while. She knelt down to the ground, shifting her fingers through the dirt. Closing her eyes, she expanded her senses to hear up ahead. Energy flowed through her and spread from her fingertips into the mountain. With fewer guards making a ruckus, she heard clearer.

A deep, disapproving voice shouted from the other hallway. The voice that answered made her jump. A sound that was familiar and easy to identify.

*Arick,* she realized. She jumped back up to her feet. She quickly grabbed her dagger out from the golem and the wall before racing down the last hallway. Her heart pounded as she ran out of fear and anticipation. Would they all be able to escape this time?

She didn't have to run far. The hallway grew dim, but she could make out a cracked door at the end. She lifted her dagger a little higher. She changed her pace from a run to a soft creep. Keeping her steps quiet and weapon ready, she leaned her ear against the door.

"What?" a slightly familiar voice said.

"Let's destroy this now." This one was Arick. Excitement washed over her, like a wave. She grabbed the door to jerk it open some more when Arick's next words made her freeze. "Before he tries to use this for that crazy convergence idea."

*Use what?* she thought.

"Let's do this," Arick said. His tone was firm and held no humor.

She kicked the door open and gasped at the room before her. Bodies lay scattered everywhere. Bodies of angels drained of everything. They looked more like skeletons with skin than the lively Gabriel angels they used to be.

A putrid stench hit her nose next, causing her to double over and gag. She covered her nose and mouth as tears formed in her eyes from the smell. With her mouth and nose closed, she continued to taste the awful, rotting smell on her tongue.

"By the trinity!" She coughed. She attempted to right herself. "This smell is awful!"

Arick and Canaan—wait Canaan? What was he doing here?

"I'm here because my brother sent me," he answered without missing a beat. His eyes darkened. "And you're right about the smell."

"Atarah?" Arick's voice sounded amazed, but Atarah couldn't look at him. She dry heaved, leaning on the door for help. Her enhanced senses were now a double edged sword for her. How did she not smell this earlier? She wiped the tears from her eyes to peer around the room. Arick was there, leaning down with concern marring his face.

"What are you doing here?" he asked as he patted her back. "I thought you and the others were able to get away? Wait a minute—Are you by yourself?!"

Atarah lifted a finger as she heaved one more time. If she had some water to wash away the stench from her nose and mouth, that would be great.

"Here, give this to her." Canaan's voice drifted closer. A canteen dropped within her eyesight, and she snatched it greedily. She tilted her head back and poured the water down her face, sputtering. Much to her relief, the water cleared the horrid smell. She coughed once before covering her nose once more.

"What's this about destroying something?" she fired off her question, tilting her head back to look at Arick. He frowned at her.

"Hey, I asked you questions first," he protested. He crossed his arms, and Atarah rolled her eyes.

"And I asked you second. Now give me the main points of what happened," she said back.

"Answer my questions first and then I'll answer yours," Arick challenged.

"Trinity! Can you not act like a child right now?"

"I'll stop when you stop, little cricket." Arick's lips twitched as if he fought against a smile. A grin crept up against her own will too. They both released the building chuckle and hugged.

"I missed you too, you big baby." She gave a soft jab to his side.

"Also guard your left side more or you'll get knocked down."

Another chuckle rumbled above her head.

"Sorry to break up the family reunion, but we have other things to worry about right now," Canaan called out.

She stepped away to get a better look at the room they were in. The bodies stacked high up against the walls and hit the ceilings. In the center of the room, a huge container, as high as the ceiling, stood filled to the brim with blood. A machine emanated the sound of a fiddle playing around them as Canaan pressed random buttons along the wide work board.

"I think one of these buttons will release all of the blood in this tank." Canaan pressed another button with shaking hands. Nothing happened. "But I am scared to press a button Matthew would want pressed."

Atarah moved closer to the control panel. The board was small with a dozen buttons. Half of the buttons appeared to be color-coded while the others were black. Canaan hands hovered above the panel, unsure.

"Why not just break the glass and have the blood be spilled?" Atarah inquired.

"The blood will have nowhere to go," Canaan answered. He froze for a moment as his eyes stared at the keyboard. "No, Azazel" Canaan continued. "We can't just leave this be."

"Azazel?" Atarah furrowed her brow.

"Up here, little cricket." Arick pointed to his head. "That watcher we made a deal with."

"Azazel…" Atarah murmured. "You mean the watcher who was dealt the worst punishment for his crimes against angels and humans? That Azazel from our history books?"

Arick winced and covered his ears. Canaan raised an eyebrow beside her. Whatever was being said inside Arick's mind must've been loud.

"All right, old timer," Arick scoffed. "It's not our fault you have a bad reputation."

"Does he know of any other way out from here?" Atarah heard desperation in her own voice. "I took down a guard and some sort of weird statue thing. I think it was a golem."

Stunned silence followed. Arick's jaw dropped open while Canaan's eyes widened.

"You took down the golem?" Arick huffed. "That's amazing! You've gotten stronger, cricket."

"Charlotte's been healing me for over a week now." Atarah rubbed the back of her head. "I think her healing power did something that made me stronger in some sort of way."

"I didn't know Raphael angels could do such a thing," Canaan said behind her. His eyes tracked her.

"Nah." Arick waved a hand. "I knew you'd be a late bloomer."

She opened her mouth to ask him further, but Canaan intercepted her.

"Was my brother with you?" His brown eyes searched hers for answers.

Atarah's heart constricted at the thought of Ben. Where was he? Why hadn't he stayed by her side?

"I don't know." Atarah frowned. "My last memory of him was when we were escaping the human realm. He pulled all of us to safety while Arick held Matthew back."

"You haven't seen my brother since?" Canaan's eyes widened more as she shook her head. Concern marred his face for a second before he wiped away all emotion. "Never mind that for now," Canaan continued. "Atarah is right. Azazel do you know of another way out of here?"

Arick's eyes went blank before the pupils oscillated side to side rapidly. His posture changed from slouched and relaxed to upright and tense. The slightest shift in his facial expression alerted her. This was no longer her brother speaking.

"There may be another tunnel down this way of my memory serves me correct." The voice speaking from Arick's body sounded gruff. "Matthew altered a few tunnels here and there, so I'm not sure if this tunnel still exists."

"Why didn't you mention this in the first place?" Suspicion leeched into Canaan's voice.

The vibrating eyes rolled up to the ceiling.

"Because you asked me to help you get in the mountain, not how to get out of the mountain." Seeing Azazel speak with Arick's body was disconcerting. All of the mannerisms and facial expressions were wrong. Atarah winced when Azazel spoke.

"This is why I hate working with angels," Azazel grumbled. "You give them a rope and suddenly they want to be a cowboy."

"Cowboy?" Atarah said, tilting her head in confusion. Azazel shook his—their shared head.

"Never mind." He walked to the back end of the large container. "You two keep trying to figure out the panel. I will feel around bchind here to see if the tunnel is still there."

"This huge thing is practically up against the wall. You might not fit behind there." Canaan followed him around the side of the blood container.

Canaan had a point. There was maybe eight inches or so of space between this large contraption and the wall. Arick's huge body wasn't going to fit.

"Let me try," Atarah volunteered. "What should I be looking for?

Azazel grunted. "Try feeling along the wall for any whiff of fresh air or a breeze. We should be close to a mountainside cliff."

"Cliff?!" Atarah exclaimed. "That's perfect! We can get Mom, Charlotte, and the others out of here!"

"Others?" Canaan turned to face her.

"Mom is here?" Arick's voice erupted out from the depth of his body. He gripped his head as Azazel and Arick fought for control. Their body jerked and flinched until one of them won. Arick ended up winning control over the body.

"Please tell me Mom is *not here! Please.*" His voice cracked with desperation. His hands gripped the sides of her arms. "Was this Matthew's doing? What's gone on since I've been here?" Arick shook her as he fired off questions.

Her answers rattled in her brain as she was shaken again. She winced as his grip tightened some more.

"Come on, Atarah, answer me!" Arick roared.

She swung her leg around and kicked him in the side. He released her, his eyes widened in more surprise than any real pain. She delivered enough force for him to be caught off guard but not enough to cause any injury or pain.

"I need you to stop shaking me around if you want answers to your questions," Atarah said, crossing her arms. "First of all, when I woke up. Mom and Charlotte were the only ones there in my room. Very shortly after that Matthew showed up and said he'd come to 'take us all home.' The psycho then transported us here." Atarah pointed to the door. "He brought us to this dungeon-like room with Gabriel angels hanging from the walls in chains upside down to drain their blood. He said the convergence plan was almost completed. We were all locked up in separate cells, and then Matthew left. I don't know where he went, but I managed to escape and free Mom and Charlotte. When I left to go search for *you,*" she pointed to Arick, "Mom and Charlotte were healing the Gabriel angels. One of the angels said with all of their combined strength, they might be able to gather enough energy to transport all of us out of here."

"If Ava and Charlotte are able to heal them," Canaan chimed in. He leaned against the wall with his hand grabbing his chin in contemplation. "They may be able to do it. How many Gabriel angels are still alive?"

"Thirteen, if you include Makoto."

"Makoto?" Arick asked, rubbing his side.

"Makoto was the one who told us the way we can transport out."

"Then we already have an escape plan." Canaan kicked off the wall. "Where are they at? Let's reconvene with the others and get out of here."

"Wait!" Arick protested. "We can't just leave this here for Matthew to use. You heard her; he said he was nearly done with his plan. That must mean all this blood he's gathered."

"Arick, our priority needs to be getting those Gabriel angels out of here," Canaan argued back.

"No, Arick's right. We are already here, and we can delay Matthew's plan a little longer if we destroy this thing." Atarah put her hands on her hips. She stuck her chin out in determination. Arick mirrored her position and narrowed his eyes at Canaan.

"You can either help us or leave," Arick said.

Canaan glanced between the two of them and sighed.

"Fine," Canaan conceded. "Let's destroy this thing and get the hell out of here as fast as possible." Canaan peered back at the space behind the container. "When we destroy the container, let's push the blood out through the tunnel Azazel pointed out. Liquid will have an easier time moving through the rock than we will."

"Atarah, can you squeeze through to open up the tunnel a little to ensure the blood goes out and not in here."

"Yeah." Atarah removed her dagger from her side before moving closer to the wall. The space between the wall and blood container was small. She had to wiggle and squeeze her way through. She shuddered.

The thought of being so constricted made her stomach clench and threatened to make her throw up. She shook her head.

No, she needed to do this. Anything to delay Matthew's plan and get everyone to safety. She wiggled her shoulder through the narrow space, with her back to the container and her front facing the rocky wall. She moved her hands along the wall, feeling for any breeze Azazel mentioned earlier. She shimmied another few feet down, feeling the wall for air. Sweat gathered along her palms and brow as her heart raced. The further in she moved, the tighter the space felt. Her heart thundered in her chest as her body pleaded for escape. Her breathing became irregular as she pressed on. She gasped for air when her hand felt a cool brush of air. She paused. She stuck her hand out again, along the middle of the wall. Another breeze blew around her hand.

"I found it!" she yelled.

"Great!" Arick shouted back. "Azazel said to move as many rocks as you can around it, until you feel the breeze grow stronger or see a light at the end of the tunnel."

She felt along the wall and noticed a few loose rocks. She knocked them away as much as she could in the cramped space. She pushed and pulled rocks along the wall. Piece by piece, she broke the rock barrier, allowing a glimmer of light to beam through the wall. A stronger gust of wind came through and blew against her sweating face. She sighed in relief as she breathed in the fresh air.

"I think that's enough," she said as she felt one more breeze against her face. More light shined through. She could hear the rushing wind outside.

*Soon,* she thought. She wiggled her way back out from behind the tank. Once free, she shook herself free from rocks and pebbles as she stretched her wings.

"That should give the blood enough space to leak through." Canaan peered through the narrow space. He nodded in approval.

"Perfect!" Atarah picked up her dagger. She opened her wings, enjoying the stretch before launching herself into the air. Arick followed right behind her. He had picked up a large, loose rock from the wall as his weapon. Once they were high enough, Canaan shuffled out of the way.

"Aim for the back of the container, so that the blood spills toward the back wall. If we're lucky the blood will flow out of here."

Arick and Atarah nodded.

"Let's see if I have better aim than you, cricket." Arick pulled back his arm and twisted his body. She witnessed each individual muscle tighten, like a spring getting ready to launch. With a grunt, Arick shot the rock forward with all his might. The rock catapulted, like a bullet, and hit the container with a loud boom. Arick's aim was good. He'd hit the backside of the glass tank. The puncture hole from the rock spewed blood in waves.

"Let's see how big of a hole I can make," Atarah murmured as she swung her dagger back. She tucked her wings in tight and dove down. She waited until the last second to swing her weapon with all of her weight and momentum. She heard the loud crashing of glass echo around her in a loud explosion.

She flapped herself higher into the air to get a better view. Blood poured out of the container, like water bursting from a dam.

*Yes!* she thought. A direct hit. She gave a smug grin to Arick, who rolled his eyes.

"Don't let all this newfound strength go to your head now, cricket," Arick drawled.

"None of those angels back at training camp will mess with me now!" Atarah cheered. She couldn't help the smile on her face. Now, she could go home accomplished. The Gabriel angels and Arick would be rescued, and Matthew's plan had been reduced to rubble. She glowed with pride that she was finally achieving something. She couldn't wait to tell everyone. Her father, mother, and especially Ben. Her heart flipped. Yes, she wanted to see Ben.

They landed by Canaan, who watched the tank drain. They heard the splashing of the liquid following down the hidden tunnel, to the outside world.

"Let's hurry and get out—" Canaan's words were cut off.

"What have you done?" A dark voice sent chills down Atarah's back.

They whirled around to see Matthew, dressed in a red robe, standing at the door. His face contorted with horror and rage.

"What have you done?!" He roared again. His eyes narrowed on Atarah. Blood dripped from the dagger in her hand.

Her limbs shook as she raised her weapon again. Matthew's gaze followed her dagger.

"YOU." A single word filled with so much hatred she shuddered. Matthew threw off his robe to flared his wings out wide. "I should have dealt with you sooner."

Arick flared his wings out wide and stepped in front of her.

"Atarah, get out of here now!" Arick shouted. Atarah flapped herself into the air, determined to defend with Arick.

"No, you don't get to escape this time." Matthew's cold voice was her warning before he moved.

Matthew moved so fast she didn't have enough time to react. One minute he stood in front of the door, the next he launched himself in front of her with a drawn dagger she didn't see coming.

"ATARAH!"

She gasped as Matthew slammed the dagger into her chest.

His body smashed into hers, careening her back to the far wall with so much force the entire mountain shook. Rocks collapsed and fell around her as her heart sputtered and stopped. Blood flowed around her as her body crumbled through the tank and into the ground. She felt no pain, only shock and mild recognition that she was dying. His cruel sneer was the last thing she saw as darkness closed in.

*Ben...Mother...Charlotte...Arick...I'm sorry....*

# Chapter 10

The sounds of clattering swords died down. Energy flowed throughout Ben's body as he lifted a fallen ax from one of the guards Mikael dispatched earlier. He swung hard as another guard ran at him, blade drawn. Another tiefling guard roared as it attacked. He dodged and delivered his own blow. The tiefling cried out in pain as his ax cut into its shoulder.

He brought down his weapon again, this time cutting the head cleanly off. Waves of energy flowed through him, powering him. Like a runner's high, Ben felt unstoppable. His body moved with little effort as he pulled his ax free from the corpse.

They had flown to the front gate of the prison Beelzebub suspected was Matthew's hideout, no guards were posted out front. Several loud booms rang out when they landed in front of the entrance gates, alerting them. Within a few steps of entering the prison, Ben knew something was wrong. With minimal effort, he heard the sporadic thoughts of the guards gathering below due to some prison break. A large angel with golden eyes had broken in. Ben recited the information to Elijah and Mikael, the latter sprinted like a bat out of hell down the prison tunnels. Leading them into chaos.

Panting, he peered over his shoulder to see Elijah's glowing hands, the staff hung around his waist. Elijah fought a little when stray guards ran past both Mikael and Ben. However, the Raphael leader never faltered in his concentration when extending a hand out to revive them while attacking with the other arm. Ben had never seen Elijah in combat like this. Elijah moved with grace and elegance. His swings were strong and his reach of power great.

Mikael fought ahead of them both, attacking the bulk of the guards, yet Elijah's cooling touch reached the warrior angel. Sweat dripped down Elijah's brow as he took down another guard. The onslaught of guards wore down on them. Ben advanced further ahead to help Mikael.

Mikael's aura remained dark and full of worry for his children. Ben burned with the desire to use his powers to read Mikael's mind but waited. The staff, tied around his waist, grew heavier as they made it deeper into the mountain. Ben wanted to travel further in the mountain before activating the staff.

*Soon,* he clenched his ax tightly. He didn't know how much time they would have and wanted to cherish every moment of it. Until Beelzebub cashed in on their deal.

He shook his head. Now was not the time to think about the bargain. He needed to get to Matthew now. The booms distracted the guards earlier, giving them an advantage. Mikael led the way, cutting down all in his path. They ran into a couple of golems, but they were no match against Mikael. Within minutes the golems crumbled to his feet. Sweat poured down his face and back as Mikael powered forward. His eyes were wide and searching down every hallway they came across. They made it so deep into the mountain, light was limited.

"Ben," Mikael panted. "It's time to use your powers so we can find the others."

"Agreed," Ben huffed. He reached back for the staff and grabbed a hold of it. Lifting the red staff in front of him with both hands, Ben concentrated his power. He focused on the thoughts around him. A sharp, stabbing pain through his skull brought him to his knees.

"AH!" Ben cried out as hundreds of thoughts shouted across his mind, all at once.

*Get the prisoners!*

*Do the elders know what's going on?*

*What the hell is going on?*

*Please! Someone help us!*

*The pain— the suffering is just too much. Please let me die already, Trinity! I don't want to live anymore!*

*Who defeated the golem by the blood bag prisoners?*

*Why hasn't the Great One returned yet? Does he know about the princeling's escape? Or that he returned?*

*What happened to the red cloaked elders?*

*Why are the guards all running around? Oh, well. Whatever keeps them away from me.*

*I...am soooo hungry. No food in almost seventy-two days....*

Dozens more voices filled his head, relentless. As the power from the staff surged, so did the thoughts. Energy funneled around him, like a growing typhoon. So much power gathered around him, so quickly, the weight was too much. Ben fell from his knees onto his face. Gravity was somehow stronger than before. While his power was greater and he heard hundreds of thoughts all at once, he had no control.

"Ben!" someone yelled.

He couldn't discern who. Everything was developing too fast. The more energy pulled to him, the more thoughts he heard. The more thoughts swarmed, the greater the weight of power grew. He screamed in pain as he struggled to hear any voice. He could have been in a rioting stadium for all he knew. There was only noise and the crushing weight of energy. A tornado swirled with him at the center.

"Ben!!" The voice sounded further away this time. Muffled.

Excruciating pain radiated down his head and his back, rendering him useless. He curled in on himself, as if he could be shielded from the pain. The staff burned in his hand as it remained activated. He tried to release the staff, but his fingers were too weak to uncurl themselves. The agony spread from his back and to his arms.

He screamed again as his back locked up. He gritted his teeth as a hammer of energy came down on his head. He needed to do something fast or else he would die this way. Ben struggled to hear his own thoughts. Anything to come up with a way to escape this hell. His breathing became erratic as he tried to keep his panic at bay. He gasped for air then froze as pain radiated every further across his body. His lungs burned for more air, but he couldn't open his throat.

He was sinking. He was suffocating. He was going to die.

Despair crawled through the depths of his mind as he realized why Beelzebub and Leviathan had been so willing to hand over their staffs. The demon lords were never worried about their staff getting in the wrong hands. They had known that the power of the staffs would be too overwhelming for anyone other than them. Ben cursed himself, for his own stupidity.

*"Beelzebub will always twist the deal in his favor. Leviathan only*

*cares about having fun and being amused."* The memory of Mikael's voice whispered through his mind.

Self-pity swallowed him as he drowned. The reality was he had been no match for the demon lords, not close. Tears swelled in his eyes as he reflected upon his own greed. Anger burned at his own helplessness. Ben closed his eyes as he accepted his fate. This would be where he died, because of his own stupidity.

He stopped fighting for breath or for control. He knew it was futile. The power from the staff continued to surge and grow. Soon the energy gathering around him would crush him into oblivion. Giving in to death was much more disquieting than he anticipated. There was now so much noise in his mind, it turned into a ringing. A high-pitched ring from a harp.

That was when he heard the most beautiful sound ever. The roaring ocean of thoughts calmed.

*Ben...*

He forced his eyes open. He knew that voice. The swarming crowd in his head couldn't stop him from hearing that voice.

*Mother...*

Gritting his teeth against the pain, he gripped the staff tighter.

*Charlotte...*

His body cried out, but he forced it to move anyway. He sucked in a deep breath and held it as he pushed himself up. He couldn't give up, not when he heard her voice. Not when he was this close.

*Arick...*

He yelled as he focused his power, not outward, like casting a net, but honed in. A laser to find where Atarah's voice was coming from.

*Come on!* he shouted in his own mind. *Find her!*

He concentrated all the energy coming to him and thought of all of the people he loved. Everything went quiet and then fell together. Like an off-key instrument coming into the right tune, he found everyone.

While his eyes were closed, he saw more than he could ever dream of. He didn't just hear Atarah's voice; he saw through her own eyes. He saw Arick, Canaan, Charlotte, and Ava. He heard all of their memories, feelings, and desires. He listened to everything about them. Their lives flashed through his eyes, outside of time as he understood it.

His body didn't feel like his own as he stood up. He watched with a roar echoing through his mind as Matthew viciously stabbed

Atarah through the heart. Her mind, consumed in shock, grew quiet. The mental screams from Canaan and Arick muffled as Atarah's vision turned dark.

...*I'm sorry*... Her last thoughts.

Ben dropped the staff.

The gravitational wind that had been building up around him, pulling down Mikael and Elijah, came to a sudden stop. Blood dripped from his ears, but he hardly noticed. A single tear fell down his face and he looked at Mikael. Elijah crawled up to his feet. His eyes widened in horror as he stared at the side of his face where blood pooled along his shoulders and chest.

Shock was the only expression showing on Mikael's face as he moved his mouth. Ben heard no words. Mikael opened his mouth again; this time he appeared to be shouting. Again, Ben heard nothing. His lungs burned as they begged for air, but he couldn't find it in himself to care.

*Atarah.*

"Atarah." He didn't hear his own voice but felt the vibrations in his throat. He knew he spoke loud enough, for Mikael's eyes widened. "Arick, Charlotte, and Ava," Ben continued. He turned to the south facing hallway. "Follow me." More vibrations humming in his throat signaled his voice.

He sprinted down the tunnel he knew would lead to Atarah. His body moved mechanically again, but this time it was different. Instead of a runner's high and the feeling of strength flowing through him, his body was numb. It was as if his brain disconnected from his body. He knew his feet touched the ground when he looked down at them. He couldn't hear or sense the others around him. From his peripheral vision he saw Mikael and Elijah running beside him, but nothing else. As if every sense was taken from him. The world turned gray.

He turned left.

Anytime a guard came into view, Mikael charged forward and slammed them into the wall. The force was strong enough to render them unconscious. Ben didn't slow down or stop for any reason.

The high pitched ringing in his mind continued as he ran past the chain door. Dozens of knocked out guards littered the tunnel. A slumped over golem with missing arms lay broken. They were almost there. He slowed once.

"Ava and Charlotte are down the tunnel to the right," Ben sensed himself saying. He didn't hear any response and didn't look to see if they had spoken either. Once they reached the fork in the hall, Ben turned to the left. Not wanting to waste any time in getting to Atarah, he pushed his body faster.

His heart constricted while his lungs burned. His first real sensation since letting go of the staff, and it was nothing compared to the stabbing pain inside his heart.

He noticed a wetness on his chest as he realized tears were streaming down his face. Tears that grew heavier with each step closer to Atarah. A flash of movement alerted him to Mikael's presence. Elijah was nowhere to be seen. Ben guessed he went down the hall that led to Ava and Charlotte while Mikael followed him.

It didn't matter. They were too late. Everything he had done: blackmailing Barmen, bargaining with the demon lords had all been for nothing. The door came into view, and Ben sprinted harder. He didn't feel the impact as he burst through the iron door. Nor did he feel the blood fall from his mouth. His throat vibrated as he released his pent up scream at the sight before him.

Canaan's jaw dropped in horror as Atarah's small body crumbled from the falling rocks. A pain-filled scream echoed in the area, as Arick attacked Matthew. Their bodies collided like boulders. Canaan felt the impact, like thunder rolling over him.

He scrambled out of the way and attempted to make his way over to where Atarah crashed. However, the falling rocks prevented him. Blood pooled around where he had last seen her body. There was no way she could have lived after such an attack, but Canaan tried to listen for any glimmer of life from her. He saw and heard nothing that resembled life from where her body lay beneath the rocks.

Another roar of anger filled the space. He glanced up to see Arick raining down punches on Matthew. The young Arch's face twisted in a way Canaan had never seen before. The laid back, sarcastic heir was gone. Canaan wondered if he would ever return. Arick's whole face flushed with blood and his eyes looked wild. Canaan heard no decipherable thoughts, only a red aura covering his entire body. Azazel's voice in their shared body was drowned out by Arick's unsettled state.

Arick screamed as he landed punch after punch. Matthew struggled against him. Canaan heard Matthew's whispering thought, wondering if he could contain Arick. Or if he would have to kill him too. Canaan's stomach lurched as he heard a strange snap in Arick's mind.

Matthew lifted an arm to defend his face, but Arick crushed it in half. Matthew cried out in pain, but Arick wasn't done yet. He snapped the other arm as well but this time he twisted it cruelly and jerked. With a sickening sound, Matthew's arm popped right off. The luciferian's cries turned into wails of pain.

Trembling with wide eyes, Canaan watched as Arick lost it. Not just physically. His power leaked out of him and slammed into Canaan. He grunted against the constriction. Once the shock fell away, he noticed thundering footsteps and a loud, sharp ringing. Not from his own mind but from someone approaching. He jerked his head to the door as he scrambled to his feet.

They were about to have more company. Canaan gripped a fallen rock, as his weapon. He pulled his arm back, just as a figure burst through the door. Canaan dropped the rock in his hand.

Bloodied, and battered, Ben came through the door. Blood ran down from his ears and painted across his torso. His eyes were so red and sunken in, Canaan wondered how he could see. His body shook while his eyes stared at where Atarah's body lay beneath the rock.

The scream Ben let loose was something Canaan never heard. Agony and sorrow were the only ways to describe the sound that emanated from his little brother. Canaan's heart clenched as Ben crawled to the rocks where Atarah's body fell. Canaan moved to grab onto his brother when he noticed Mikael and his chaotic thoughts.

*Where's Atarah and Ava? Why were they here in the first place?* Mikael's gaze moved to Arick, who thrashed Matthew's now still form. *My son! What's happened?*

Mikael moved fast and grabbed Arick from behind and pulled him off Matthew. Canaan saw all of Mikael's muscles flex while he strained to hold Arick off. Arick roared and reared back, trying to dislodge his father off of him. Arick's eyes appeared wild and crazed as he flailed.

Arick threw his head back, smashing into Mikael's nose. Mikael grunted as blood poured from his nose, which was no doubt broken.

"Arick!" Mikael shouted. "I am here now, son! I am here!"

Another wail drew Canaan's attention. Ben dug through the rumble, looking for Atarah's body. Blood stained his hands as he lifted boulder after boulder. Canaan moved to his brother's side as he frantically searched for her body. Tears threatened to spill over as Canaan gripped Ben in the same fashion that Mikael held Arick.

"No, no, no, no, no, no, no, no, no," Ben murmured over and over again. Canaan held his brother close as the painful memories of their parents' death came to his mind. Ben pushed against him to get free, but Canaan tightened his hold. He didn't want Ben to find her body the same way he found their parents. He heard the devastation it had caused his little brother. He would do everything he could to spare Ben the same image.

"I am here, bean," Canaan grunted. His nickname for Ben rolled off his tongue as he tried to soothe. Normally, Canaan instantly heard all of the thoughts flowing through his little brother's mind but not now. Silence reverberated through his mind. It disturbed him at how muted Ben's thoughts were. While Canaan couldn't hear Ben's thoughts, it appeared that Ben couldn't hear the words Canaan had spoken. The only sound that echoed through Ben's mind was that strange ringing sound. It was endless.

Ben continued to try to break free of his hold. Canaan held firm.

"I am so sorry, bean," Canaan choked over his words. "She's gone. It's too late."

"No, no, no, no, no, no!" Ben cried.

Canaan wasn't sure how long he clutched Ben like this. Or how long Mikael wrestled with Arick. Only that, this was how Charlotte, Ava, and Elijah found them. Ben and Arick were inconsolable while Canaan and Mikael fought against them.

It was Ava who tipped the scale for control. She walked over to Arick first. She knelt down beside where he fought to get free from Mikael.

"Ava stay back!" Mikael shouted. "He's not himself."

She didn't glance at her husband, her eyes glued to Arick. She reached her hand out and placed them over Arick's head. Arick froze.

"Come back to us, Arick." Her voice sounded so gentle and light, Canaan was soothed just by hearing it.

Arick's eye came into focus as he stared up at Ava.

"Mom—" he gurgled. He slumped against Mikael. His body deflated as all of the fight inside of him left. "I—I tried. I promised I tried to stop him." The rest was indiscernible as tears fell down his face.

Ava's brows furrowed in confusion.

"What do you mean?" She got her question out before Ben jerked in his grasp.

"Please, Atarah," Ben pleaded loudly, attempting to crawl back to the rumble. "Don't leave me!"

Ava and Mikael both turned to heads to where Canaan struggled to hold Ben. Their faces paled while their minds grew frantic.

"Atarah?" Ava mumbled as she stepped closer.

A strangled cry erupted from Charlotte as she fell to her knees, her eyes on the blood around Canaan and Ben.

"She's dead?" Charlotte's voice quivered. Elijah picked his daughter up and held her by her shoulders for support. His eyes also locked on the spot where her body was last seen. Canaan gave a solemn nod when Ben slumped forward. His hands still reached for her, separated by fallen rocks in their way.

Their minds, collectively, changed to an off key orchestra. One sound was the deep bass of a cello, while another was the sound of a trumpet playing off tempo. Another was a clarinet being played out of tune. Someone else's mind sounded as if warning bells rang. They all banged out of tune and sync. Canaan winced as such an awful symphony.

Despite the jarring sound, Canaan grew more concerned by the lack of sound he heard from Ben.

"Elijah, Ava, and Charlotte," His voice grew thick. Ben's body remained limp in his arms. "Please come closer. There's something wrong with Ben."

The three Archs moved closer. Their tear-stained eyes still fixed on the rubble.

"Are you sure…she's…" Charlotte's words drifted off.

"I don't hear any of her thoughts and…" He hesitated. "I saw Matthew stab her right through the heart."

Ava knelt by the rocks, her arms outstretched.

"This can't be happening," she murmured. She shook her head as tears swelled in her eyes. Charlotte stumbled to where Ava sat. Silence stretched between them outwardly while Canaan heard the cracks of their grief taking root.

# Chapter 11

The fine-tuned sound of a fiddle crescendoed to the forefront of Ben's fractured mind.

"Oh my." A soft, feminine voice drew their attention.

Within the doorframe, a curvy woman leaned against the side and peered at them. She wore a ruby dress that hugged her hips and chest, matching the red lipstick she wore. The dress straps hung off the shoulders, with a slit coming up her left thigh. She wore no shoes and held a martini glass in her right hand as she regarded them.

Shiny, thick, blonde hair cascaded down her head and neck, curling around her shoulders. Her nails were painted red, and even her aura appeared red. Her diamond shaped face possessed high cheekbones with full lips and bright green eyes. Her eyes were so vivid, Ben thought they were emeralds. She was breathtaking. An exceptionally gorgeous specimen that commanded the room as soon as she entered.

*How disgusting.*

Her thoughts reverberated in his mind, along with her strong disdain for them. On the outside, her face showed a serene, welcoming appearance, but in her mind she grimaced.

*What are all of these pests doing in my domain?*

"What is going on here?" She directed her question to Mikael.

Mikael's face paled as he gaped at her. Elijah jerked Charlotte behind him, flaring his wings to cover her.

Canaan tightened his grip to the point of pain, but Ben didn't care. The pain in his heart was so strong, no physical pain could ever match it. The high pitched ringing in his ears lessened but remained ever present.

Her green eyes skimmed over Mikael and landed on Matthew's still, unconscious body. She raised an eyebrow and lifted her drink to her lips. She gave a small groan.

"Oh my goodness," she moaned. "What an absolute mess it is in here!"

Blood coated all of their clothes, with the stench of rotten bodies filling the air, which he failed to notice. More pain laced through his body from the after effects of using the staff. If it wasn't for Canaan, he would have collapsed.

"Oh no!" Her green eyes stared at the destroyed canister of blood. "Look at how much trouble you've caused me. I don't deserve to be put through any of this!"

Her narrowed eyes whirled back to Mikael and Arick's kneeling forms.

"You should be ashamed of yourselves."

As she spoke the words, a heavy burden of shame swam through him. He shuddered as thoughts swirled in his head.

*Unworthy. Disgraceful. Hated.*

He clutched his chest as his heart tightened. An overwhelming amount of guilt flooded him at the state of the room, though he had nothing to do with its destruction. Why was he feeling this way? He saw the same effect it had on everyone around him. All of their faces screwed together as if they were in physical pain.

*Oh bother,* the strange female's thoughts drifted toward him again. *Now I have to start all over again. No matter, at least I could use them to do my bidding. That'll be an easy illusion.*

Confusion coated his mind as he listened to her words. What was going on?

"You're…" Mikael sputtered. Tears appeared in his eyes, threatening to spill over. "Her…You're Satan."

She narrowed her eyes further at him.

"How rude of you to talk directly to me." She gasped. She raised a hand to her chest, furrowing her brow, offended.

The feeling of shame sharpened, cutting through him like a knife. They winced and groaned in pain. More of Satan's thoughts swirled around him.

*Hmmmm, what a disappointment.* Her high-pitched voice floated around his head. *Why must I always have to deal with these problems? I never get anything I want!* She puckered her lips in a pout.

She tipped her head back as she took another sip of her drink. She drained the contents of her glass and threw it at the wall. Ben expected the glass to shatter when it hit the rocks, but instead it dissolved like smoke. Wisp to the wind within seconds. Was that an illusion? He glanced back at her. Was she an illusion? He winced against another wave of remorse flooding him. What was going to happen to them?

*Besides, I know I sensed my staff somewhere around here. One of these filthy creatures had their paws on it!*

Ben's blood ran cold. That fast! She had tracked them down that quickly since he used the staff. He thought he would've had more time before she hunted them down, but it was too late. He turned to Canaan to warn him to get away but saw glittering anger in his eyes. Ben saw his older brother move his mouth in speech but heard nothing. Beside him, Arick's mouth opened wide as if he was yelling but Ben heard none of it.

He froze.

The ringing in his ears had lessened, but he couldn't hear any spoken word. He heard Mikael and Satan as clear as day, but why couldn't he hear Canaan and Arick? He lifted his hands to his ears, probing. When he pulled his hands away all he saw was more blood staining his hands.

He tried to focus on what Canaan and Arick said, but he couldn't decipher the words from their lips. After failing to hear what was spoken, Ben attempted to read their minds. His stomach dropped as he heard nothing again.

Not an aura accompanied them to give him a clue as to what they were feeling. In fact, Satan was the only one with an aura and it filled the room. He shifted to face his brother head on. He grabbed Canaan by the collar and searched for that calming blue aura he carried with him. Nothing surrounded him. No color, no discern-able emotion, nothing. What was happening?

Canaan furrowed his eyebrow together as he glanced down at Ben's distraught face. Was that confusion on his face? Concern? What did that expression mean?

"You." A single word made the hairs on the back of his neck rise. Ben turned his head to Satan, with wide eyes. She pointed a single, manicured finger at him with the other hand on her hip.

*Gotcha,* she thought to him. *It was you who took my staff. Clever boy.*

He realized too late that she had thought the word to him. She hadn't spoken it out loud, leaving him the only one who heard her. He paled as she walked forward. He couldn't hear the steps she took, but sensed her frustration.

*I don't have time for little brats to be taking my stuff!*

She reached down to grab him, but Canaan moved faster. He jerked Ben behind him and stretched his wings out wide, covering him from view. Behind him, Ben couldn't tell what he was saying but guessed it was infuriating Satan.

*How annoying! Can I kill them all or do I need to keep some of them alive? Let's see, who all is here?* Her thoughts moved from words to images as she looked from face to face. *They must be of the Michael clan.* Images of Arick and Mikael floated through her mind. Suddenly the image changed to Elijah, Ava, and Charlotte. *They're of the Raphael clan.* The next image was of Canaan with his arms outstretched with his wings. *A Selaphiel angel judging by the wings. That younger one is someone important to him.*

Her mind moved fast as she analyzed each of them.

*They must be Matthew's prior family. So he must be Mikael or Arick.* She rolled her eyes. *It's hard to tell them apart after a while, and it doesn't matter. Some of the Michael clan, Raphael, and Selaphiel clan. Hmmmm,* she pondered. *I think I can work with that. I really wanted a Gabriel or Raziel angel but these little pests will do for now.*

"Why?" His vocal cords vibrated as he spoke.

*Why does this little brat think I'll entertain such a question?*

"Why do you need angels?" he pleaded again. He gripped Canaan's shoulder for support as his pain spread.

She narrowed her eyes at him. *The arrogance on this brat!*

A tidal wave of depression washed over him as memories of Atarah flooded him. He was back on that balcony, in Urbs Antiqua, about to get married. Atarah's face twisted with disgust as she wiggled out of his arms.

*I could never marry you.* She screeched at him.

His mind grew fuzzy as another memory came to the surface. The one of him digging through the rubble of Chrysi Poli. He froze when his hands brushed by a cold body. A strangled sound left his throat when he saw his mother's eyes glaze over. Dead. Both of his parents dead before him.

*Why must I have a failure of a son?* His father's voice echoed around him. Ben's stomach twisted as shame and grief consumed him.

"Stop that!" Elijah cried out. "Whatever illusion you're showing him, stop!"

Elijah's shouts broke him out of his spiral. Ben slumped forward as residual despair carved into his heart. Canaan wrapped his arms around him once more.

"Ben?" Canaan shook him lightly. "Little bean?!"

*I don't have time for this. Where is Matthew?*

Satan swiveled to where Matthew's body lay, next to Mikael and Arick.

*I'll take all three of them for now.*

The red staff that dangled by Ben's waist side, jerked away from his belt and into Satan's waiting, outstretched hand. A glow emanated from the staff, stretching up her arm. A red line surrounded Mikael and Arick, pulsating.

Satan paused for a second and regarded Ben's crumpled form.

"I'll be back to deal with you later." Her voice turned to ice, sending shivers down his spine. Mikael moved fast. He flung the staff given to him by Beelzebub toward Elijah. A big red light flared around them, and they were gone. Mikael, Arick, Matthew and Satan were nowhere to be seen. Except for a hand. Mikael's hand flopped to the ground, splattering blood as it made impact. The hand he used to throw his staff out of the way before Satan could take it. Beelzebub's staff clattered at Elijah's feet. The ringing in Ben's ears blared louder than before. He winced, the sound of nails scratching against metal cycled in his head.

Ava's mouth opened wide as she cried out. He deciphered one word as the suffering on her face painted a clear picture.

"Noooo!!"

She scrambled to where Mikael and Arick had been, wailing. Elijah was there. He cradled Ava to his chest and held her tight while she sobbed.

"This isn't the end, Ava!" he whispered in her ear. "We will get them back. They're not lost."

She continued to sob on Elijah's shoulder. Charlotte fell to the floor, covering her face with both hands. Her shoulders quivered as she cried. They all sat there, defeated. Emotionally and physically crushed.

A withered voice caught his attention.

*Whatever happened here, it didn't end well.* The thought came abruptly.

Ben turned to see Gabriel angels, with shaking limbs and sunken eyes, standing by the door. Their black wings appeared withered to the point where he doubted they could fly. Their minds strung like out of tune guitars that blended in with the ringing in his ears. There must be a dozen or so gathered.

The angel standing in front spoke, but Ben didn't hear a single word. He hung his head and clutched his ears as if it would stop the pain and ringing. Elijah and Canaan both nodded as they listened. Ben drowned them all out, tempted to let the closing in darkness consume him until he heard Elijah's reply.

"Barmen was here?" Elijah asked with his eyebrows raised. Ben jerked his head up as a fire blazed in his chest.

*That lying bastard,* Ben thought with venom. Rage built up within him. *If it weren't for him, Atarah would still be alive and safe!*

He clenched his fist as he lifted his head. Anger twisted in his gut as he gurgled.

"Where is he?" His throat vibrated as he spoke. He didn't mind not hearing his own words but was infuriated by his inability to hear the reply.

The Gabriel angel in front widened his eyes as he saw Ben. A few others behind him took a step back away from him. He saw the fear and hesitation in their eyes, but he didn't care.

"Where is he?" His face twisted with a sneer. His voice must have grown in volume for the vibrations in his throat grew stronger. If pain hadn't rendered him immobile, he would have grabbed the angel by the collar and shaken him.

The angel lifted his hands up and shook his head. He moved his lips in a reply, but Ben growled in frustration.

"I can't hear any of you!" he roared.

Hands grabbed him as red swam in his vision. He jerked away from the hands, but they held on. Canaan came into his view. A frown marred his face, but Ben couldn't discern anything else from his expression. Canaan turned his head to Elijah, who looked at Ben with a keen interest.

"Makoto's right. We need to get out of here and regroup." Elijah gathered both of his daughters close before looking at Ben. "And we need to get Ben treatment as soon as possible. Something's very wrong with him." Elijah turned back to Makoto. "Get us out of here now."

Makoto nodded as he beckoned the other Gabriel angels behind him. One by one, they each placed their hands on each other's shoulders, all linking together. Makoto's hands glowed as he pulled apart a portal.

Ben roared and flailed weakly in his brother's arms. He was not leaving until he stomped Barmen into the ground. Canaan bound both arms around him as he walked them forward to the blazing portal.

"No!" he cried out this time in panic.

Atarah's body was here somewhere. He couldn't leave her. He struggled to break free but failed due to his weakened state. Kicking and screaming, Ben stared back at the pile of rubble as he was thrown through the portal.

Despair and anger swirled around him. Destroying him.

Amos pressed his lips together as thousands of thoughts swarmed him. The chilly air was a welcomed distraction to his burning head but not enough. Without a word to Joshua or Gabriel, he ducked into one of the washrooms in Joshua's estate. He growled against the sharp pain stabbing into his temple while he filled the sink with cold water.

Once full, he dunked his head into the water. The cold shocked his body and mind, giving him a blissful moment of silence. Cool relief and quiet eased the muscles along his neck and back. He slumped forward in the sink, not caring that water overflowed the sides and onto the floor.

He blew the rest of his breath out from his mouth, feeling the bubbles rise to the surface. With reluctance, he lifted his head out. Like the water rushing down his face, thoughts poured into his head. The minds of others were like the summer gnats swarming him, never-ending.

A knock on the door made him jump.

"Is everything ok in there?" Joshua's voice called out from the other side. Amos groaned as he forced himself to focus on the two males on the other side.

*Father always said focusing on a few thoughts helps against the headaches,* he mused. He never knew just how valuable this advice was until he ascended as the new Head Arch. He closed his eyes again and concentrated. Gabriel's pacing feet, which annoyed him earlier, now helped him find focus on a single sound. He took a deep inhale.

*Thoughts can be like a camera lens*, his father's words came to him. *Zoom in and find the focus on one thought, and all the rest will blur away.*

Gabriel's anxiety blared, like strings of a violin being played off-beat.

He exhaled.

He found Joshua's thoughts next. His thoughts presented louder with concealed frustration. Amos grew up hearing about Mikael and Joshua's adventures. Joshua and Mikael were fast friends while young and talked about as hot-tempered, reckless youths. Hearing the inner workings of Joshua's mind now, he understood the constant war going on within his head.

Anger, frustration, then calm and understanding. Hyper and manic to cool and monotone. The pendulum pivoted back and forth like a metronome. He wondered if the pendulum would shift to one side, if under a certain amount of weight. Would he still be the Joshua he saw today?

Another knock on the door drew his attention.

"Amos? Do I need to call for a healer?" Joshua's voice floated beyond the door.

"No," he replied. His throat itched from dryness.

He grabbed a towel from one of the cabinets off to the side and rubbed his hair. Gabriel's thoughts from earlier surfaced as he regarded his reflection in the washroom mirror. He was looking rough. His eyes were dark and sunken. His beard appeared unkempt and his skin dull. He grimaced.

Maybe a day at the villa's spa wouldn't hurt…Ridiculous!

He shook his head. He didn't have time for this!

He threw the towel off to the side and paused with his hand on the handle of the door. He took another deep breath to compose himself.

*Push everything away and get shit done*, Amos whispered to

himself.

He pulled the door open and joined the others. Joshua stood just a foot away from the door and blinked at his arrival. His eyes traveled back and forth.

"Are you good?" Joshua's steadied on his face. Amos gave a firm nod before turning to Gabriel, who paced near the windows. His black wings twitched every few seconds now instead of minutes. He opened his mouth to speak when another person's thought shot through his mind like an arrow in the night.

A word that caused him to freeze.

*Ben.*

"Wait," he gasped. Gabriel and Joshua both eyed him with apprehension.

*I think he's cracking underneath the role of Head.* Gabriel's thoughts echoed. *He's obviously not very put together.*

Amos ground his teeth together to bite back his cutting remark. He needed to stay composed. Amos closed his eyes and searched for that voice again. Where were these thoughts coming from? From who? A collection of emotion and voices came into focus, and they were close by.

*I wonder how the others are doing in the demon realm? I hope Ben makes it out alive. Making that deal with the demon lords was beyond reckless of him. I need to let my father know soon.* Gabriel Jr.'s face came into view as he shuddered. Anxiety filled his belly at the thought of disappointing his father.

Amos scoffed, opening his eyes. Like father, like son. Both riddled with anxiety.

"Is there something you want to share with the rest of us?" Joshua's blue eyes pierced him. Gabriel Sr. paused in his stance. His hands glowed with the effect of his powers.

"Your son is somewhere close by." Amos sighed. "I'm trying to pinpoint him now."

Gabriel Sr. was in front of him in the blink of an eye. An explosion of urgency poured from his mind as his hands gripped the sides of Amos' shoulders.

"Where is he?!" Gabriel asked, shaking him. Panic screamed inside his mind as his eyes traveled around the room as if his son would pop up at any moment. Images from when his son was born poured into his mind. Sights of blood and a blue, still-looking baby flashed through his mind from Gabriel's memory.

*I need to know if he's okay or hurt!*

*Trinity, my father's going to kill me when he sees me.* Junior's thoughts sounded louder.

"He is within the city," Amos answered, furrowing his brow in concentration. "I believe he's outside of the library, and he's not alone either."

Other voices floated around Gabriel Jr.'s, female voices. He opened his eyes in surprise.

"We have several unexpected guests this afternoon," Amos continued. The tension along his neck eased as their voices rang clear in his mind.

Joshua frowned. "We were only waiting for Sewall. We don't have time for any others."

"You will be interested in what our new guests will have to report," Amos answered as he opened the door.

Sewall's wings flared in surprise. His hand, which was raised to open the door, froze. His black eyes narrowed on Amos.

*What was so important that I had to come here immediately?* Sewall's voice thundered in his head.

"Your children are here," Amos spoke aloud. Sewall's reaction was instant. His wings flared once more, and his eyes widened. The angel of death gripped his collar and shook him in earnest.

"Are they okay?" Sewall asked through clenched teeth.

The lines in his face furrowed into a sneer. His grip turned tighter as anger rose to his features. Cloaks of darkness and smoke swirled around his side and wings from the emotions. The tendrils of Sewall's powers caressed him, making him feel sick. Amos' energy sapped away within seconds. His soul withered in a way he'd never felt before. Like a flower being drained dry from the sun, he had no shelter.

His brain fogged and his vision blurred as the shadows reached his head. The contact was light and brief, but it didn't take much for the angel of death to tighten his grip. Sewall hardly registered the effect his power had on Amos. Sewall's thoughts grew quieter as Amos weakened with each second. Sweat formed on Amos' brow as fear set in while his body turned cold.

"They are on their way here." His voice trembled.

His arms fell to his side, limp, while his legs threatened to cave under him. He regretted telling Sewall about their new arrivals.

"Please pull back your power before you kill me," he pleaded. His weakened heart sputtered in his chest, desperate to escape this hellish state.

Something flickered in those dark eyes. Was it realization? It didn't matter, for Sewall pulled back his darkness. The tendrils coiled around him, retreating like a slithering snake, back to their master. His energy returned within a few seconds. Amos gasped with relief as strength came back into his limbs and his head cleared. Amos swore he heard a hiss of some kind when the last of the shadows and smoke entered into Sewall's wings.

A chill ran down Amos' spine as he scurried back from Sewall. Amos' heart thundered in his chest. He narrowly escaped death itself. Sewall's black eyes appeared far more sinister than before. Feeling Sewall's power for the first time was different than hearing about it secondhand from another's mind.

"Apologies." Sewall bowed from the waist. "That was a shameful display of behavior, and I'm truly sorry. I vow to ensure none of you in this room will have to see the real me." Sewall straightened up to his full height. His eyes narrowed. "Unless you deserve it." Sewall finished. His voice sounded cold as ice.

Amos swallowed hard before speaking again.

"Apology accepted," he murmured. "Trinity help whoever's deserving of such…torture."

Sewall's face remained expressionless, but Joshua and Gabriel paled. Neither Arch Head raised their eyes to meet Sewall's. Tension lined along their wings and in their thoughts. Amos heard the fear and aversion each had for Sewall.

"Sewall has had a rod up his ass since he was born," Joshua said with a wry grin. Sewall scowled at Joshua, who averted his gaze. A whisper of smoke drifted from his wings.

"Should I have a rod," Sewall replied darkly. "I know exactly what I would use it for."

A huff erupted from Gabriel, who quickly covered his mouth with his inner elbow. Gabriel pretended to cough in his elbow to hide his laughter. Joshua's lips twitched and his wings dropped just a little.

*Damn,* Gabriel thought. *Funny come back.*

Another choir of voices echoed in his mind. Amos moved to the opposite door. His legs shook as he walked. He opened the door wide before returning to his seat. A quiver continued down each limb as he sat. Joshua made his way over to his mini bar and mixed a drink while they waited. However Gabriel broke the silence.

"As you were saying," Gabriel stood behind one of the chairs, gripping the back portions with both hands. "Our children are on their way here? That must mean they're safe, right?"

Sewall walked stiffly over to one of the chairs. He glared down at the red-colored chair for a few seconds before sitting down. He hissed as if the chair felt abhorrent. He kept his back straight and his hands in his lap, never relaxing.

Joshua came back over to where they'd gathered and handed Amos a dark colored drink.

"Here," Joshua spoke. "You'll need this after what Sewall did."

Amos gave a nod before grabbing the drink from Joshua. He took a big gulp, draining half of the glass' contents. The drink had a smoky, caramel flavor to it, and burned down his throat before settling into his stomach. A warm sensation coiled inside him as he put the glass down on the table.

The click of the glass signaled the heirs coming in. Gabriel Jr. was the first to come in the room. He walked in and froze when he saw his father. Sweat coated his shirt, especially under his arms. Next was Noah, followed by Zewal and Tariel. The last two heirs entered: Clarissa, who looked pale, and her sister Isabella. They all stopped behind Gabriel Jr., as his wings quivered.

The young heir swallowed. "Father—I," His words were cut off as Gabriel Sr. rushed to his son and embraced him. His black wings encased them. His arms wrapped around his son's torso, his fear of letting him go pounded in his heart. The hug lasted for a few seconds before he pulled away.

"Are you ok, Twenty?" Gabriel Sr. patted down the sides of his son, checking for injuries.

Gabriel Jr., or 'Twenty,' blushed bright red. He tried to step away, but his father held firm.

"I am fine, dad," Twenty murmured. "I promise."

"As for *you two*," Sewall's cold voice called out. "Both of you better be injured." Sewall flapped his wings hard and leapt to where his two children stood. Zewal flared his wings as his father landed just in front of them. His jaw clenched, and his eyes narrowed on his father.

"What made you think you could just run off like you did?" Sewall hissed. His face twisted in a sneer. "After everything you've caused your mother, now you drag Tariel into your irresponsibility."

Zewal flinched and curled in on himself as if Sewall had struck him. Just as Zewal's wings slumped, Tariel stepped forward furious.

"Don't bring Mom into this!" Tariel's volume rose. Sewall stepped back once but then took another step forward, closer to his daughter.

"Don't talk back to me, young lady! You are in just as much trouble as your brother," he yelled back. Sewall gave a scathing look to Zewal. "But I expect more from you, Zewal. You. Disappoint. Me." He enunciated each word, causing devastation. Amos heard how Sewall's words cut through Zewal's heart. Zewal's expressionless face crumpled with hurt and shame.

"Any of you," Joshua chimed in, drawing everyone's attention. "Have any of you seen my son, Barmen?"

Amos was flooded with all of their memories at once. He clenched the armrest until his nails turned white. Each of them possessed a different perspective, and a story to what happened to all of them. Images of the demon lords, Ben, Mikael, and Elijah flashed through his mind. Amos gritted his teeth as he tried to file through all of their memories.

One by one, Amos was able to order the events from each of them within his mind. Nothing was spoken out loud, as the heirs looked to one another in uncertainty.

*Who should go first?* was the common question on their minds.

Amos cleared his throat. "Gabriel—or er—I mean Twenty," he clarified as both Gabriels turned their heads, "should go first. Start there and work our way around." He rubbed his temples again as the play-by-play of his brother bargaining with the demon lord made his stomach twist. "We have a lot to cover it seems." He sighed.

Twenty nodded and started off with his story. They all sat around in a circle, the Archs listening. The only interruption was Joshua when he heard Barmen's name mentioned in the confrontation with the demon lords. His wings flared wide once but allowed the others to continue. Clarissa and Isabella confirmed everything Twenty explained. Zewal gave his story next, his eyes downcast and wings hanging low to the ground.

His voice strained with emotion as he gave his side of the story. Noah took over their version and explained how they met up with Mikael and Elijah.

While Noah and Clarissa finished off their tale, this gave Amos time to process. He wondered and worried about his brothers. Did Ben become that desperate, to approach a demon lord?

*No*, Amos mused.

Ben must have seen an opportunity and gone for it. His little brother struck him as narcissistic in his pursuits; that's why Ben made him nervous. He mused over Gabriel's last memory of Ben. His little brother appeared as disheveled as he did. Maybe Ben had changed for the better?

Amos shook his head.

He needed to focus on the plan for now. If Ben was still in the demon realm, going after Matthew with Satan's staff, how could they use that to their advantage? Amos clasped his hands together as he pondered the possibilities. Once again he had to change his plans to accommodate his little brother's antics.

Amos stared across the room, at the disentanglement puzzles Joshua had on his shelf. Mikael and Elijah were a part of his plan now, whereas prior they were not. What were the demon lords' motives? According to the heirs, the demon lords tolerated each other but were not steadfast allies. More like bickering siblings. Powerful siblings at that.

Each of their staffs were with the others back in the demon realm. Amos peered at Joshua, listening to his thoughts. Joshua knew of the staffs and understood that their power was too great for any Arch to wield. Amos grimaced. If the staffs were too dangerous then they were useless. Amos turned back to Noah and Clarissa. He heard the fire in their hearts, the urge to go back and fight.

*Nothing will stop them*, Amos thought. *They're too determined.*

However, Amos regarded Twenty again with new eyes. He'd always brushed Twenty aside as nothing more than a faithful 'daddy's boy' who barked whenever spoken to. Twenty surprised him. The young heir disobeyed his father in order to help the others and that was no small change.

Clarissa glared at Tariel and Zewal when the discussion about Arick arose. Tariel flared her wings as Clarissa gave a scathing remark about the halfling. Noah's wings flared as well. Their motive to prove him innocent was ridiculous but powerful enough for them to go to the demon realm without a word to their families. Amos almost scoffed when Noah came to Arick's defense. It didn't matter anyway. Amos wasn't going to allow that halfling back in his realm any more than he would a demon.

"Enough," Amos huffed out. "That is the whole story? After which, Elijah and Mikael kicked all of your asses back to our realm, correct?"

A few hesitant nodded.

"Very well, then," Amos stood up from his chair. "Now comes our plan that all of you will help with," he indicated to the heirs.

Sewall bristled. "No, they will return home at once!" He argued back.

"Why bother when they can make a difference here and now, with minimal risk?" Amos retorted.

"What do you need help with?" Noah asked. He leaned forward from his seat. His eyes looked hungry for action.

"In fact," Amos glanced at Sewall with his two children. "With everyone here, we could do more damage than the first plan." He turned to Gabriel Sr./Nineteen. "Hear me out before saying anything." He pointed a finger at Sewall and Nineteen. "Gabriel—I mean Nineteen, You will open a portal for us to the demon realm, specifically to Ianua. There Sewall, along with your two kids, can weaken everyone within the vicinity while Joshua creates an illusion that renders them into an infinity state within their mind, keeping them stuck in a loop, immobilizing them. When that is going on, Clarissa and Isabella, I want you to destroy everything you see but most importantly, destroy the portal within the city center." Clarissa raised an eyebrow, but Amos nodded. "I know you and your sister can create a fire tornado; do that and burn the entire city to the ground. Leaving nothing left of Matthew's little assimilate cult stronghold. Once that's done, Nineteen and Twenty can open another portal so we can escape."

"What about my people?" Nineteen asked, his mind filled with reluctance.

"I can go and get them back up." Noah stood up with his wings flared. "I know where they were going. I can join them."

"The jail cell the demons are holding everyone in is a maze, idiot," Clarissa said from where she sat. "There's no way you would know your way around."

"Silence." A cold hiss came from Sewall. His black eyes narrowed onto Amos. "We aren't doing your plan."

Zewal and Tariel stood up to protest, but their father silenced them.

"I will not allow you to go back to such a barbaric place."

"Those monsters and guards back there tormented our mother," Tariel said with venom. Her face skewed into a scowl. "We deserve to go back there and fight for her!"

At his daughter's words, Sewall jerked up with his wings wide and a thunderous expression. He glared at his daughter, who held his gaze.

"You have no idea how hard I'm fighting for your mother," Sewall whispered. "This kind of fight is one of support and gentleness that your mother needs. Not running off to the place that caused her the most pain."

"Sewall." Joshua's blue eyes glinted dangerously. He moved to Sewall's side and whispered in his ears. No one heard except for Amos. It was impossible to keep a secret from him.

"Let the beast out. I know it's twisting and roaring to let loose. Do it *for Fatima.*" The shadows rippled from Sewall's wings again. Zewal pulled his sister a step back from their father as the smoke swirled around him. Amos saw the beast Joshua whispered about for a brief second. Within Sewall's dark eyes, something with sharp teeth gazed back out. Something with a dark desire that promised pain and suffering to all who met it. Amos shuddered at Sewall's thoughts.

The urge to tear apart every demon he saw. The sight of his crying wife when she arrived back at home, broken in a way no healer could fix. Sewall clenched his fists. Destruction and death was the only thing he wanted to bring to the demon realm.

Sewall turned his head to Amos and gave the smallest of nods.

*We will do it*, Sewall's voice came as a hiss in his mind. Another chill ran down his spine. He pitied whatever poor demon should meet the true Sewall.

"What shall I do then?" Noah drew his attention.

"You can fight, or you can help destroy the city." Amos frowned. He hadn't really thought of the young Raphael's role in the plan. "Or help heal whomever gets injured."

Noah pursed his lips together. "What about my father and Mikael? Don't they need backup?"

Joshua scoffed. "Mikael needing backup?" He chuckled. "Don't be ridiculous. He's the best one out of all of us suited to take on any demon."

Right when Joshua finished speaking, a sharp sound of a new voice caused Amos to jump. A few seconds rolled by before Amos could identify the newcomer. How did he get here so quickly without him noticing?

Suddenly the door kicked open. Everyone was on their feet, wings flared and weapons drawn facing the door. Amos froze as he received a plethora of information from their new sunrise guest. Thoughts, images, and emotions slammed into him like a battering ram. Amos lifted a hand to his head, wincing at the new arrival.

*Barmen*, Amos grimaced. *The last missing heir in this puzzle.*

Barmen walked in the room with squelching sounds. He was covered, head to toe in so much blood his shoes squeaked. Joshua's eyes widened at his son's sudden arrival. None of the heirs knew where he had gone or if he had been there at all to begin with. Now here he stood, covered in blood with an overwhelming account of what took place from *his* perspective. He held Atarah's slumped over body in his left arm and something else in the right arm. Jaws, all around the room, dropped at Barmen's arrival. Amos heard several gasps but kept his eyes on the Raziel heir.

"Glad everyone is here," Barmen panted as if he had been running. He threw the thing in his right hand that landed with a sickening, wet sound. It plopped on the small coffee table before them.

It was a hand. No—not just any hand, Mikael's hand! Amos' stomach curled.

Barmen grabbed the glass, Amos drank from earlier. Barmen shot back the last of his whiskey, cradling Atarah's pale form.

"There's something you should know before you go into the demon realm."

# The End

**Thank you so much for ordering True Strength!**
**If you enjoyed it, please consider leaving a review.**

**Want more of Atarah's and Arick's story? Sign up for my newsletter to get early access to cover reveals, discounts, sales and more!**
**http://graciemitchell.com**

GRACIE MITCHELL

# ACKNOWLEDGEMENTS

Thank you so much for continuing to read the stories of Arick, Atarah, Charlotte and so many others. I hope you have enjoyed reading their journey as much as I enjoyed writing their adventures. I am truly grateful for the opportunity to share their stories and I couldn't have done it alone. I express my deepest gratitude to the people below. I want to say thank you to my husband, Malcomn, for cheering me on from the sidelines. You have been my number one fan and supporter. Thank you to my cat Zeus for cuddling by my side as I stay up late to write this book. Thank you for my amazing and supportive family! Love ya'll so much. Every like or share on social media has meant the world to me. Thank you for everyone who has purchased my book, whether by ebook or by paperback.

Thank you to my editors starting with Connie Dowell for copyediting. Thank you Nichole Heydenburg for developmental editing. Thank you Catherine Kopf for proofreading True Strength! I appreciated all the attention to detail from the feedback given. Thank you every ARC reader for your amazing feedback and hard work.Thank you Terra Hitzing for formatting my book! You are an amazing genius! Thank you Jessica Slater for all of the amazing work you have done for my book cover and design! The cover art looks great! Lastly I want to thank you—the reader. Thank you so much for reading my book and I truly hope you enjoyed this story! If you did, please let me know by leaving a review. I would greatly appreciate it!

GRACIE MITCHELL is a yoga-loving, caffeine addicted writer currently based in Georgia. When she is not working endlessly as an Indie author, she can be found curled up on the couch, with her husband, reading a new book or watching a new tv series. On top of her love to read and write, Gracie enjoys going on adventurous hikes, painting, spending time with her cat and traveling to different countries.

Follow her for more at: https://graciemitchell.com/
Insta: @clanofthearchseries
@gmitchell505

**Also by Gracie Mitchell**

**True Wings (Book 1)**

**Amazon:**
https://a.co/d/eBsedXw

**Barnes & Noble:**
https://bit.ly/3WlINlY

**Apple Books:**
https://books.apple.com/us/book/true-wings/id1574054011

**Kobo:**
https://www.kobo.com/us/en/ebook/true-wings

**All other vendors:**
https://books2read.com/u/3R82yY

**True Spirit (Book 2)**

Amazon:

https://a.co/d/fg1uhfy

Barnes & Noble:

https://www.barnesandnoble.com/w/true-spirit-gracie-mitchell/1142638747?ean=9781735457543

Apple Books:

https://books.apple.com/us/book/id6444295492

Kobo:

https://www.kobo.com/us/en/ebook/true-spirit-5

All other vendors:

https://books2read.com/u/4AvlaJ

**True Vengeance (Book 4): Coming 2023**